SHAUN
HUTSON
The REVENGE *of*
FRANKENSTEIN

HAMMER™

AN EXCLUSIVE MEDIA COMPANY

Published by Hammer Books 2013

2 4 6 8 10 9 7 5 3 1

First published in Great Britain in 2013 by
Hammer Books
Random House, 20 Vauxhall Bridge Road,
London SW1V 2SA

www.randomhouse.co.uk

Addresses for companies within The Random House Group Limited can
be found at: www.randomhouse.co.uk/offices.htm

The Random House Group Limited Reg. No. 954009

A CIP catalogue record for this book
is available from the British Library

ISBN 978-0-099-55623-7

The Random House Group Limited supports The Forest Stewardship
Council (FSC®), the leading international forest-certification organisation.
Our books carrying the FSC label are printed on FSC®-certified paper.
FSC is the only forest certification scheme endorsed by the leading
environmental organisations, including Greenpeace.
Our paper procurement policy can be found at:
www.randomhouse.co.uk/environment

Typeset in Palatino by Palimpsest Book Production Limited,
Falkirk, Stirlingshire
Printed and bound by CPI Group (UK) Ltd, Croydon, CR0 4YY

The REVENGE of
FRANKENSTEIN

Author's Introduction

In my humble opinion *The Revenge of Frankenstein* is the finest of the seven Frankenstein films that Hammer produced between 1957 and 1974.

It has complexities within its central characters not seen in the other films in the series and it shows probably more acutely than any of the others the fascinating dichotomy between the two sides of its leading figure, Baron Victor Frankenstein.

It is also one of my favourite horror movies so when the chance came to transform its script into a novel I had no hesitation.

The main problem from the writing point of view was that Frankenstein as a character isn't particularly terrifying. His obsession with creating life and his ruthlessness in the pursuit of his goal certainly make him a sometimes dangerous man. But he isn't a frightening figure in the sense that Dracula, the Mummy, the Werewolf or many of Hammer's other stalwarts are. He's in the same company as Doctor Jekyll, I suppose: a man who thinks that his work will ultimately benefit mankind but who falls foul of his own ambition. In the films it is the monster he creates that is the source of the horror and the fear, not the Good Doctor himself.

But in *The Revenge of Frankenstein* the monster is also different from the usual stitched-together monstrosities that the Doctor creates. Strictly speaking, there is no monster in this film. What we're presented with is an unfortunate man who helps Frankenstein and seems to be rewarded for that help.

Needless to say, it's not quite as straightforward as that but the character of Carl, the subject of the Baron's experiments in the story, is completely different from the creations in the films that both preceded (*The Curse of Frankenstein*) and followed (*The Evil of Frankenstein*) this particular outing. The monsters in those two films were the more horrific beings that one tends to associate with Frankenstein movies. Indeed, the creations in *Frankenstein Created Woman* in 1967 and also in *Frankenstein Must Be Destroyed* in 1969 were also much more than the mindless freaks one normally associates with the Baron. Only in the final film, *Frankenstein and the Monster from Hell*, did Hammer trot out a true monster. A lot of the time there was an attempt to create sympathy for the being that Frankenstein had fashioned.

What Hammer did quite brilliantly right from the beginning, however, was to shift the focus from the monster to its creator.

In the old Universal films of the 1930s and 1940s the name Frankenstein was always thought to refer to the monster itself (the flat-headed, bolt-necked creation portrayed by Boris Karloff). Hammer quite correctly changed the public perception of the name and concentrated on the scientist himself rather than the terrifying entity that he made. They were aided in this by the brilliance of Peter Cushing who played the Baron in the six main Hammer Frankenstein films. (We can discount here *The Horror of Frankenstein* from 1970, by the way, when Ralph Bates played the Baron, because this was more or less a remake of *The Curse of Frankenstein* and was probably intended to reinvent the character. It didn't work.)

Peter Cushing was the embodiment of Baron Frankenstein. He made the role his own just as Christopher Lee did that of Count Dracula for the same studio. The two men starred in many Hammer films and were superb in them all. Frankenstein as played by Cushing was suave, sophisticated, brilliant and totally ruthless. These were some of the aspects of his character I wanted to get across when it came to doing the novelisation but, important as the Baron is, the creation, particularly in *Revenge*, is a pivotal figure and in this film is also one of the most complex in any of the Hammer Frankenstein movies. Carl is not just some reanimated corpse with a fresh brain stuck in his skull. He is a sympathetic human being who wants Frankenstein's help.

What the film couldn't show and what I had the time and opportunity to explore in the novel was exactly why the two men were so drawn together. It was important for me to demonstrate how the two of them needed each other but more importantly to show Carl as a truly sympathetic individual with whom audiences (or readers, in my case) would want to empathise. As with the other novelisations I've done for Hammer I added extra scenes, in this case to underline (or bang home without the slightest hint of subtlety, some might say!) his alienation and loneliness. There are more new scenes involving Carl than there are for any other character in the film. I've also changed slightly the role of Margaret Conrad, the nurse, as she was originally just the common or garden 'damsel in distress' figure so beloved of horror films. I wanted to make her stronger and more essential to the plot. Whether I've managed it or not you'll have to decide.

This brings me back to the whole business of novelisations and what the writer should do when confronted by a script that was written more than fifty years ago. Should I update it? No, the very idea of Frankenstein in a modern setting is ridiculous. Modern medicine has overtaken the Baron in all but brain transplantation. Should I re-imagine the character? Again, no. Why mess around with something that works perfectly well to begin with? It would be like changing Dracula into a vegetarian! Look at the subject matter from a different angle? Why change the structure when it already works? There was also the temptation to go a little over the top with the later cannibalistic scenes but, unusually for me, I resisted that. Hammer fans may well be relieved; my own regular readers may be disappointed!

Hammer films have always had a recognisable stamp of quality about them but they also have a recognisable style and I felt that any novelisation of the movies concerned should display the same kind of respect with which the original was presented to its audience. For instance, the character of Margaret *could* have been seen as a bit of 'female interest' lusted after by patients and doctors alike – but I couldn't bring myself to do that. Similarly, the scene when two potential young lovers are preparing for a carnal interlude *could* have been the occasion for some gratuitous sex – but I couldn't bring myself to do that, either! Inserting sex scenes into some of the older Hammer stories would be like catching your grandparents in bed! It's just wrong. But more importantly it would have detracted from the overall feel (excuse the pun) of the film and the characters and I was never going to do that.

There is something sacrosanct about the structure and characters of each Hammer film and trying to put a modern spin on it just doesn't work when you're dealing with a film that is set in the nineteenth century to begin with. Fans of the films want, in my humble opinion, to read adaptations of movies they've known and loved, not some re-imagined stuff churned out by a writer who thinks they're smarter than the original screenwriter. Also, I think my admiration for the films has also prevented me from tampering too much with their framework and plots. Characters have to be explored more deeply and new ones introduced (as long as they don't stick out like sore thumbs from the character types that inhabited the original films, of course). The joy of a novelisation is that the author has more scope than a scriptwriter to explore their thoughts and motives and that is what I hope I've done here and also in the novelisations I've done of those other Hammer films: *Twins of Evil* and *X the Unknown*.

I first saw *The Revenge of Frankenstein* on a black and

white television late one Friday night when I was about ten. It was a joy to me then and has been ever since so to be given the chance to novelise it was a great honour. I just hope I've done it justice. The only people who can decide that now are you, the readers.

SHAUN HUTSON

'To destroy is always the first step in any creation'

e. e. cummings

One

Victor Frankenstein could see the castle from the window of his cell.

Perched on the peak of one of the mountains that surrounded the small town of Innsbruck it dominated the skyline and was visible for miles around. Even in this stinking prison cell where Frankenstein had been incarcerated for the last three days it was possible for him to see the majestic building that he had called home for all but six of his thirty-eight years. It had been the residence of his family for three generations. When his father had died Victor himself had become master of the place and also recipient of the family fortune. He had become the new Baron Frankenstein. The master of all he surveyed. Such wealth had enabled him to pursue his dreams and ambitions with a ferocity that others had found intimidating. He kept his gaze fixed on the gaunt edifice of the castle, his mind filled with sobering thoughts.

How he wished he were there now instead of shut up inside this reeking room that was less than twelve feet square with nothing inside it except some straw – strewn haphazardly on the dirty stone floor – and a crude wooden bed. Frankenstein scratched at his forearm and glanced irritably at it. He was convinced that the filthy mattress he had been forced to sleep on had fleas in it. Just the thought disgusted him and he ran a hand through his hair, rubbing and shaking his head as if to dislodge any more of the tiny parasites that might be lurking there.

He turned away from the window now and wandered over to the heavy metal door on the far side of the cell. He was a tall man and it took him just two strides to cross the room. There was a barred window in the door – little more than an observation slot, in fact – and Frankenstein peered through it now, looking along the corridor that stretched away from his cell and the others like it. The flagstoned walkway led to an office, then beyond to another large door and then to the courtyard of the prison. Beyond that lay freedom. It was such a short journey but it might as well have been a million miles.

Freedom. The word seemed redundant and worthless to Frankenstein for he was sure that he would never again know that particular joy. He would never be able to return to his castle and, above all, he would never be able to continue with his experiments. He took a deep breath, wincing slightly as he inhaled the rancid odour of the prison. From one of the other cells he could hear the low muttering and grumbling of another prisoner. A common criminal, he thought, not a man of learning like himself. He didn't belong here. He had no place here among scum like this. Thieves, robbers, rapists and drunkards. The dregs of humanity.

Baron Victor Frankenstein was a man of wit, intelligence, determination and ambition but it was because of his all-consuming drive that he now waited in this cell. The fools who had placed him here could never understand the way his mind worked. They could never hope to fathom or comprehend his goals. Not with their small closed and uneducated minds. He felt he should pity them for their lack of knowledge and their apparent insistence on ignoring the kind of secrets that he had striven to unlock. But it wasn't pity that he felt – it was hatred. He hated them because their inability to understand him and what he had worked for had caused them not only to place him in this stinking cell but also to condemn him to death.

Frankenstein sat down wearily on the wooden bed, his head in his hands. Death.

The word reverberated inside his mind. In two days' time he would be dead, executed by the guillotine that was being erected in the courtyard outside. Even in this most dire of situations he managed a smile because the irony of his position was apparent to him more than anyone. He, the man who had conquered death, was now facing an end to his own life. Instead of lauding and praising what he had done, the small-minded ignorant fools who called themselves judges and jurors had sought to condemn him because they were too stupid to see beyond the casualties that had ensued as a result of his experiments. And to Frankenstein that was all the deaths had been. The people who had died had been unfortunate *casualties* in a march towards a greater and more meaningful good that none but he seemed to appreciate. He shook his head wearily. How many had died?

Two? Three? But to what end? The education of mankind, the changing of dogmatic thought that had endured for five hundred years or more. What were two or three lives in comparison with the knowledge that he had gained? They were drops in the ocean barely worth consideration but now he himself was to become a casualty of his own work and research, another life given – but for what? There was no one to continue his work. No one who would seek to enhance the knowledge he had worked so hard to attain. When he died his work and his dreams would die with him and that thought filled him not with fear but with even more seething hatred for the men who had condemned him. They neither knew nor cared that they were destroying what he had striven for because their feeble minds could not ever begin to comprehend the genius of his. They could never hope to see into his thoughts and share even a fraction of the inspiration there. A brilliance that in time might even have helped those who had condemned him so easily.

He got to his feet and began pacing back and forth as best he could within the constricting confines of the cell. Occasionally he would pause to look at the barred window or the thick metal door and each time the thought was the same. There had to be some way out of this place. He stood still in the centre of the room, his keen gaze travelling over every inch of the stone walls and floor.

Are you looking for a crack that you could slip through? Are you a phantom who can walk through walls?

Victor Frankenstein smiled bitterly at his own fanciful

thoughts. The thick unyielding brickwork offered no hope of escape. Even with a sledgehammer it would take him days to smash his way out. He knew that if he were to escape this cell and also to evade the ultimate punishment then he would have to use the most powerful weapons he possessed.

His brain and his intellect. If they failed him now he was finished.

Two

Frankenstein glanced up to one corner of the cell and watched as a fat spider advanced slowly towards a fly that it had ensnared in its web. The fly struggled helplessly on the sticky strands as if realising that it was about to be devoured. The Baron knew that this was impossible because insects had no capacity for that kind of intelligent thought. Man was the only animal able to comprehend and consider his own end. But he watched nonetheless, fascinated by the slow approach of the corpulent arachnid.

You're a fly caught in the web of the fools who put you here.

He shook his head as if to drive such a strained and melodramatic metaphor from his thought processes.

The fly can't escape its fate and neither can you.

The Baron's musings were interrupted by the sound of footsteps in the corridor outside. He crossed to the door and peered through the observation slot.

One of the guards was making his way slowly from cell to cell. He was carrying three metal bowls somewhat precariously in his thick-fingered hands. He placed them on the stone floor, unlocked the first room and pushed a bowl inside before slamming the door and locking it again. He did this until he had just one bowl left and Frankenstein watched him as he approached. The guard was a small man, his body twisted and disfigured by the very noticeable hump on his back. The ill-fitting dark blue uniform that he wore was stretched almost to bursting point by the physical aberration. Frankenstein had decided that the deformity was caused by some kind of bone disease. Whatever the true nature of the affliction it had also caused a withering of the left arm and there was poor movement in the man's left leg also. He shuffled along the corridor towards the Baron's cell, his progress slow and cumbersome. He was probably in his early thirties but the nature of the condition that had left his body so twisted and wasted had also taken its toll on his facial features. His skin was dry and pale, his eyes sunken deep into the dark pits of their sockets. His lank black hair hung as far as his collar.

Frankenstein retreated to his bed and lay down upon it as he heard the key being pushed into the lock.

Seconds later the door swung open, the hinges squealing protestingly. The guard was silhouetted in the doorway for a moment. Then he took a step inside.

'Some food for you, Baron Frankenstein,' he said and shuffled towards the bed, bending to place the bowl on the floor near the Baron.

'Food, Carl?' Frankenstein murmured. 'Is that what you call it? I wouldn't honour the slop you serve here by calling it food. I wouldn't have given that to my dogs.' He sat up slowly and looked unblinkingly at the guard.

'You don't have to eat it,' Carl Lang said almost apologetically.

'And if I don't eat I'll starve to death. You don't want that, do you? You don't want to cheat the executioner. What would the townspeople say?'

'I don't care what they say. I have no love for any of them.'

Frankenstein reached for the bowl and glanced dismissively at the contents. But despite his contempt for what was being offered he took the metal spoon protruding from the bowl and began picking out pieces of vegetable that he could identify within the thick broth. He chewed on a piece of potato and ran an appraising gaze over the guard.

'It isn't easy being different, is it, Carl?' he said, quietly. 'I know that. People are afraid of anything other than what they know to be normal.'

'I don't care what they think of me,' Carl grunted. 'What they say about me.'

'What do they say, Carl?'

'They point at me. They mock my appearance. Their children laugh at me.'

'They're fools. They understand nothing but their own worthless little lives and they care for no one but themselves.'

'It's been the same all my life. I should be used to it by now. After all, it isn't going to change.'

'It could.'

Carl looked questioningly at Frankenstein.

8

'How?' he demanded. 'I was born with this body.'

'Just because you were born with it doesn't mean that you have to keep it,' the Baron said, raising one eyebrow. 'I could help you.'

'How? You're to be executed in two days. What could you do for me?'

Frankenstein picked out a piece of carrot and ate it.

There was a heavy silence in the room for a second. Then Carl spoke again.

'How could you help me, Baron?' he asked.

'I have knowledge that no other man has, Carl,' Frankenstein announced. 'Knowledge I acquired during the course of my work. That knowledge could help a man like you.'

'Is it true what they say about you?'

'That I'm a wizard?' Frankenstein smiled. 'A sorcerer in league with the Devil?'

'That you stitched the parts of corpses together and made a monster.'

'There were flaws in my work,' said the Baron, with a twinkle in his eye. 'I don't deny that. But what I achieved was unlike anything that anyone has ever done before. I gave life where there was only death. And for that I am condemned.'

'But you killed people.'

'Not I, the creature I created. The man I made. He was the one who killed but when his body was destroyed in acid there was no one to blame but me. I sit here accused of crimes that I didn't commit, Carl. I murdered no one.'

'All murderers say they are innocent.'

Frankenstein eyed him unemotionally.

'You say you gave life. Only God can do that,' Carl went on.

'Do you believe in God, Carl? Do you believe that He gave you the body you have now? Because if you do you should hate Him for it.'

Carl gently touched his left arm, stroking the gnarled flesh on the back of his hand.

'What would you give for a new body, Carl?' Frankenstein asked, his gaze never leaving the other man. 'If that were possible? Your mind inside the perfect unblemished body of another. It would still be you but without the problems that afflict you and that have made your life so difficult.' He raised a finger and pointed lazily at the hump on Carl's back.

'You could do that?' Carl asked softly.

'If what they say about me is true then why doubt it?'

Frankenstein picked out a small onion and chewed it for a moment before replacing it in favour of a piece of carrot.

'But that argument is academic, isn't it?' the Baron went on. 'If I die in two days then my expertise will be no use to you or to anyone else.'

Carl hesitated for a moment. Then he glanced at the Baron once more and saw that the other man's attention was focused more fully on the bowl in front of him.

'I will be back later, Baron,' Carl said, falteringly. 'Perhaps we could talk more then.'

'Why not, Carl,' Frankenstein responded without looking up. 'After all, I have nothing else planned.'

Carl backed out of the cell almost deferentially,

closing the large door and locking it. He peered through the observation slot at the Baron for a moment longer, then headed off back down the corridor.

In the cell Frankenstein heard his shuffling footfalls receding. He managed a thin smile.

Three

'How's your new friend?'

Carl Lang heard the words but he didn't turn towards the man who had spoken them.

Instead he crossed to the line of small hooks on one side of the guardroom and hung the keys he'd been carrying on one. They clanked loudly as he placed them in their customary position and only then did he turn to glance at the source of the words. The other guard was a tall man in his late forties. He had pitted skin, a legacy of smallpox, and he was losing his hair. He was puffing on a pipe, creating a small cloud of smoke around himself and the desk where he sat with his boots propped on the top.

'I said how's your new friend?' the guard insisted, grinning crookedly at Carl.

'I heard what you said,' he answered.

'How's the Baron adjusting to his new surroundings?' the other guard went on. 'I bet he doesn't like it, does he? Having to mix with the likes of us, the commoners. He's used to having all the best things in life. To being surrounded by luxury – but now he's come to this. Still, he won't have to concern himself with his surroundings for much longer, will he? The executioner will have his head in two days' time.'

'He's a very intelligent man,' Carl said, moving towards the large metal stove in one corner of the room. He stood there warming himself for a moment.

'He's a monster,' the other guard snapped. 'A murderer. You know what he did.'

Carl didn't answer. He was gazing off into space, lost in his own thoughts.

'Why do you think he cares what you've got to say?' he went on dismissively.

'I don't judge people the way you do,' Carl responded.

The guard laughed. 'He was judged,' he grunted. 'Your new friend down there was judged by the magistrates and he was convicted. That's why he's sitting in that cell, waiting for the executioner.'

'What do you know about him other than rumours and gossip?'

'I know that he's a rich bastard who's going to get what he deserves.'

'Do you want him dead because he's rich or because of what you think he did?'

'Both. He and all the other rich bastards should be treated the same way. People like Frankenstein don't care for the likes of you and me.'

'It's not his fault that he was born into a rich family.'

'To hell with him and all those like him.'

Carl shook his head and reached for the large black overcoat that was hanging from one of the hooks near the door of the guardroom. It was made of rough material and it needed washing. He dragged it on, wincing when it wouldn't close at the front because of the large protuberance on his back.

Carl pulled open the heavy door that led out of the guardroom into the courtyard of the prison.

'If you're going into town bring me some tobacco,' the other man insisted. 'I'll pay you when you get back.' He sucked at his pipe.

'Like you did last time?' Carl grunted and headed for the door.

'I'll make sure your new friend is kept happy while you're gone,' the guard called mockingly. 'If he needs you I'll tell him you'll be back soon.'

Carl shook his head and slammed the door behind him. He shivered slightly as he felt the wind whipping around him and he pulled up the collar of his heavy coat as best he could to offer some additional protection from the elements. He looked across the prison's main courtyard, the centre of which was occupied by a wooden platform reached by three steps. At the top of this small flight stood a guillotine, dominating the courtyard. The machine was only partially complete. The main frame had been assembled but the release handle, bascule, mouton and blade had yet to be added. Each part of the device was assembled separately and the final touches that turned a simple frame of hardwood into a killing machine would be added in due course either by men who worked at the prison or by assistants sent by the executioner himself. The man who would pull the lever to end the condemned man's life also owned the guillotine. Death was a business to him and nothing more.

Carl had seen the formidable-looking device used before and the sight of those two upright posts above the lunette always sent a shiver down his spine. He tried to imagine what it would be like being strapped to the bascule, your head forced between the two pieces of wood that formed it. Lying there waiting for the blade above you to drop and slice your head from your body. What thoughts, he wondered, went through the mind of the condemned man, firstly when he emerged into the courtyard to see the instrument of his execution and then when it was all too late and he was lying there? The knowledge that death was now inevitable and unavoidable must be unbearable.

This thought would be occupying the mind of Baron Victor Frankenstein, Carl mused as he headed past the gaunt frame of the guillotine towards the main gates that would lead him out of the prison and on to the main road leading into Innsbruck. On top of the high wall that surrounded the courtyard Carl could see another guard plodding back and forth in the icy wind, a rifle gripped in his cold hands. Occasionally he would glance down into the courtyard and, indeed, as Carl reached the main gates the man did just that. But he afforded Carl only a perfunctory look and continued with his vigil, shivering visibly in the cold that was made worse by his elevated position.

There was a small gatehouse beside the main entrance and Carl entered to find another man seated at a desk, poring over some paperwork. He looked up as Carl came in, his expression darkening.

'What do you want?' the man said sharply.

'I'm going to the inn,' Carl informed him.

'The keys are there,' the man told him, jerking a thumb towards a large ring of them hanging on the wall to the right of the door.

Carl selected the one he needed. He inserted it into the lock of the door beside the two wide main gates and opened it before returning the keys swiftly to their appointed position.

'And don't bang too hard when you want to get back in,' the man told him sharply. 'You nearly knocked the door down last time. You don't know your own strength.'

Carl ignored the comment and headed off towards the road.

The prison was situated about a mile from Innsbruck itself, further isolated from the town by the dense forest that grew around it and formed another natural barrier between the monolithic building and the population. A single road ran through the forest to the town and as Carl made his way along it he was careful to keep to the edges of the muddy thoroughfare. It was deeply rutted by the passage of wagons and coaches and the recent rain had left it looking more like a quagmire. Puddles of filthy water had formed in the ruts and Carl saw several birds drinking from these makeshift pools. They flew off, rising high into the cloudy sky as he passed. He walked on as briskly as he could, almost slipping a couple of times on the glutinous mud.

Away to his right there was a thin plume of smoke rising into the air and he knew it came from the small hut inhabited by a woodsman. There were several small dwellings within the confines of the forest itself. The one belonging to the woodsman was closest to the road but Carl knew there were others. Within them dwelled people who either couldn't afford to live within the town itself or who simply chose to keep away from the other inhabitants of Innsbruck. Carl could understand their way of thinking. He himself lived in a tiny attic room on the outskirts of the town and many times he had wished that he was further away from the prying and contemptuous eyes of the townsfolk. But another part of him remained defiant. Why should they drive him away? He had done nothing to harm them and he never would. He didn't deserve their scorn and their derision. He was as good as any of them. Carl nodded to himself as he walked on, pulling his coat as tightly around himself as he could. They were too quick to judge and to make those judgements purely on physical appearance. His own body wasn't perfect but did that give people the right to stare at him and mock him? No, it didn't. Carl felt that he should pity those who scorned him for their ignorance but it was difficult to feel anything other than hatred for these people who were so quick to condemn those who were different. He had always been taught that what was inside a man was the most important thing. It was one of the few things he could remember his mother telling him when he was growing up and it had stayed with him.

She had been dead for more than twenty years now and sometimes he had trouble remembering her face or the way her voice had sounded. She had been the only person in his life who had ever shown him love, who had never judged him for his appearance. Her love had been unconditional, as had been her acceptance. His father had left the day after Carl's birth, repulsed and disgusted by the misshapen appearance of his son. Carl wondered if he too was dead, or was he out there somewhere in the world, still ashamed of the child he'd fathered? He pushed the thought to the back of his mind and walked on, approaching a fork in the road.

The left-hand fork led directly into Innsbruck, the right curved slightly towards a small inn. Carl took the right fork.

From behind him he heard a low rumbling and he turned to see a coach moving along the road, the driver flicking the horses with his whip to force them on through the thick mud. The four animals neighed and whinnied as they pulled the coach along the road and Carl stepped away from the track as the coach passed, narrowly avoiding the water that sprayed up from beneath the coach's wheels. The vehicle swept past, heading for the inn, and Carl saw it stop outside, the occupants climbing down carefully and moving inside the building.

He walked on.

Four

Frankenstein heard the rattle of the key in the cell-door lock and he turned towards the sound, looking bored.

A tall guard was standing on the other side of the heavy door, peering at him through the observation slot.

'A visitor for you, Baron,' he said, not attempting to hide the contempt in the last word.

Frankenstein eyed him expressionlessly and got to his feet as the door of the cell swung open. Beyond, in the corridor beside the guard, stood a well-dressed man with bushy sideburns and a moustache. He was a year or two younger than Frankenstein but his hair was already receding. When Frankenstein saw him he got to his feet with barely disguised delight and smiled.

'I'll be just down the corridor if you need me,' the guard said to the newcomer. 'Call if you want anything.'

The other man nodded and stepped inside the cell, allowing the guard to close the door behind him.

'Paul,' Frankenstein said, smiling and taking a step towards the man, who recoiled slightly and met the Baron's delighted greeting with a look of disdain.

Paul Krempe pulled nervously at one sleeve and regarded Frankenstein hostilely.

'I knew you'd come,' the Baron told him. 'How is Elizabeth?'

'She's fine, considering what she's been through,' Krempe told him flatly.

'Is she here?' Frankenstein wanted to know.

'Do you think I'd bring her to a place like this? She's at my house where she'll be safe.'

'She was never in any danger.'

'She was almost killed, Victor. Killed by the creature you created.'

'You helped me. Don't forget that. You helped me stitch that creature together. You helped me give it life. And you can help me now.'

'How?'

'By telling them the truth. Tell these fools who locked me up what really happened, then they'll have to release me. You can do that, Paul. You know that it wasn't me who killed those people. You have to tell them that.'

'I don't *have* to do anything, Victor.'

'Tell them the truth and get me out of here.'

'So you can begin all over again? Never. You're a menace, Victor. I'm not going to help you.'

'Then why did you come here?'

'To say goodbye.'

Frankenstein shot the other man a withering glance and kept his gaze fixed on him. Krempe couldn't maintain eye contact and looked down at the straw-covered floor.

'You're as guilty as I am,' the Baron hissed. 'You knew what we were doing. You knew what we were trying to achieve and we did it, we succeeded. If it hadn't been for you there would have been no deaths.'

Krempe opened his mouth to protest but Frankenstein went on angrily.

'You damaged the brain that we put inside the skull,' he snarled.

'Yes, the brain of a man you murdered.'

'The brain of a genius,' Frankenstein snapped. 'Your meddling destroyed it. You're the one to blame for what happened. Without your interference that creature would have been perfect. A creation that God Himself would have envied.'

'It was a monster.'

'The facial disfigurements could have been rectified in time. But you damaged the brain beyond recovery. You turned it into a madman by what you did to it.'

Krempe turned towards the door. 'I'm not listening to any more of this,' he grunted.

Frankenstein grabbed his shoulder and pulled him around, glaring into his eyes again.

'Tell Elizabeth I never meant to put her in danger,' the Baron said, his tone softening.

Krempe didn't answer.

'Paul, promise me you'll tell her that,' Frankenstein persisted.

'She cares nothing for you now, Victor,' Krempe said quietly.

'Then let her come here and tell me that herself.'

'I wouldn't let her anywhere near this place or near you. Not again. You destroy everything you touch with your obsession, Victor. There's a fine line between madness and genius and you stepped over that line a long time ago. I won't allow Elizabeth to be exposed to any more of your insanity.' He looked back at Frankenstein for a moment, then called: 'Guard.'

They both heard footsteps approaching along the corridor outside.

'Goodbye, Victor,' Krempe said emotionlessly.

'I know why you came to look at me for one last time, Paul,' Frankenstein said quietly. 'You came because we're alike. You wanted the knowledge we discovered as much as I did; you wanted that power as much as I did. The power to create life.' He smiled. 'But you lacked the courage that I had. You're a coward, Paul, you always were. And you know it.'

The cell door opened and the tall guard looked at both men.

'I'm finished here,' Krempe said and brushed past the guard as he left the cell.

'A man has to know his own limitations, Paul,' Frankenstein called. 'Remember yours. Remember what you are.'

The cell door slammed shut.

Five

Carl Lang felt the pleasing warmth inside the inn envelop him as he walked through the front door.

He glanced around and saw that there were a dozen people inside the hostelry, some gathered close to the roaring fire that was the source of the heat, others standing or sitting at the long L-shaped bar. There were three tables draped with red-and-white-checked tablecloths close to the bar and more people were sitting there eating meals prepared by the innkeeper's wife. All eyes turned in his direction as he entered, shuffling across the wooden floor towards the bar.

'Ale,' Carl said, digging deep in the pocket of his overcoat for some money to pay for his drink.

The innkeeper regarded him warily for a moment, then filled a stein and pushed it across the bar for him. Carl took a hefty swig and wiped his mouth with the back of his hand.

He was aware that several of the other customers were looking at him but he was used to the stares of others and found it relatively easy to dismiss their unwanted attention. However, that didn't stop him feeling irritated by their needless gazing. The innkeeper walked away to serve someone else and Carl was left gazing into his drink, looking as if he was seeking something within the dark depths of the ale. He took another swallow, then rubbed his stomach and raised a hand to beckon the innkeeper back towards him. The man returned and looked at him blankly.

'Could I have a bowl of soup and some bread?' Carl asked.

'I suppose my wife could get some for you,' the innkeeper muttered a little reluctantly. 'Two crowns.'

Carl nodded and dug in his pocket for more money as the innkeeper beckoned to his short, tubby wife. She looked at Carl, then nodded and headed off into the kitchen.

'What are you doing here, anyway?' the innkeeper asked him. 'I would have thought there was plenty to do at the prison, what with the execution coming up.'

'Everything is in hand,' Carl said.

'The sooner that madman is executed the better,' the innkeeper muttered.

'Do you mean Baron Frankenstein?'

'Who else would I mean? Who else has been terrorising the countryside for miles around?'

Carl didn't answer.

'If we'd had any sense we'd all have gone up there to his castle and burned it to the ground with him in it,' the innkeeper went on vehemently. 'I heard he'd been robbing graves and the charnel house. What kind of man is he?'

'He's a very intelligent man,' Carl said. 'Educated.'

'How would you know?' the innkeeper snapped. 'What do you do up there at the prison, anyway? Take the prisoners their food? Empty slop buckets? How can you know anything about a man like Frankenstein?'

'I have spoken with him,' Carl explained.

The innkeeper raised his eyebrows, then turned away dismissively, stepping aside as his wife appeared beside him carrying a wooden tray with a bowl and some bread on it. The innkeeper nodded towards Carl, and the woman placed the steaming fare down in front of him. Carl took a large piece of bread and dipped it in the soup before pushing it into his mouth.

'It's good,' he said appreciatively. But the innkeeper's wife seemed oblivious to his compliment and bustled back towards the kitchen.

Carl took another mouthful, then prepared to get to his feet.

'Where are you going?' the innkeeper asked.

'I'm taking my food and drink over by the fire where it's warm,' Carl said.

'Don't disturb my customers,' the innkeeper told him.

'I'm one of your customers too,' Carl said sharply and ambled across to the roaring fire, managing to carry his soup and bread in one hand and his drink in the other.

As he approached, three of the people near the fire ran appraising stares over him. A fourth, a little girl no older than three, looked at him and smiled. Carl smiled back at her, touched by the warmth in her expression. He saw her mother snake out an arm and pull the child closer to her as if to protect the girl as Carl moved nearer to the fire. He nodded dutifully to the other people, put his ale, bread and soup on an empty table and settled himself in a seat close to the leaping flames.

The girl's mother and father and the coach driver were seated at a table on the opposite side of the fire, eating from the plates that had been placed before them by the innkeeper's wife who now returned to the table to check on her guests.

'The food is excellent,' the man announced, dabbing at his mouth with a napkin.

'Thank you, sir,' the innkeeper's wife replied. 'I expect you're glad you stopped here.'

'We didn't have much choice,' the coach driver said, cradling his drink in his hand. 'This is the only place between here and Carlsbad.'

'Is it far to Carlsbad?' the woman asked, letting her hand slip from the little girl's shoulder. 'We wanted to get there before it got too late. We're visiting relatives.'

'We'll be there before nightfall,' the driver assured her.

Carl could see the little girl gazing raptly at the fire, watching the flames dancing wildly. As her mother continued to talk with the driver she slipped from her chair and moved slowly towards the fireplace, smiling conspiratorially at Carl who watched her in fascination. He supped more of his soup and thought what a beautiful little girl she was. Her long blonde hair was in two plaits and she wore a red-checked dress and shiny black shoes. Carl thought she looked like a doll. He waggled his fingers at her and she smiled even more broadly at him before coming closer to the fire.

When a small piece of burning coal dropped into the hearth the little girl looked at it in amazement, struck by the glowing bright red colour of the fuel. Mesmerised, she reached out a hand to pick it up.

Carl realised what was happening and jumped up from his seat as quickly as he could. He grabbed the child and lifted her away from the fireplace seconds before her fingers connected with the red-hot ember.

Surprised by this sudden intervention the child cried out.

All heads turned towards the sound.

'What are you doing?' the father snarled.

'Get away from her,' the mother snapped angrily.

Carl put down the child.

'She was going to burn herself,' he explained.

'How dare you touch her!' rasped the innkeeper's wife.

'I stopped her hurting herself,' Carl said, watching as the little girl was pulled into her mother's arms.

'Get out.' Another angry voice came from behind him, that of the innkeeper himself who had come out from behind the bar and was standing defiantly a yard or two behind Carl. 'Get out of here now. I told you to stay away from the other customers, didn't I?'

Carl hesitated a moment, then realised the futility of trying to explain what had happened. He grabbed his drink and downed what was left in the stein, some of it dribbling down his chin. Then he headed for the door, not meeting the glares of the other people as he passed.

'Don't come back here,' the innkeeper called after him. 'We don't need custom from the likes of you.'

Carl pulled open the door and paused there with his back to the others. Then he stepped across the threshold, closing the door behind him as he walked out into the biting cold once again.

Six

Victor Frankenstein stood at the window of his cell, gazing out into the darkness that had fallen over the land.

With that darkness had come a biting cold and the Baron shivered slightly as he remained immobile, his hands gripping the bars as if he were about to tear them away.

He managed a humourless smile. If only it had been that simple to escape this place. If there had been any way by now then he would have found it. He moved away from the window as he heard the bell in the prison clock tower tolling midnight. Another six hours and they would be coming for him. The escort would arrive to march him out into the courtyard where the guillotine would be waiting to snuff out his life for ever.

Six hours.

He swallowed hard, wondering if the emotion he was feeling was fear. It wasn't one that he was familiar with. Fear had never been a part of his life until recently. But then, he reasoned, in just over six hours' time nothing would ever bother him again. He banged helplessly with one fist on the thick stone wall of the cell. What a stupid way to die. It was the way common criminals met their end, not men of superior intellect like him. It was wrong that his life was to be ended with the pull of a handle by some illiterate fool. Anger overtook any vestiges of fear lurking within his mind and despite himself he couldn't help but see the supreme irony. He, Victor Frankenstein, the man who had given life to an inanimate corpse, was to be killed. The giver of life was to lose his own. Frankenstein shook his head. It was like someone killing God. He smiled to himself. How those fools in the town would have cursed and berated him if they knew he held himself on a level with God. How their small and ignorant minds would rebel against such a statement. And yet, when that guillotine blade fell in six hours' time, they would win. They and their outdated, moronic beliefs would have triumphed. That thought alone was enough to send him shaking to the other side of the cell.

He could still picture the men on the jury who had convicted him and he wished now that the creature he had created had killed them all. He wished that it had run amok in their village and slaughtered every last one of them and their stinking families. He closed his eyes, squeezing the lids together so tightly that white stars danced in the blackness before him.

'Fools,' he snarled aloud. 'Stupid ignorant fools.'

He sucked in a deep and angry breath and stood with his back pressed against the cell wall.

'Baron Frankenstein.'

The sound of his name caused him to jerk his head to one side and face in the direction from which the words had come.

Carl Lang was standing there, looking in at him. 'I heard you say something,' he confessed. 'I thought you called.'

'Just talking to myself, Carl,' Frankenstein told him. 'I find it's the only way to get any sensible conversation around here.'

The hunchback nodded and smiled. 'I can imagine, Baron,' he conceded. 'Especially a man of your intelligence.'

'You'd be alone in thinking me to be anything other than a crazed monster, Carl,' the Baron said.

'The people in the town call me a monster too,' Carl said quietly. 'I hate them for it.'

'And so you should. Ignorance should always be despised.'

'I don't understand the things you did but—'

Frankenstein cut him short.

'How much do you know, Carl? About me and about my work – other than the rumours and the pathetic talk of those in the town? Did any of them stop to think of the intellect, the sheer will involved in what I did?' Frankenstein shook his head. 'No, of course they didn't, because they could never countenance such intellect or will. How could they ever hope to understand what I did? They're frightened children, Carl. No more than that and yet because of them I will die six hours from now. And I tell you this: when that blade cuts through my neck any hope you ever had of leading a normal life will die too.'

'But it's impossible, what you said to me before,' Carl protested. 'My brain inside the body of another.'

'Not just a body, Carl. A better one. A *perfect* body. Imagine that. I learned so much the first time – there would be no mistakes if I tried again. There would be only perfection.'

'I can do nothing to help you, Baron. I wish I could.'

Frankenstein took a step towards the door, where Carl stood on the other side.

'Oh, but you *can* help me, Carl,' he said calmly. 'And if you do then I promise you I will use all my powers and my knowledge to help you. Get me out of here and two men will begin new lives. I promise you that.'

'How will you help me? You cannot put right what God has done to me.' Carl touched his withered arm with something close to revulsion. 'You cannot rid me of these burdens that I have carried since I was born.'

'Yes, I can, Carl. If you could see the laboratory in my castle you would see the equipment with which I would change not just your body but your life.'

'But even if I help you get out of here, if you return to your castle you will be discovered again before you can help me.'

'Do you think I would remain here? Surrounded by the same ignorant fools who have condemned me? The same men who condemned me have sentenced you too, Carl. They have ensured that by my death you will suffer for what is left of your life.'

'So where would you go?'

'We would travel to a place far away from here where I could work without hindrance and you would help me, Carl.' Frankenstein shrugged. 'But all this talk is pointless because when dawn breaks that is the end of me. Of both of us.'

Carl gripped the bars on the door and looked through at Frankenstein who had turned his back and was gazing in the direction of the window and the night sky beyond it.

'Do you ever think about death, Carl?' the Baron asked. 'Man is the only creature on this Earth able to contemplate his own mortality. I thought about that for years – that was why I began my work. I intended to conquer death, to banish it, and I succeeded.' He turned towards Carl. 'And I could succeed again with your help.'

Carl didn't speak. He merely looked at the Baron as he stood motionless in his cell.

Seven

Frankenstein hadn't expected to sleep that night but despite himself he had fallen into an unexpectedly deep slumber, propped in one corner of his cell. It was the sound of keys turning in the lock that now woke him.

As he blinked myopically and sat upright he realised that there was dull grey light filtering into the room from the barred window. It was the light of dawn and that realisation caused him to suck in a deep and racking breath. Dawn signalled the time of his execution and that time had finally come.

He scrambled to his feet, trying to maintain some kind of dignified appearance as the cell door was pushed open.

The Baron saw a small man clad in black priest's robes standing there, with Carl just behind him.

The priest was clutching a Bible and he took a couple of steps into the cell while Carl retreated back down the short corridor towards the guardroom.

'Good morning, my son,' the priest said quietly. He even managed a smile.

Frankenstein regarded him with a mixture of contempt and indifference. The cleric was in his forties, his face pudgy and ruddy-cheeked. He was losing his hair and there was a sizeable patch of bare skin visible at the top of his head, surrounded by greying strands.

'I thought you might want to talk,' the priest began, 'before . . .' He trailed off.

'Talk about what?' Frankenstein said.

'I wondered if you might want some spiritual comfort.'

'Keep your spiritual comfort for those who might think they need it. I have no use for it.'

'At this time, my son, all men should turn to God.'

'Why? What is God going to do for me, father? Is He going to reach down from Heaven and lift me out of this cell? What can God do that I can't?'

'That is blasphemy,' the priest said breathlessly. 'A man in your position would do better than blaspheme, my son. God will not look kindly upon that.'

Frankenstein shook his head. 'What do you want me to do – confess?' he sneered. 'Unburden my conscience before they cut my head off?'

'If that is what you wish to do then I will hear your confession.'

'Confession is about apologising, isn't it? Seeking forgiveness for wrongs that one has committed? Well, I did no wrong. There is nothing I want to apologise for. If I had the chance I would do the same things over again. The quest for knowledge should not be regretted and I regret nothing that I've done.'

'Not even the deaths you caused?'

Frankenstein exhaled wearily. 'If I told you what happened you wouldn't believe me,' he said. 'If I

35

attempted to explain what I did you would not be able to comprehend.' He looked directly at the priest. 'Do what you must, father. Do your duties and leave me in peace.'

The priest looked helplessly at Frankenstein and reached out a hand to touch his shoulder.

'I will pray for you, my son,' he intoned.

'Don't waste your breath, father,' the Baron told him.

There was movement near the door of the cell and Frankenstein looked up to see Carl shuffling into the room.

'It's time, Baron Frankenstein,' he said somewhat apologetically.

Frankenstein felt a slight shiver run the length of his spine. Then he swallowed hard and took a couple of paces towards the doorway where Carl was waiting. The priest followed, murmuring words that Frankenstein couldn't make out.

'Where are the other guards?' the Baron enquired.

'I volunteered to supervise your execution,' Carl told him. 'I'm the only one on duty until the others arrive in an hour's time. Everything is ready.'

Frankenstein nodded and began walking, leading the forlorn little procession along the short corridor to the guardroom and then beyond, into the prison courtyard. He faltered momentarily as he looked up at the guillotine that stood before him, the blade already hauled up and waiting between the two uprights. Beside the machine a tall man waited, his face hidden by a black mask. He had his hands clasped in front of him and his head was bowed as if in prayer. He didn't even look up when he heard the footfalls on the wooden steps that led up on to the platform.

Frankenstein saw a cheap wooden coffin at the bottom of the steps, its lid open to reveal bare wood within. It looked as if it had been hurriedly hammered together the previous night. Not that the quality of the box which would contain his earthly remains should trouble him, he mused. They could dump his body in a freshly dug hole and it would make no difference to him. Again he paused, his foot on the last of the five steps that led up to the wooden platform. He glanced again at the guillotine, then at the executioner who was still standing there with his head bowed.

Carl moved past him, up on to the platform, and the priest followed, still murmuring words of comfort, absolution and forgiveness.

Frankenstein joined them, standing close to the bassinet.

He glanced at Carl and the humpbacked guard held his gaze for long seconds.

Only now did the executioner raise his head.

Frankenstein looked at the hooded man. Then he glanced up at the gleaming slanted blade of the guillotine and, in spite of himself, he smiled.

A chill breeze swept across the prison courtyard.

Eight

'We'll do it tonight,' Fritz Hoffer grunted, slamming his half-empty stein down on the table.

Kurt Friesler took a swallow of his own ale and looked warily at his companion, both of them seemingly deaf to the raucous sounds that filled the tavern where they had both been sitting for the past two hours.

'What do you say?' Hoffer insisted.

'I don't know,' Friesler answered. 'I don't like it.'

'What's wrong with it?'

'There's nothing wrong with it, I just don't like it.'

'Look here, my old friend,' Hoffer said, leaning closer and prodding his companion's shoulder. 'You *are* my friend, aren't you?'

'Yes,' Friesler said quietly.

'Would I suggest it if it might go wrong?' Hoffer went on.

'Yes. Remember last time? You were supposed to watch in the street.'

'How was I to know they had dogs?' Hoffer said apologetically.

'I've still got the scars,' Friesler said, pulling at his jacket sleeve and trying to haul it up to display what he spoke of.

'We don't have to break in anywhere this time,' Hoffer persisted. 'It's all in the open – nothing can go wrong.'

'Last time I got six months. I can't do that again. I've had enough of it.'

Hoffer shrugged. 'All right, forget I ever mentioned it,' he sighed, sitting back. 'If you don't trust me I'll just have to do it on my own.'

Friesler got to his feet. 'Fine,' he belched. 'I'm going home.'

Hoffer gripped his arm and rubbed his own chest delicately. 'Of course, the doctor did say that I wasn't supposed to do anything to strain my heart.' He managed a thin smile and continued rubbing his chest.

'I'll see you tomorrow,' Friesler grunted, unimpressed by his friend's charade.

'And of course I would have the whole ten marks to myself,' Hoffer continued.

Friesler shot him a quizzical glance.

'Ten marks?' he slurred. 'You said six.'

'Six or ten – what does it matter? You're not coming with me, anyway.'

'Ten marks,' Friesler breathed, sitting down again. 'Ten.'

'I'm not creeping about in some graveyard in the dead of night,' Kurt said nervously.

'Why not?' Hoffer demanded. 'It wouldn't be the first time and it'll be worth our while, I promise you. Besides, where else are we going to find a dead body but in a graveyard?' He supped more ale, wiping froth from his bushy moustache when he'd finished.

'But why him? Why his body?' Kurt went on.

Hoffer looked at his thin-faced companion and then put a large hand on his shoulder and squeezed.

'They cut his head off this morning, Kurt.' He grinned. 'Frankenstein can't hurt you any more.'

'Then why not just leave him where he is? Let him rot in that grave.'

'He was a rich man,' Hoffer said, leaning closer to his companion. 'He'll have been buried with all manner of possessions on him. Possessions we can sell for good money.'

'What kind of possessions?'

'We won't know until we go and dig him up, will we?'

'And what if he's got nothing worth taking?'

'Then we'll have wasted our time, won't we? But I'm telling you, he was a very rich man and even if we only take his clothes we'll make enough to keep us in drink for another night at least.'

Hoffer took another huge swig of ale and then belched loudly.

'I bet the guards from the prison took anything worth stealing before they buried him,' Friesler grunted, gazing into the depths of his own stein. He remained in that contemplative pose for a while as Hoffer looked wearily at him, then smiled crookedly.

'Just because that was what you used to do when you worked at the prison,' he said, chuckling.

'I never stole anything,' Friesler said defensively. Then his face softened into a smile. 'Well, maybe one or two things.' Both men laughed.

'We'll finish these drinks, then we'll go and pay

Frankenstein a visit,' Hoffer said. He belched again and massaged his stomach with one grubby hand.

'I thought they would have buried him in the family vault up at his castle,' Friesler offered. 'Not in the graveyard outside the town with everyone else.'

'He was a criminal when he died. It doesn't matter if he was a baron, a count or a king. He broke the law and he suffered for it.'

Friesler nodded.

'Perhaps we should take a trip up to the castle another night,' Hoffer suggested. 'See what's up there that's worth taking. We could steal enough to make us both rich.'

'I'm not going near that place,' Friesler told him. 'I've heard too many stories about what he got up to there. I heard that he made some kind of pact with the Devil, that he was a black magician who could summon the dead.'

Hoffer grunted dismissively. 'Well, the Devil didn't help him much this morning, did he?' he snorted. 'If he had then Frankenstein would still be alive, not buried in some shallow grave for us to dig up.'

'Keep your voice down,' Friesler snapped, leaning closer to his friend and glancing around at some of the other denizens of the tavern. 'We don't want anyone to hear what we're going to do.'

Hoffer shrugged, downed what was left of his drink and once again belched loudly. Then he got to his feet.

'Come on, then – let's get it done,' he said, waiting as Friesler too stood up.

They headed towards the tavern door, picking their

way past the other drinkers. As they stepped outside into the chill night air both of them shivered involuntarily. The moon was hidden by thick banks of cloud; they would have the shelter of the darkness to hide them.

The journey to the graveyard would take less than thirty minutes.

Nine

'Slow down.'

Hoffer was gasping for breath by the time he and Friesler reached the cemetery. He was a big man and years of inactivity had contributed to the large gut that strained against his shirt and coat as he walked. Despite the chill of the night air he was sweating, wet beads popping onto his forehead and cheeks as he and his companion headed towards the small hut that stood just inside the main entrance of the necropolis. It was towards this structure that he now headed.

Friesler watched him as he paused at the door, sliding something metallic from his coat pocket. He snapped the lock holding the door shut with ease and slipped inside, emerging a moment later with two shovels. He tossed one towards Friesler who tried to catch it but missed. The metal clanged against the ground and the noise seemed to reverberate in the stillness.

Friesler turned, looked at his friend and muttered something under his breath before snatching up the shovel and brandishing it in both hands.

'Come on,' he said, agitated. 'I don't want to hang around here any longer than I have to.'

Hoffer caught him up, putting a hand to his chest as

he stood motionless. He coughed loudly and hawked, the lump of phlegm just missing a nearby gravestone. He pointed towards the far side of the graveyard, then started walking again, sticking to the narrow pathway that led through the centre of the large expanse of land.

The cemetery was surrounded by a low wooden fence, hedges and the low-hanging branches of trees, all of which combined to create a formidable barrier. The hedges needed cutting and some of the branches hung down as far as the dark earth – in fact, the whole place reeked of neglect. Grass grew knee-high in many places and Hoffer thought that the gravedigger should have taken his scythe and cut it down to make the place look more presentable. Some of the graves were marked only by bare wooden crosses, others by headstones. A few had fresh flowers on them, placed there by grieving relatives, but many were bare and unattended. Once you were in the ground no one remembered you, Hoffer thought as he and his companion trudged on.

The land sloped downwards slightly and at the bottom of the gentle incline there were several more graves but these were little more than mounds of earth: piles of dirt that covered shallow resting places, only a handful of which were marked by rudimentary crosses, some just by single pieces of wood jammed into the dirt to record the fact that someone lay beneath. The overgrown perimeter hedge seemed to be creeping across the land here too – these graves lay at the very edge of the cemetery. It was as if the remains of their inhabitants were not wanted near the bodies of the others who filled the place.

'There,' Hoffer said, pointing to these forlorn heaps of soil. 'That's where they put the ones from the prison.' He swung his shovel ahead of him and advanced towards these pitiful resting places, glancing at each of them. The dirt covering one looked particularly dark and rich and there were footprints in the mud around it. He drove his shovel into it, hurling earth away in an effort to reach the coffin below.

'Come on, help me,' he urged, gesturing to Friesler. 'It's this one. This one is Frankenstein's grave.'

'How can you be sure?' the other man wanted to know. 'We could be digging up anyone.'

'The dirt's freshly turned,' Hoffer assured him. 'No one else has been buried around here for months. Come on – dig.'

Friesler waited a moment, then started shovelling, muttering to himself under his breath.

The moon, which had been hidden behind thick cloud for most of the night, chose this moment to emerge and the cold white light it gave off illuminated the efforts of the two men as they dug deeper, piles of earth accumulating on either side of them as they struggled on with their task. Hoffer smiled triumphantly as his shovel finally struck something solid and he nodded at Friesler as he realised that they had reached their objective.

The cheap coffin had been buried only a couple of feet below the surface and Hoffer dropped to his knees now to scrape away the last of the soil with his hands. Friesler hurled his shovel to one side, his interest suddenly heightened by the actual sight of the box, and he stooped to help. Both men dragged the remaining clods away from the coffin lid. When it was clear Hoffer pulled from his pocket the same piece of metal he'd used to force the door of the gravedigger's hut and slid it beneath the lid. He used all his weight and it came free with ease, the wood groaning and snapping.

The two men looked at each other excitedly for a second and then Hoffer dragged the lid away. They both stared down into the box.

Friesler got to his feet and took a couple of steps backwards, his eyes bulging as he fixed his gaze on the contents of the coffin. Hoffer too stumbled away, taken aback by what he saw.

'What kind of game is this?' he gasped.

The body that lay in the coffin was that of a small man clad in black priest's robes that were stained with blood from top to bottom. Beside the corpse lay a severed head with a thin covering of grey hair. The eyes were still open and staring sightlessly at the two men who had disturbed it.

'A priest?' Friesler stammered. 'Where the hell is Frankenstein?'

Hoffer merely shook his head, his gaze still riveted on the decapitated body.

'Where is he?' Friesler repeated, raising his voice in anger and frustration.

Hoffer had no answer.

'Good evening, gentlemen.'

The words caused them both to turn.

'Oh my God,' Friesler gasped, gazing fixedly at the well-dressed tall man who stood close to the perimeter hedge, looking as if he had emerged from the dense foliage itself.

Victor Frankenstein smiled at the two men.

Hoffer merely shook his head as he backed away, trying to comprehend what had happened, wondering why such a sharp and crushing pain was building so quickly in the centre of his chest.

Frankenstein took a step towards him.

Hoffer felt incredible agony lance through him and he clutched at his torso as, inside his ribcage, his heart seemed to swell and then simply stop. He dropped to his knees before falling backwards into the grave, covering the body of the decapitated priest. Friesler turned and tried to run but he never saw the other figure looming up behind him.

Carl Lang snatched up one of the discarded shovels and swung it with tremendous power, bringing it down on the head of the terrified Friesler. The metal edge sheared effortlessly through the cranium and buried itself, the splintering of his skull clearly audible in the stillness of the night. Blood and tiny fragments of brain and pulverised bone flew into the air as Friesler fell hard, landing on his back, his body twitching.

Carl dragged the shovel free, then swung it down again, this time smashing in most of the man's forehead and driving one of his eyes back into its socket. Greyish-pink brain matter slopped onto the dark earth as the blood soaked into the dirt around Friesler. Carl prepared to strike again but when he looked more closely he saw that there was no need for a third blow.

Frankenstein looked down emotionlessly at the two

bodies, then at Carl who was still holding the shovel in front of him, blood dripping from its edge. Carl looked from the corpses to Frankenstein who merely nodded sagely and then pointed one finger at the bodies before him.

'Bury them, Carl,' the Baron said flatly. 'They wanted to see the inside of my grave and now they will.'

Propelled by the chill breeze, clouds scudded across the moon and the entire cemetery was once more cloaked in darkness.

THREE YEARS
LATER . . .

Ten

Professor Edward Brandt removed his metal-rimmed glasses and used the bottom of his long white coat to wipe away the smears on the lenses. He continued diligently and unhurriedly with his task, finally inspecting his work by holding the spectacles up in front of him. A shaft of light that was spearing through the large window to his right showed that the glass was now clean again. Brandt pushed the spectacles back onto his nose and turned towards the occupant of the bed nearest to him.

She was a woman in her mid-twenties. A thin scrawny specimen with tangled brown hair. Like most of the residents of the hospital she had bad skin and Brandt had concluded long ago that this was the product of bad nutrition. Bad food and not enough of it was the cause of many of the complaints suffered by the occupants of Carlsbruck's Hospital for the Poor. Any number of diseases that afflicted the needy, as well as accidents and violence, brought patients into the building. But all were cared for with the kind of expertise and compassion that people of such limited means could scarcely dream about normally. Good medical care had been the province of the rich in this large town until as recently as two years ago. Before that the poor had been forced to seek help from apothecaries if they could find one but even then they were usually unable to find the money to pay for the remedy that was recommended for them.

The foundation of the Hospital for the Poor had changed all that and Brandt had been a member of its staff since it had first opened its doors to unfortunates such as those it was now full of. Exactly how much the hospital had cost to set up he didn't know. Just as he didn't know where the benefactor who had initiated the purchase of the building had accumulated the necessary wealth. All that mattered to Brandt was that he personally had been able to help in this noble venture.

Of course, he still administered to the wealthy of Carlsbruck. But Brandt found his work with the poor more fulfilling and more in keeping with what had drawn him to medicine in the first place. The financial rewards of his profession might have been considerable but before coming to work at the Hospital for the Poor he had not felt so necessary to the common good. He felt that he mattered to these unfortunates to whom he gave his time. If not for men like himself many would surely have died, he mused. He felt now as if his work had meaning and worth – and not many men could say that as they went about their daily duties.

Brandt was a rotund man, some would have said fat, who moved slowly and with great deliberation as if every movement had to be given consideration before it was made. His face was red even when he was resting and the colour always deepened when he was working hard as he was this particular day. He looked at the young woman in the bed and smiled, his chubby cheeks swelling like rising bread.

'And how do you feel this morning, my dear?' he asked.

The girl coughed by way of reply.

Brandt handed her some water and she sipped it gratefully.

He reached for his stethoscope and pressed it to her chest and then her back, satisfied that the sounds he heard were consistent with a recovering patient.

'I think you'll be able to go home soon,' he told her. 'The fever you had has gone and you seem to be in much better health. I'll have to let my colleague examine you as well, though, before you can be allowed to leave.'

'Thank you, doctor,' she said softly. 'You're very kind. Not like the other doctor.'

Brandt looked puzzled.

'He never says much to me,' the girl went on. 'He always seems as if he's in a hurry.'

'He's a busy man,' Brandt told her.

'He's a cold-hearted bastard.'

The words came from behind Brandt and he turned to see a man in his thirties glaring at him.

'I agree,' someone else added. 'He always seems as if he's doing us a favour by helping us. He's not like you, doctor.'

Brandt was about to say something when another man spoke up.

'What about me?' a loud voice called from the next bed. 'When can I go home?'

Brandt turned and saw a man lying there with his left leg in plaster from the hip to the ankle.

'Not for a while, my friend,' the doctor said, turning his attention to him. 'You broke your leg in three places when you fell from that roof. You'll be with us for some time, I fear.'

'If he hadn't been stealing lead from that roof he wouldn't have fallen off it,' another voice from the other side of the ward called and there was a chorus of raucous laughter to accompany the remark. The shout had come from a large man with lank brown hair who was moving none too busily between the beds, sweeping up.

'Shut up, Meyer, you fat pig,' the man in plaster called back.

Meyer raised his broom menacingly and snorted loudly.

'You should be thanking me,' he grunted. 'I'm the one who keeps this pigsty clean.'

'You call this clean?' the man in plaster retorted. 'It's about as clean as you.'

A number of the other patients laughed.

Brandt held up his hand for quiet and was rewarded eventually with a low murmuring of conversation within the ward.

'People are trying to rest in here,' he said. 'Please keep your voices down.'

'Sorry, doctor,' the man in plaster said. 'But I don't like it here in hospital.'

'And where would you rather be?' Brandt asked.

'I'm a sailor,' the man told him. 'I've been at sea since

I was a boy. I don't like being shut in like this. It smells in here, too.'

'*You* smell,' Meyer shouted.

'Well, you won't be going back to sea until you can walk out of here on your own,' Brandt said to the man in plaster.

The man nodded and Brandt moved to the next bed.

There were twenty beds in each of the wards that made up the hospital and a total of forty patients could be accommodated at any one time. On the lower floor of the building there was a surgery that doubled as a consulting room, an operating room and several offices where Brandt and his colleagues also worked. On that same floor was the office of the head of the hospital, the man who had been responsible for its opening. He was down there now, as far as Brandt knew. He worked longer hours than anyone else at the hospital as if he needed to set an example to the others who toiled there. He was always first to arrive in the mornings and invariably the last to leave at night. Brandt knew little about his background and the two men had not socialised much during the past three years. There had never seemed to be time. There was always so much work to do at the hospital. And yet Brandt was fascinated by the man about whom he knew so little. Intrigued by his enthusiasm and drive and captivated by his devotion to his work. There was, he guessed, much more to this man than he knew.

He came from a different part of the country, that much Brandt did know, but from exactly where he had no idea. He had arrived in Carlsbruck and within six months of his arrival he had purchased the building that had become the Hospital for the Poor. After that he had approached various local physicians and asked them to help him in his work with the needy and, unlike Brandt, many had refused. For them the financial rewards were the only ones they needed. They had no burning desire to help those less fortunate than themselves. There was nothing altruistic in their motives. But Brandt was different and he had been only too willing to offer his expertise even if it had incurred the disapproval of the Carlsbruck Medical Council.

Brandt smiled to himself as he thought about that august but somewhat pompous and self-important group of men. They seemed to hold no fear for the benefactor of this Hospital for the Poor. He had been unimpressed by them from the time he'd arrived. That was another of the things that Brandt liked about him if he was truthful.

He moved from bed to bed, speaking with each patient and examining them when he had to.

He paused at the end of the ward and looked back at the patients, satisfied that he had once again been able to help them. His rounds would continue in the ward on the floor above.

Brandt nodded warmly to the nurse who bustled past him and she smiled back.

'How are you today?' he wanted to know.

'I'm very well, doctor,' she told him, disappearing into the ward he'd just left.

Brandt was about to say something else when he became aware of a figure on the stairs to his left.

'Professor,' the newcomer said. 'Have you a minute to spare, please?'

Brandt nodded. 'Of course I have, Doctor Stein,' he said and walked towards the man.

Baron Victor Frankenstein smiled broadly at him.

Eleven

Frankenstein's office in the hospital was reached by descending a flight of broad stone steps that led down to another level mostly occupied by storerooms – apart from the operating room, the surgery-cum-consulting room and several other offices.

It was in this office that the Baron and Professor Brandt now sat, Frankenstein seated behind his large desk with his back to a wooden door.

Beyond the door there was another flight of steps that led down to a cellar which was kept locked and was the domain solely of Frankenstein and those he deemed worthy to enter it. Brandt himself had seen the laboratory that lay below them once or twice but not for at least three months. Despite his admiration for the Baron's concerns for the needy he had little or no interest in his work beyond that.

Perhaps that was just as well.

Frankenstein crossed to one side of his office and poured himself a small glass of wine, gesturing towards the other glass there.

Brandt nodded and accepted the claret when Frankenstein handed it to him.

'Thank you, Doctor Stein,' he said, sipping the wine and nodding approvingly. 'An excellent vintage.'

Frankenstein smiled and took a sip of his own before reseating himself behind his desk.

'I've had an invitation from the Carlsbruck Medical Council,' the Baron began. 'They want me to address their next meeting.'

'That's interesting. On what subject?'

'My dear Brandt, they have no interest in my views on any subject.' Frankenstein smiled. 'They have invited me purely and simply so they can question me about my work here in Carlsbruck.'

'Perhaps they're thinking of asking you to join them.'

'Even if they did I would refuse. I have no desire to mingle with men like that. I certainly don't care for their blinkered views on medicine.'

'I think they're more concerned with the fact that you've taken half their patients since you arrived here,' Brandt chuckled.

'If I offer a better service than they do I cannot be blamed,' Frankenstein said. 'Besides, you know that my work here is financed by what I earn from administering to those with more resources.'

'So will you attend?'

'I'll see. If I can spare them an hour or so from my work here then I might. But I have far more important things to do than spend my time in the company of such a collection of pompous, self-serving windbags.'

Brandt grinned.

'If only they could hear what you say about them, Doctor Stein,' he said, 'they'd force you out of Carlsbruck.'

'They'd try,' Frankenstein murmured. 'But what have I to fear from any of them? The hospital is flourishing. The poor are as well cared for as any of the rich and privileged whom the Medical Council chooses to treat.' He took a sip of his wine. 'I need nothing from them.'

'Couldn't they stop other doctors or nurses from joining you here?'

'They couldn't stop *you*.'

'I'm an old man coming to the end of my career,' Brandt said quietly. 'I have retirement to look forward to. I chose to work with you because I admired what you were trying to do. Younger doctors may feel differently. If the Medical Council blocks their attempts to help you or threatens their careers you may find yourself working alone – even a man as skilled and driven as yourself would find it hard to maintain this hospital with the limited number of staff you have now.'

Frankenstein didn't answer; he merely gazed down at his wine glass as he ran one index finger around the rim.

'Go and speak to them,' Brandt went on. 'What harm can it do? They may even offer to help you.'

Frankenstein raised an eyebrow questioningly.

'I have all the help I need,' he said, raising his glass in salute. 'As long as I have you, professor, I can continue. The workload is manageable. If you decide to desert me I shall simply find someone else.'

Both men laughed.

'I'm sure you would find many willing to be of service,' Brandt said.

Even if they knew who I really was?

Frankenstein smiled thinly.

How many would be eager to aid me, professor, if they knew I had escaped the guillotine for performing experiments that even you would find shocking and blasphemous?

'Well, I trust you have no plans to leave me in the near future, professor,' the Baron went on.

'None at all,' Brandt assured him, finishing his glass of wine and setting down the empty receptacle on the desk.

There was a knock on the office door and Brandt turned.

'Come in,' Frankenstein called and the door opened slightly.

Carl Lang stuck his head inside, saw Brandt and then retreated again.

'I'm sorry to bother you, Doctor Stein,' he said apologetically. 'I'll come back when you've finished.'

'That's all right, Carl,' Frankenstein said. 'You have nothing to say to me that I don't want the professor to hear.'

Carl nodded and shuffled into the room.

As he normally did, Brandt looked at the humpbacked man with a combination of pity and professional curiosity. He and Frankenstein had discussed the man's deformity before and also the possibility of some kind of surgery that might lessen the disfigurement. But Brandt was convinced that the poor man was doomed to remain misshapen and crippled until the day he died. Frankenstein had insisted there was a way to help him but had never been too specific about the matter as far as the professor remembered.

'Is there a problem, Carl?' Frankenstein asked.

'A man was here earlier wanting to speak to you,' Carl told him. 'A young man. Well dressed and well spoken.'

'What did he want?' Frankenstein asked.

'He wouldn't tell me,' Carl replied. 'He said that he had to see you personally and that it was important.'

'And he didn't leave his name?'

Carl shook his head.

'I told him you were busy . . .' The humpbacked man let the sentence trail off.

'Well, if it's that important he'll come back, won't he?' Frankenstein offered. 'You didn't recognise him, Carl?'

'No, Doctor Stein.'

Brandt looked at each man in turn and wondered why both their expressions had darkened a little.

'If you see him again, let me know immediately,' Frankenstein instructed.

Carl nodded dutifully.

'Was there anything else?' the Baron went on.

'Some more of the equipment you ordered has arrived,' Carl said.

'Tell them to leave it at the back of the hospital; we'll move it down to the cellar tonight.'

Again Carl nodded, then turned and headed back out of the door.

'More equipment for your private research, Doctor Stein?' Brandt mused. 'When are you going to share it with others?'

'It's nothing worth talking about,' Frankenstein said quietly. 'Just some work I've been conducting.'

'Concerning what?'

'When I feel the time is right I'll share my findings with you, professor.'

'You're a secretive man sometimes, Doctor Stein.'

'Not all secrets are to be shared.'

He smiled and poured the professor another glass of wine.

'Carl has been with you for some time now, hasn't he?' Brandt observed, cradling the wine glass in his hand for a moment before sipping from it.

'Ever since I arrived in Carlsbruck,' Frankenstein acknowledged. 'He's been a great help around the hospital.'

'If you don't mind me asking, how did you become friendly with a man like him?'

'It's a long story, professor, and I'm not about to bore you with it now. As I said, he's been a great help to me in many ways over the last three years. It's probably safe to say that without him I wouldn't be here now.'

'His condition is irreversible, I suspect. The deformity and the skin problems look severe.'

'A time may come when something can be done for him. I think he realises that.'

'Perhaps your secret research may help him,' Brandt said, laughing.

Frankenstein smiled. 'It may well, professor,' he said, raising his glass in salute. 'It may well.'

Twelve

The underground laboratory was huge.

Worktops and benches, operating tables and display units filled the vast subterranean room, almost all of them crammed with equipment or specimens. Most of the equipment would have appeared alien to the untrained and less than expert eye but Frankenstein knew every inch of the laboratory and everything inside it. He had spent the last three years assembling the array of material that he needed for his experiments and now he stood surveying the underground domain like a self-appointed monarch.

This was where his true work was carried out. Work that he could share with no one. What lay down here was the product of his own specialised genius and would, in time, see the culmination of everything he believed in and strove for.

He glanced across to where Carl was dragging a large glass display case into position.

'Be careful with that,' he snapped, jabbing an impatient finger towards the humpbacked man and the heavy load he was struggling with.

Carl merely nodded and succeeded in lifting the case up onto a worktop nearby. Then he turned and looked towards Frankenstein as if awaiting further instructions.

'That's the last of it, doctor,' he said, wiping sweat from his forehead with the sleeve of his jacket.

'Good,' Frankenstein said quietly, nodding to himself.

Carl moved closer to the doctor and glanced around the laboratory, his eyes focusing on several of the display cases and the rows of test tubes on view.

'Doctor,' he began, quietly. 'You said that the time would come—'

'And it will, Carl,' Frankenstein snapped, cutting him off. 'But not yet. You must be patient.'

'I've been patient for three years, doctor. How much longer do I have to wait?'

'My work takes time, Carl,' Frankenstein reminded him, his tone even. 'You know that. When the time is right I will act. Didn't I promise you I would help you?'

'You promised me three years ago.'

'If you are tired of waiting, Carl, then I suggest you leave here. Walk away – but who else is going to help you? Who else can free you from that twisted, deformed body you inhabit? Do you think there are any other doctors in Carlsbruck who can do what I can do?' He sucked in a deep breath. 'No one else in the world can do what I can do, Carl. No one else can help you – and why would they want to?'

Carl clenched his fists but kept silent.

'I just thought—' he said finally. But again Frankenstein interrupted him.

'Well, don't think, Carl,' he hissed. 'Leave the thinking

to me. You are here to help me and in time I will help you. Didn't I always promise that?'

Carl didn't answer.

'Well, didn't I?' Frankenstein pressed, his tone darkening.

Carl nodded.

'There is more work to be done yet, Carl,' the Baron went on. 'If you are to have the kind of life you dream of then you must trust me.'

'I do.'

'Then don't question me,' Frankenstein rasped.

The two men regarded each other silently for a moment. Then Carl spoke again.

'Does Professor Brandt know what kind of work you are doing here?' he asked.

'Brandt is a good man but what I will accomplish here in this laboratory will be beyond even his considerable intellect and understanding,' Frankenstein stated. 'But when it's finished the whole world will see and it will marvel, Carl. The medical profession will look in awe at what I have achieved, as will the rest of the world. And you will be there with me, Carl.'

The hunchback nodded. 'So the professor doesn't know about your work?' he enquired.

'What I do in this laboratory is private. That privacy extends to Professor Brandt.'

'What would he say if he knew the truth?'

Frankenstein fixed the hunchback with an unwavering stare.

'He won't know the truth until I choose to reveal it

to him, Carl,' the Baron said. 'And that is how it must remain. Do you understand?'

Carl nodded.

'You may go now,' Frankenstein told him. 'I have some work to do here.'

'Yes, doctor,' Carl murmured.

The Baron turned towards the worktop nearest to him and Carl shuffled towards the flight of stone steps that led out of the cellar. When he reached the top he paused and looked back at Frankenstein. He waited there for long moments, his gaze fixed on the Baron who was peering through a microscope. Then, slowly and almost resignedly, he left through the single door out of Frankenstein's office, closing it quietly behind him. He stood in the darkness outside the office for a moment, then trudged slowly away.

As he walked along the corridor outside the office he glanced around, the silence of the hospital at night closing around him like an invisible glove. Somewhere he could hear guttural snoring coming from one of the wards and also what seemed to be a low weeping.

It sounded as if someone was in pain.

Carl knew how they felt.

Thirteen

Professor Edward Brandt sipped at his wine and looked down at the remains of the meal on the plate before him.

He rubbed his chest lightly and belched quietly.

'I do apologise, my dear,' he said, looking across the dining-room table at his wife who smiled as reproachfully as she could.

'I hope that isn't a comment on my cooking,' she said.

'Your cooking is as good now as it was when we were first married twenty years ago,' Brandt told her, pouring himself more wine and sipping it. 'I just have a touch of indigestion.'

'Are you eating properly at lunchtimes?' his wife asked. 'I hope that Doctor Stein isn't making you work too hard at that hospital of his.'

Brandt smiled thinly and touched his chest again, clearing his throat too before downing more wine.

'You should ask him to dinner again sometime, Edward,' Martha Brandt suggested. 'He seemed very charming the last time he was here.'

'That's one thing Doctor Stein isn't short of, my dear: charm.' Brandt coughed lightly again. 'And he's going to need all the charm he can manage when he goes before the Carlsbruck Medical Council. They've invited him to speak at their next meeting.'

'They've been against him since he arrived here in Carlsbruck. Why? As far as I can see he's done nothing but good with his treatment of the poor.'

'That's the problem. Stein's Hospital for the Poor and his care for them merely highlight the lack of care that the Medical Council afford to the same people. What he does out of the kindness of his heart they see as a slight against them.'

'I just hope that he remembers how much you help him in his work.'

'He's a good man and he appreciates what I do at the hospital.'

'Be careful you don't anger the Medical Council by helping him, Edward.'

'There's nothing they could do to me, my dear. I have my own patients outside the hospital just as Doctor Stein does. And the Council can't prevent me from treating them. The money that those patients pay me is more than enough.'

'I heard that Doctor Stein is to call on Countess Namarov. She says that she is plagued by pains in her back and she wants him to help her.'

'For the right price I'm sure he will. His motives are less than altruistic when it comes to dealing with the rich of Carlsbruck.' Brandt smiled and rubbed his chest again.

'But he's a wealthy man himself, isn't he?' Martha observed. 'How else could he have set up the Hospital for the Poor? Where did his money come from?'

'I don't know. If I'm completely honest I don't even know which part of the country he's from. He never speaks of his life before he came to Carlsbruck.'

'You must know something about him, Edward. You work with him every day and I'm sure that he spoke of some family in the south of the country when he was here that night.'

'Then you have a better memory than I have, my dear. What was said at a dinner party three years ago is beyond my powers of recall, I'm afraid.' Brandt sat back in his chair. 'No, he never speaks of anything other than his work at the hospital and his research – and he's rather guarded about that, now I come to think of it.'

'What kind of research?'

'As I say, he doesn't speak of it. All he'll say is that when it's finished it will be something to marvel at.' Brandt shrugged. 'We shall have to wait and see.'

'But he doesn't ask for your help with the research?'

'No. He prefers to work alone where that's concerned. The only other person involved is Carl, the hunchback who works and lives at the hospital. They seem to be good friends, although it's difficult to see how two men so different came to be companions in the first place. But Doctor Stein won't talk about that, either.'

'He sounds like a very secretive man.'

'I'm sure he has his reasons, my dear.'

Martha looked across at her husband as he sipped his wine once more. She smiled at him.

However, that smile vanished a second later when she saw his face contort with obvious pain. He let out a gasp and clutched at his chest with both hands, the wine glass dropping from his grip and shattering to spread the red colour of its contents over the expensive white tablecloth.

'Edward!' she said, getting to her feet in alarm.

He could only groan by way of reply.

'What is it?' she cried, reaching out to him.

Brandt's face had turned the colour of milk and his eyes rolled upwards in their sockets as he clenched his teeth together so hard that it seemed they would shatter. He let out another low groan and pitched forward, his head slamming into the table as his heart finally gave out.

Martha screamed.

Professor Edward Brandt was dead before she even reached him.

Fourteen

From the window of his room in the attic of the hospital, Carl Lang could see the lights burning in the house across the street.

And he knew what those lights meant. They glowed behind the thick curtains set at each window but, even so, Carl knew what went on inside that house. He was aware of the reasons why so many men arrived at the house, especially during the hours of darkness.

Many a night he had sat at his window and watched visitors as they came and went. He had seen the women leave too, sometimes climbing into waiting carriages with the men who had paid for their company. Yes, Carl Lang knew what went on behind those dimly lit windows and he realised that the girls inside that house would be prepared to spend time with any man if the price was right.

Any man? Even one as grotesque and twisted as you?

He looked at his bedside table and the coins that were there. There were five gold crowns laid out and it had taken Carl months to save such a sum. He reached for them with a shaking hand and pushed them into the pocket of his coat. He hesitated for a moment, then turned and headed for the door of his tiny room. There was barely enough space to fit anything in apart from the single bed wedged up against one wall but to Carl this tiny dwelling was his home and it was, he remembered, considerably better than most of the places in which he had spent his life so far.

He made his way out of the attic room and down the narrow flight of wooden steps that led to the second floor of the hospital. From inside one of the wards he could hear loud snoring interspersed with coughs and groans. The usual night-time symphony of suffering and slumber. Two of the nurses would make their rounds in less than thirty minutes and Carl wanted to be gone by then. He didn't want to see anyone and he didn't want anyone to witness him leaving. Especially not the nurses. He didn't want them to know where he was going. What would they think of him? Would they understand how appallingly lonely he was in his tiny room every night and look kindly upon his need for companionship with a woman in the house nearby? No, they would despise him for his base appetites, he was sure of it. Carl did not want that.

He made his way down the broad stone steps that would take him to the hospital exit at the rear of the building.

'Where are you going?'

The voice echoed through the corridor, bouncing off the walls and reverberating in Carl's ears.

He turned to see the source of the voice.

The man who was walking towards him was in his mid-fifties. Overweight and with pockmarked skin, he was carrying a long wooden stick that was secured to his wrist by a thick length of leather twine that had been threaded through one end of the stick and then wound around the lower end of his arm.

Carl hesitated for a moment, then shambled on.

'I asked where you were going,' Meyer rasped. He was a large hulk of a man who had been janitor at the hospital for the last year. He had a small office on the ground floor of the building where he sometimes slept, usually drunk after his nightly rounds.

'None of your business,' Carl told him.

'Sneaking out at this time of night,' Meyer went on. 'You must be up to no good.' He laughed throatily. 'Are you going to see your girlfriend?'

Carl eyed him with a mixture of disgust and anger.

'But then again,' Meyer added contemptuously, 'what kind of girl would go near you?' He laughed again.

'Why don't you just do your job and mind your own business?' Carl snapped, stepping away from the big man.

'I *am* doing my job. Perhaps I should report you to Doctor Stein; he might wonder where you were going at this time of the morning.'

Carl held the big man's gaze for a moment longer, then turned and made his way down the wide flight of steps towards the hospital exit. Behind him he could hear Meyer's derisive laughter echoing loudly.

Carl hurried out onto the street and stood motionless for a moment, sucking in the night air as he struggled to control his fury. He clenched his fists until the nails dug into his palms, his breathing gradually slowing as he leaned back against the door.

It was cold and he shivered involuntarily as he stood gazing at the buildings near the hospital, in particular the house with the lights burning behind its curtains. That was where he knew he wanted to be but there was something inside him that prevented him making the short journey to the building. Carl knew that it was fear he was feeling. He dug a hand into his coat pocket and felt the coins there.

They won't care what you look like if you give them money. Money is all they care about.

He swallowed hard and moved out into the street towards the front door of the house he sought. There was a short path leading up to the door and Carl paused again, gazing up at the building, watching the windows where lights burned and wondering exactly what was going on behind the thick curtains that masked that light.

What are you going to do, stand here all night?

Again he touched the coins in his pocket as if they were some kind of lucky charm that would imbue him with the strength and courage to approach the door of the brothel. A cold breeze swept down the street and Carl shuddered again, hesitating.

Come on. They don't care what you look like. You've got money and that's all they want.

He walked to the house and knocked loudly. From inside he heard the sounds of movement and a woman's voice muttering, then the sound of the door being unlocked. The door swung open and he found himself confronted by a large woman in her forties. Her pitted skin was covered by a layer of pale make-up so thick that it looked as if it had been applied with a trowel.

Even then it wasn't thick enough to cover the wrinkles around her eyes and the corners of her mouth.

'What do you want?' she asked, sniffing loudly.

'I want to come in,' Carl said. 'I want a girl.'

The woman grinned crookedly.

'I know you,' she said. 'You work over at the hospital, don't you? I've seen you around here before.'

Carl nodded.

'I've got money,' he said, thrusting his hand into his pocket to pull out the coins.

The woman regarded them indifferently, then nodded.

'Come in,' she said.

Carl hesitated on the doorstep, his mouth dry and his hands trembling slightly.

'Well, come on,' the woman urged. 'You're letting the cold in.' She pushed the door open wider and urged him to enter, which he finally did.

As he stepped inside the brothel the first thing that struck Carl was the overwhelming smell of perfume. The air was heavy with it. A scent so strong that it was difficult to breathe at first. He felt as if he was choking. The woman motioned towards a door on his right and almost shoved him in that direction.

'What kind of girl do you want?' she asked as she bustled along behind Carl. 'I don't suppose you're too fussy, are you?'

Carl didn't speak but instead allowed himself to be ushered through into the room beyond the door that the woman had indicated. It was a salon with red carpets and curtains and in here the gas lamps were turned down low, unlike the ones in the hallway. There were several chairs and a chaise longue upholstered in red velvet that matched the thick curtains. The whole room looked as if it had been decorated with congealed blood and, like everywhere else in the house, it reeked of perfume.

'You sit down there,' the woman suggested, motioning to one of the chairs. 'Do you want a drink while you're waiting?' She pointed towards some decanters set on a dark wood sideboard near the open fireplace.

Carl shook his head.

'I'll go and find out which of the girls is free,' the woman told him. 'What kind did you say you wanted?'

Carl could only shrug helplessly.

'I know who you'd like,' the woman cackled. 'I'll get Heidi. She's just your type.' She stepped out of the room, closing the door behind her.

Carl stood motionless in the centre of the room, looking around him. There were several prints on the walls showing naked women in various positions. He crossed to the nearest of them and ran one shaking index finger over the outline of the painting's subject, concentrating on her face. He wondered if the girl worked here in this brothel. She was beautiful. Raven-haired, slender and with a welcoming smile. Carl was more entranced by the smile than he was by the bare breasts that were on show in the picture. It was as if the girl in the painting was smiling just at him. He touched the painted lips with his finger, then brushed that digit against his own mouth.

He looked at the other paintings on the walls. He looked at the breasts and the legs but he was most fascinated by the faces. Carl touched one hand to his own face and felt the shrivelled skin there.

You don't belong here.

He tried to swallow but his throat was dry.

He looked down at his withered arm, the fingers clenched into a claw, the skin blemished and rough.

Carl turned towards the door of the salon. The eyes of the girls in the paintings suddenly felt as if they were burning into him. They weren't welcoming any more – they were accusing and angry. There was no warmth there now, just disgust and revulsion. Carl stood in the centre of the room and bowed his head.

He heard movement on the stairs. He could hear raised voices. Women's voices.

He dragged open the salon door and hurried towards the main door of the brothel, dashing out as quickly as he could into the street and the cold night air. The blackness closed around him. It welcomed him because he knew that was where he belonged. In the shadows, hidden from others. He heard the woman shouting something after him but he couldn't make out the words. He knew he had been a fool to go to the brothel in the first place. He didn't belong there.

Behind him he heard the brothel door slam shut.

Fifteen

Frankenstein stood by the graveside, glancing around surreptitiously at the other mourners and studying each one individually.

As he had known, Professor Edward Brandt had been a popular man and that popularity was evident in the number of people who now clustered around the grave to pay their respects to the dead man and to his widow. Frankenstein stood close to Martha Brandt, as he had done throughout the funeral service during which she had barely stopped crying. An understandable reaction, the Baron thought, but nevertheless her persistent weeping was becoming a little wearing now and nothing that anyone had said or done had been able to stem the flow of tears. If he was honest, Frankenstein would be pleased when the ceremony was over, even if only to rid himself of this poor distraught woman and her wailing.

More than once during the ceremony he had contemplated an idea that had been with him since he was much younger. The whole idea of a funeral seemed pointless as far as he was concerned. Losing someone close was bad enough but then, a few days later, the pain that might have eased slightly was reignited when the funeral took place. How much easier it would be simply to transport the deceased straight to a graveyard upon their death, bury them then and there, and allow those who wished to pay their respects to do so at a later date, rather than have to endure the archaic and painful ritual that was a funeral. Looking again at Martha Brandt and her tear-streaked face, Frankenstein grew even more fervent in his belief that all funerals should be abolished. And the pointless words uttered by the priest did nothing to help, either. No amount of consoling words could ever bring back the deceased and that was what caused the grief, after all. That knowledge of the complete and utter finality of death.

Frankenstein suppressed a smile. A finality that he himself had managed to conquer. His work had allowed him to defeat death. His years of research and dedication had ensured that. Perhaps in time everyone would learn that the inevitability of death was only apparent and was not something to be feared. There was something beyond it – and he didn't mean the pathetic promises of Heaven or the perceived threat of Hell. One life would end and another would begin in a different body. It was that simple.

He lowered his gaze briefly, peering down at the dark earth of the graveyard, earth that very soon would be shovelled onto the coffin of Edward Brandt. When he looked up again he was aware that someone on the other side of the grave was looking at him.

It was a man in his late twenties. He was smartly dressed and when Frankenstein caught his eye the younger man touched the brim of his top hat in salute almost reverentially. The Baron nodded by way of acknowledgement, wondering who the man was.

He was standing with several members of the Carlsbruck Medical Council who Frankenstein did recognise. Pompous fools. He wondered how genuine their grief was at the passing of Brandt. Perhaps they were merely here to gloat, to rejoice in the fact that Frankenstein himself had lost his one true ally in the town.

Again he held back a wry smile. If they imagined that was going to handicap him then they were even more idiotic than he had originally thought.

The priest was still droning on, murmuring platitudes and speaking of how Heaven awaited Brandt. But Frankenstein only looked contemptuously at the black-robed man as he stood at the head of the grave murmuring his practised words. There was nothing awaiting Brandt except decomposition, Frankenstein thought. His company from this point on would not be angels – it would be the graveyard's worms and rats. Martha Brandt began weeping with fresh gusto as if she knew that Frankenstein was right. There would be no joyful reunion with her husband in Heaven, only the lonely chill of her own grave when that time came.

It wasn't a smile that Frankenstein had to stifle now but a yawn. He covered his mouth with one gloved hand and leaned closer to Martha, sliding his arm around her shoulders.

'I'm afraid I must leave now,' he said softly. 'I must get back to the hospital.'

'Thank you for coming, Doctor Stein,' she said tearfully. 'Edward always thought very highly of you.'

'And I of him. He will be sadly missed.'

Frankenstein's words triggered another flood of tears and he stepped back to allow a relative to take his place as support to the grieving woman. The Baron nodded affably and moved away from the crowd of mourners, heading towards the dirt track that led through the centre of the graveyard and towards its main entrance. He had taken barely ten steps when he became aware of someone striding after him.

'Doctor.'

Frankenstein turned to see that the young man he had noticed on the other side of the grave was heading towards him.

The man was smiling warmly as he extended his right hand. 'Doctor, my name is Hans Kleve,' he announced.

Frankenstein shook the offered hand and nodded.

'*Doctor* Hans Kleve,' the man added.

'I'm very glad to meet you, doctor,' Frankenstein said. 'I wish I could stop and talk but I have to get back to my hospital.'

'I imagine that the death of Doctor Brandt is a blow to you in more ways than one. He helped you at your Hospital for the Poor, didn't he?'

'Yes, he did. He was a good man. I shall miss him and so will my patients, I'm sure.'

'I assume you'll be looking for someone to replace him.'

Frankenstein eyed the younger man warily for a moment.

'I'd like to volunteer my services,' Kleve went on.

'What would the Medical Council say, Doctor Kleve?

I noticed you standing with some of their members – surely they wouldn't approve of you offering to help me. I'm not exactly welcomed by them here in Carlsbruck, you know.'

'I don't care what they think.'

Frankenstein smiled. 'I'm afraid I haven't the time to discuss this now, doctor,' he said, turning away.

'At least say that you'll consider me for the position,' Kleve said, a thin smile on his lips. 'I may be young but I'll be of great help to you. I've already called at the hospital trying to speak to you but I was told you were busy.'

Frankenstein nodded and turned away, walking quickly towards the graveyard entrance.

Kleve watched him go, the smile slipping from his face.

'You should consider me, you really should,' he muttered darkly. 'For your own sake.'

Sixteen

The estate of Countess Maria Namarov was a twenty-minute carriage ride from the town of Carlsbruck. It was approached via the narrow roads that led from the town into the surrounding country-side and then, once those had been negotiated, by a wide driveway that led through the grounds to the house itself.

As the carriage trundled along the driveway, Frankenstein glanced out of the window and peered towards the looming edifice of the house. It was a magnificent structure, its many windows reflecting the morning sunshine and forcing him to shield his eyes briefly.

To the right, shaded by widely spaced trees, lay a huge ornamental lake that stretched away into the distance, while on the rolling hills that rose towards the rear of the house there were stables. Frankenstein could see several of the horses that were kept in these buildings being exercised on the slopes as he looked more closely. A veritable army of gardeners was swarming over the grounds, engaged in tasks that ranged from raking away fallen leaves to trimming the many topiary animals that lined the driveway and decorated the ornamental gardens like so many green-clad sentinels.

The scent of flowers and cut grass reached his nostrils as the carriage swung around towards the front of the house. Frankenstein let himself out as the conveyance came to a halt and he stood for a moment admiring the opulent building before he made his way towards the short flight of broad stone steps that led up to the oak doors.

The similarity to his old home was not lost on him. The Namarov estate was no more grand than his own family's had been and for a few fleeting seconds Frankenstein felt a twinge of an emotion that he couldn't readily identify. Was it regret or sadness that he would never see his home again? He shook his head. His home was here in Carlsbruck now and, once his work had been seen and acknowledged, then the time might well come when he could return to his ancestral home and all its magnificence. The fools who had condemned him three years earlier would be forced to apologise and to accept his genius. When the time came it would be his choice whether or not he returned. He smiled to himself as he approached the house. Perhaps he would just buy this place and live here, he mused. The old Countess wasn't much longer for this world as far as he knew. The property might well be vacant soon.

Frankenstein pulled the long metal chain that hung beside the front doors and heard a bell ring inside the house. Moments later a flustered-looking butler opened the doors and bowed courteously.

'I'm here to see Countess Namarov,' Frankenstein stated. 'My name is Doctor Stein.'

'If you'd follow me, please, sir,' the butler intoned. 'The Countess is expecting you.'

Frankenstein nodded and allowed himself to be led through the vast hallway of the house towards a set of double doors that opened into an equally cavernous drawing room.

Seated near a set of wide French windows was Countess Namarov. From her vantage point she could see across the wide lawn at the rear of the house and up onto the hills where the stables lay. As she heard the doors of the drawing room open she turned and saw the butler approaching with Frankenstein close behind. She prepared to rise but Frankenstein shook his head.

'Don't get up, Countess, please,' he said, smiling as he ran an appraising gaze over her. She was in her mid-seventies, possibly even older, her face pale partly due to the amount of make-up she wore but also, he suspected, because of the illness that she had summoned him to treat. The skin of her hands and arms was almost translucent and he could easily see the dark threads of her veins through it.

'Doctor Stein, madame,' the butler declared.

'You may leave us,' the old woman said, waving a dismissive hand. When she spoke Frankenstein detected the hint of an East European accent.

'Good of you to come, Doctor Stein,' she said. 'I have heard many good things about you from those in the town and from other friends of mine whom you have treated.'

Frankenstein nodded sagely.

'My husband always used to say that a person needed two things in life,' the Countess went on. 'A good accountant and an even better doctor.'

'Your husband was a very astute man,' Frankenstein conceded. 'And a very rich one too, by the look of it. You have a beautiful home, Countess.'

'Thank you, doctor, but unless you can rid me of what ails me I fear I will not be here to enjoy it for much longer.'

There was a large oil painting hanging over the marble fireplace and it showed the Countess and her husband, the latter looking resplendent in a military uniform. Frankenstein guessed it must have been painted thirty or forty years earlier and the old woman was not slow to catch his interest in the painting.

'If only we could turn back time,' she said wistfully. 'I would give my entire fortune for another twenty years,' she said.

'Who's to say you won't have them?' Frankenstein exclaimed.

'My friends whom you have treated say you can work miracles, Doctor Stein. You would need to do so to give me another twenty years.'

'We shall see, Countess,' Frankenstein said quietly. 'Now, if I am to help you I must examine you.'

The Countess nodded.

She was about to speak again when the doors of the drawing room opened and Frankenstein turned to see a slender young woman with dark brown hair enter.

She hesitated when she saw him and was about to withdraw from the doorway when the Countess held up a hand to beckon her in.

'It's all right, my dear, you can come in,' she called. The young woman nodded demurely and stepped inside the room, closing the doors behind her.

'I didn't mean to interrupt. I'm sorry,' she said, walking towards Frankenstein and the old woman.

As she drew nearer he could see how attractive she was and he guessed her age to be somewhere around thirty, perhaps a year or two younger. She smiled at him and then looked warmly at the Countess.

'I've been out riding,' the younger woman said apologetically. 'I didn't realise you had company.'

'That's perfectly all right, my dear,' the Countess told her. 'I would like you to meet Doctor Stein. Doctor, this is my niece Margaret Conrad.'

'Miss Conrad,' Frankenstein said, nodding to her and shaking her outstretched hand gently.

'My aunt has been singing your praises all morning, Doctor Stein,' Margaret told him.

'Let us hope she is still doing so after I leave,' Frankenstein said.

'Margaret has been living here with me for the last ten months,' Countess Namarov said. 'Since the death of my sister.'

'Are you from this area?' Frankenstein asked, looking more deeply into the eyes of the younger woman.

'From Ingolstadt, in the south,' she told him. 'Do you know it?'

'I have heard of it,' he told her.

'I was a nurse at a hospital there,' Margaret went on. Frankenstein looked more intently at her.

'Perhaps the doctor would have a position for you at his hospital, Margaret,' the Countess said.

'I am always on the lookout for young ladies of quality to aid me in my work there,' Frankenstein conceded. 'Would you really be interested in working there, Margaret? I have some good staff but more experience is always welcome. If you come and see me tomorrow you can have a look around and meet some of the patients and the other staff.'

Margaret nodded enthusiastically. 'Thank you, Doctor Stein,' she replied, beaming.

'You have my thanks too, doctor,' the Countess added. 'Margaret has a low threshold for boredom and I fear sitting around here talking to me all day and night does little to help her.' She squeezed the young girl's hand warmly.

'You know what my hospital is there for, don't you, Margaret?' Frankenstein asked. 'We tend to the poor and the underprivileged. It may be something of a shock for you, considering your present surroundings.'

'I doubt it, doctor,' Margaret assured him. 'The hospital in Ingolstadt where I worked had little money. I'm sure the patients you treat can't be that different. After all, medicine is the same for all, isn't it?'

'But money normally buys better care,' Frankenstein said, smiling down at the Countess. 'And some of my patients are – how should I put it? – less than cultured.'

All three of them laughed.

'I will see,' Margaret said, and smiled.

Frankenstein nodded, his stare still fixed on the young woman.

Seventeen

The severed hands that floated in the tank on the worktop had exceptionally long fingers.

Frankenstein had thought that when he'd first amputated them and now, looking at the appendages suspended in preservative fluid, he was reminded of his initial impression once more.

They could have been the hands of a surgeon like him. He smiled to himself and looked down at his own hands admiringly, flexing the fingers. Then he glanced back at the hands floating in the tank. They had been severed just above the wrist and the stumps had been sealed and cauterised quickly and efficiently upon removal. There were no other marks upon the hands other than the redness around the flesh where the initial cuts had been made. Frankenstein had found in the past that speed was of the essence when amputating if the severed limb was to be maintained at peak quality. It should have taken no more than seven seconds to cut through the flesh of the wrists before hacking through the bone with a saw. Arms and legs were a different matter because the bone and surrounding tissue were thicker. But the removal of both external and internal organs required the same kind of haste as the hands had needed.

The same had been true of the eyes that floated in the tank next to the hands.

Organs as delicate as eyes really needed more care and time for removal – unless the skull they were being taken from belonged to a cadaver. When removing delicate organs from a dead body then the greater speed required was because of the rate at which these parts decayed. Body parts such as the liver, kidney, lungs and eyes decomposed at a much faster rate than arms and legs. They could not be kept preserved for as long, either, Frankenstein had learned. They had to be selected and transplanted within an hour or less, otherwise cells would begin to decay and that might damage the overall function of the organ once it was placed inside another body.

Words like 'transplantation' circled inside his head. He sat back from his journal for a moment and rubbed his face, aware of the tiredness that was enveloping not just his mind but also his body. He would need to leave the laboratory soon. He had to sleep. It had been a tiring day and he didn't want to continue with his work if it might suffer because of his weariness.

Frankenstein got to his feet by swinging himself down from the stool he'd been sitting on for the last thirty minutes. He crossed the laboratory to another worktop and checked that the temperature in the tank there was not too high. If the liquid inside was overheated then it could damage the specimen he wanted to place there. Satisfied that the fluid contents of the tank were suitable he moved back to the stool and sat down once more, scribbling furiously in his journal as he had been since he had first descended into the subterranean laboratory earlier that evening.

It was now well past midnight. Frankenstein yawned and took a sip of the red wine that had remained untouched close beside him.

He looked again at the severed hands and this time he allowed himself a smile. They would be perfect, he told himself.

From the far end of the laboratory there was a low grunting sound and the Baron turned towards it as if that simple act alone would stop the noise. When it didn't he got to his feet and walked towards it as it grew louder.

There were several large cages in this part of the laboratory, the largest of which was occupied by an orang-utan. The large primate was sitting, sullenly picking at some leaves and nibbling on a banana. The grunting, however, was coming from a chimpanzee in another cage opposite the orang-utan. When it saw Frankenstein it jumped against the bars of its cage and stuck a furry hand through a gap at him.

Frankenstein smiled and touched the offered paw affectionately.

The chimpanzee remained close to the bars as if wanting to be near to its keeper. The orang-utan remained resolutely in the corner of its own cage, apparently uninterested in either Frankenstein or the other primates housed in cages around it. A rhesus monkey moved distractedly back and forth, occasionally sipping from its water bowl, while a smaller chimp was curled up in a ball in another cage, apparently asleep and deaf to the sounds around it.

Frankenstein stood looking at the apes for a moment longer. All of them seemed to be staring at him with a kind of pleading in their wide black eyes. Perhaps they wanted to be freed from their cages, perhaps they wished there was some way they could communicate with him. If it was true what some scientists said and that man had evolved from monkeys then they should have a lot to tell him, he mused. As he continued to look at the chimpanzee nearest to him he thought how he would make the entire theory of evolution redundant. His work would render such thinking obsolete. He would create an entirely new set of scientific and ethical principles and his contemporaries would look upon his work with awe and envy.

They would be forced to admit that all their backward archaic ideas were useless. They would be forced to embrace the knowledge and visions that he laid before them. Textbooks would have to be rewritten when they saw what he had done. Those who had condemned him would be forced to acknowledge his skill and his brilliance. They would be exposed for the ignorant fools he had always thought them to be. They would be forced to bow down to his superior intellect and ideas. No man alive would be able to challenge him.

Frankenstein felt a chill of excitement run through him. It was a shudder that he had experienced before. When he had looked upon the completed body of his first creation he had felt that tingle.

Even now in his mind's eye he could picture it floating in the clear fluid, waiting for him to give it life again. Not God, nor some other manufactured deity, but *him*. He had been the one who had assembled it from dead body parts and he would be the one to reignite the spark of life within it. And he had succeeded and, he told himself, his success would have been total but for the meddling of others. The creature he had assembled had not been perfect but it had been just the first attempt.

The next time there would be no mistakes.

Frankenstein turned away from the monkey cages when he heard banging coming from somewhere nearby.

It took him a moment to realise that someone was knocking on the rear doors of the hospital.

Who wanted entry at such an hour? he wondered irritably.

The banging continued and Frankenstein moved agitatedly towards the flight of stone steps that led up out of the cellar laboratory. Why wasn't Carl or the janitor dealing with this interruption? The noise carried on as he reached the office and then strode on into the corridor beyond that led to the doors.

There was a moment's pause and then more urgent banging.

Frankenstein wiped his hands on his waistcoat and unlocked the rear doors of the hospital.

Immediately he recognised the young man who stood there gazing back at him.

'Doctor Kleve,' Frankenstein said.

Kleve nodded.

'My patients are trying to sleep,' Frankenstein went on. 'You seem intent on waking them.'

'It's you I want to speak to,' Kleve told him.

'Well, whatever it is, I'm sure it can wait until the morning.'

Frankenstein pushed the doors but Kleve put his hands against them and held them open.

'No, sir, it can't,' he insisted.

Frankenstein ran an appraising stare over the other man.

'Persistence is usually a virtue I value,' he said wearily. 'But not at this time of the night. If the Medical Council sent you then they have as little idea of good manners as they do of medicine.'

'The Medical Council don't know I'm here,' Kleve snapped. 'I came because I wanted to, not because they sent me. I need to talk to you, doctor.'

'Tomorrow,' Frankenstein insisted.

'I know who you are.'

The words hung in the air like a bad smell and Frankenstein eyed the younger man a little more intently.

'Everyone in Carlsbruck knows who I am,' Frankenstein said, smiling.

'I mean I know who you *really* are – Baron Frankenstein.'

Eighteen

Frankenstein held Kleve's gaze for what seemed like an eternity, his face expressionless. Then he smiled thinly.

'My dear doctor, do you have any idea what you're saying?' the Baron said quietly.

'I know it's you,' Kleve told him. 'I knew from the first time I saw you at Professor Brandt's funeral.'

Frankenstein shook his head slowly and dismissively.

'You can deny it all you like – I know that you're Baron Frankenstein,' Kleve went on.

'How do you even know that name?'

'Any doctor who wishes to advance the theories of science and anatomy knows and reveres that name.'

Frankenstein didn't speak.

What kind of bizarre trap was this?

'You are mistaken, Doctor Kleve,' he said as convincingly as he could. 'My name is Stein.'

Still Kleve remained where he was, blocking the doorway and determined, it seemed, not to move until the Baron had confirmed his identity. Frankenstein was equally adamant that he would not reveal it and he merely shook his head again as if that simple gesture would discourage this newcomer.

'I am here because I wish to learn from you, to help you,' Kleve went on.

'If you want to work here in my Hospital for the Poor then come back at a reasonable hour of the day and we will discuss your credentials and—'

Kleve cut him short.

'I want to learn from you, Baron Frankenstein,' he snapped. 'I want to know how you work and I want to assist you in any way I can.'

'You can assist me by not mistaking me for someone else,' Frankenstein said. 'My name is—'

'Baron Victor Frankenstein,' Kleve rasped. 'Why do you deny it? Why pretend? You should be proud that I recognise you. Am I the first?'

'Do you recognise me for what I am or what you would have me be?'

'Your activities here lead to only one conclusion.'

'You really must stop this madness now,' Frankenstein said.

'Let me in,' Kleve insisted. 'Let me talk to you. I'll show you how determined I am to help you, how much I respect the work you've done.'

'I appreciate that, Doctor Kleve. I like to think that what I've done here for the poor of Carlsbruck is appreciated—'

Again Kleve cut across him. 'To hell with your work with the poor,' he snapped. 'I'm not referring to that. You know the work I speak of.'

'I know that I am very tired and that I am facing a rather deluded young man who thinks I am someone other than who I really am, so . . .'

'What do you think the Medical Council would say if they knew you were Frankenstein? If I told them—'

It was the Baron's turn to interrupt. 'First of all, they wouldn't believe you,' he said. 'And secondly, they would be helpless to interfere with my work here.'

'You are Frankenstein?'

'First you tell me I am, then you ask me,' Frankenstein said. 'Why are you so interested in this gentleman?'

The two men faced each other, neither giving way.

'Teach me,' Kleve said. 'It is knowledge I seek. Share your genius with me.'

'You think that appealing to my intellectual vanity will persuade me to admit to your accusation?'

'It isn't an accusation. I have nothing but respect for what you've done. I want to help you.'

'The man you speak of was executed in Innsbruck prison three years ago. How can I be that man?' Frankenstein insisted.

'You *are* Frankenstein, I know that. Was Professor Brandt helping you with your work?'

'He had been of considerable help here at the hospital since I arrived, aiding me with the care of the poor and—'

'Not your work with the poor,' Kleve snapped. 'You know which work I speak of. Let me help you or I swear that I will expose you to the Medical Council and the authorities of Carlsbruck.'

Frankenstein held his gaze for a moment. Then he stepped back and ushered the younger man inside.

'I see there is no reasoning with you, Doctor Kleve,' he said. 'I wish there was. Perhaps we should speak inside. Blackmail threats are better delivered away from doorways.'

'I'm not blackmailing you, doctor,' Kleve protested.

'You threaten to expose me to the Carlsbruck Medical Council,' Frankenstein said sharply. 'You *threaten* me. It sounds like blackmail to me, Doctor Kleve.'

'Just hear me out,' Kleve said.

'As you wish.'

Kleve nodded and walked into the hospital, pausing for a moment as Frankenstein locked the doors behind him and then motioned towards the office a little further up the corridor. As they approached the office door Frankenstein heard movement near the flight of stairs leading down from the upper floors of the building. He glanced up and saw Carl standing there.

'Carl, could you come here a moment, please?' Frankenstein asked.

The hunchback shuffled down the stairs towards the other two men, glancing curiously at Kleve who looked back with an expression of indifference on his face.

'This is Doctor Kleve,' Frankenstein said by way of introduction. 'He seems to be a little confused. He has mistaken me for someone else. Perhaps you could enlighten him. What is my name?'

Carl hesitated, perplexed by the question.

'Tell Doctor Kleve my name, Carl,' Frankenstein repeated. 'He thinks I am a man called Frankenstein.'

Kleve couldn't help but see the flicker of concern that flashed across Carl's face. But then the hunchback merely swallowed hard and looked at the younger man.

'His name is Doctor Stein,' Carl said.

'You've rehearsed your charade well, Baron,' Kleve said, smiling.

'Thank you, Carl,' Frankenstein said quietly. 'That will be all for now.'

Carl hesitated, then watched as Frankenstein and Kleve walked into the office. The door closed behind them.

Nineteen

'Even if you are right, what do you hope to achieve?' Frankenstein sipped at his red wine and stared at the younger man across the office desk. 'What good would come of exposing a man like Frankenstein?' he went on.

'I don't want to expose you,' Kleve protested. 'I want to help you – I want you to help me, to teach me. Share with me the knowledge you've acquired, let me explore the frontiers of science and medicine with you.'

'Which members of the Medical Council sent you here?'

'No one sent me,' Kleve exploded. 'How many times do I have to tell you that? If I wanted to expose you I would have come here tonight with the police.'

'So no one knows you're here?'

Kleve shook his head.

Frankenstein regarded him silently.

'What do I have to say to prove that my only motive for approaching you is to share in your genius?' Kleve protested. 'I wish you no harm. Would I have come here at night like this if my intention was to hurt you?'

Still Frankenstein didn't speak.

'I want to work with you,' Kleve went on. 'To assist

you and learn from you. To do whatever I can to become the kind of doctor you are. I want to learn what no university could ever teach me. I want to be the pupil of the greatest doctor and the finest medical brain in the world.'

Frankenstein smiled.

'No matter what it takes,' Kleve added.

'Have you any family, Doctor Kleve?' the Baron asked.

Kleve looked puzzled by the question but then shook his head.

'No,' he answered. 'My parents died some time ago. I lived with relatives in Innsbruck until I graduated from medical school.'

'Innsbruck,' Frankenstein said softly. 'So that is how you know the name Frankenstein.'

Kleve nodded, his gaze never leaving the Baron.

'If you lived in Innsbruck then you heard the rumours and the gossip about Frankenstein,' the Baron went on. 'The ignorant ramblings of peasants and fools. You heard that and you believed it.'

'I heard that you created a monster in your laboratory,' Kleve said. 'A monster that ran amok and killed several people.'

'A man,' Frankenstein snarled, getting to his feet and leaning over the desk as he glared at Kleve. 'I created a *man*.' His nostrils flared wildly and Kleve could see fury burning in his eyes as he looked at him. The anger in his voice gradually subsided and he sat down again, gazing off into space as if lost in his own thoughts now. 'It should have been perfect,' he said quietly. 'But the brain was damaged. That was why the creature was uncontrollable.'

Kleve smiled triumphantly.

'There were other problems too,' Frankenstein went on. 'But I won't make the same mistakes again.'

'So you have continued with your work here?' Kleve said excitedly.

'Of course.'

'I knew I was right,' Kleve said, smiling.

'About my identity? Yes, Doctor Kleve, your keen eye was correct. My name is Frankenstein, I'll admit – but it is a very large family. Remarkable since the Middle Ages for its fecundity. There are offshoots everywhere; even in America, I'm told. There's a town called Frankenstein in Germany and then, of course, there are the Frankensteins who come from Silesia. But that really isn't important any more, is it?'

Kleve looked puzzled. He saw Frankenstein lean forward slightly.

The Baron slid open the drawer of his desk and from it he pulled a pistol.

Kleve stiffened, his gaze fixed on the muzzle of the weapon.

'What good will your knowledge do you now?' Frankenstein asked him, aiming the gun at Kleve's head.

'I told you I meant you no harm,' the younger man insisted.

Frankenstein thumbed back the hammer of the pistol.

'You broke in here late at night, threatening me,' he said gently, steadying the pistol with his free hand. 'You attacked me and I was forced to defend myself. That is, of course, the story the police will be told when I report your death.'

'No,' Kleve gasped, getting to his feet. He backed away, knocking his chair over in the process.

'There was a witness, naturally. Carl will have seen us arguing in the corridor. He will tell the police what happened.' Frankenstein was also now on his feet, the pistol still aimed at Kleve. 'He will tell how he burst into this office to find us struggling and in that struggle I was forced to shoot you to protect myself.'

Kleve stood motionless beside the door, his back against the wood.

'You wouldn't kill me,' he said.

'Really?' Frankenstein said flatly. 'Why not, Doctor Kleve? You know the kind of man I am. Do you think that one more life would make any difference to me? Especially the life of a man who has threatened to blackmail me or expose me to those who would destroy me.' Frankenstein's finger tightened slightly on the trigger.

'I only came here to help you,' Kleve insisted, his heart now pounding in his chest.

'You sought to help me with threats?' Frankenstein murmured, taking a step closer to the terrified younger man.

'If you kill me then the police will investigate you – they will find out who you really are,' Kleve blurted.

'The Chief of Police is one of my patients,' Frankenstein explained. 'Anyway, whose story would he be more likely to believe? That of a crazed young man who broke in here late one night and got what he deserved – or an upstanding and valuable member of Carlsbruck society? The police will treat your death the same way they would treat any other burglar's or intruder's death. I will tell them that you had been bothering me for days, following me, and that I feared for my life. I think we both know where their sympathies will lie, Doctor Kleve.' He raised his eyebrows. 'Now, enough of this, I have work to do.'

He pushed the muzzle of the pistol closer to Kleve's head.

'Goodbye, Doctor Kleve,' he said, quietly.

Twenty

Kleve closed his eyes and waited for the explosion as the pistol was discharged. He gritted his teeth, expecting the lead ball to slam into his head, and for a fleeting second he wondered if there would be much pain.

Praying to a God he didn't believe in, he stood quivering against the door of the office.

The explosion never came.

Seconds passed and he finally opened his eyes, looking towards Frankenstein, his heart hammering madly against his ribs.

'If you're going to kill me, then get it over with,' he gasped, his mouth dry.

Frankenstein held the pistol close to Kleve's face for a moment longer. Then he lowered it, clicking the hammer back into the safe position.

'I'm still trying to work out if you're a very brave young man or a very foolish one,' the Baron said impassively. He turned away from Kleve and walked across to one of the large bookcases that lined the walls. There was a decanter of red wine and two clean glasses on one of the shelves. Frankenstein poured some of the claret for himself, then some for Kleve. He held out the glass to the younger man. 'Take it – you look as if you need it.'

Kleve hesitated a moment, then accepted the offered glass, slurping down the contents quickly and noisily. Frankenstein motioned to the chair in front of his desk and Kleve sat down, beads of perspiration on his forehead and top lip. His hands were shaking almost uncontrollably.

'Now we both know where we stand,' Frankenstein told him slowly. 'You know who I am and you also know that if you attempt to expose me I will not hesitate to kill you.' He laid the pistol down and raised his wine glass in salute.

Kleve echoed the gesture and nodded. 'I thought you were going to kill me then,' he said, breathlessly.

'Would you have blamed me if I had?'

Kleve drained what was left in his glass, then accepted another as Frankenstein poured from the decanter.

'You must be very keen to learn from me if you're prepared to put your life at risk to do it,' Frankenstein observed, sipping from his own glass. 'I'm sure you appreciate my need for anonymity here, Doctor Kleve. Or may I call you Hans?'

Kleve nodded and swallowed some more wine.

'I needed to know just how far you were willing to go, Hans,' Frankenstein told him. 'The extent of your dedication, let us say.'

'And now you know?'

'I know that you're a very determined young man and determination in the kind of work in which I specialise is a necessary attribute. Some might call it a necessary evil.'

Kleve looked at him.

'Certain sacrifices have to be made in the pursuit of knowledge,' Frankenstein went on. 'Not all men are willing to make those sacrifices.'

'But I am. I told you, I'll do anything to help you, to learn from you.'

'Anything?'

Kleve nodded.

Frankenstein topped up his glass once more.

'What exactly do you know of my work?' the Baron enquired.

'I know that you made a creature from body parts and reanimated it,' Kleve told him. 'You learned secrets that only God knew.'

'I *was* God,' Frankenstein said, tapping his own chest. 'But outside influences and others conspired against me. The brain that was put into my creation was damaged. When the creature was reanimated it was . . .' He shook his head as the words trailed away. 'There was nothing I could do to improve it.'

'Could a new brain have helped?' Kleve wanted to know.

'Many of the internal organs needed work too. I was obsessed with building a man from nothing. I tried to assemble a living being as one would assemble a jigsaw. This time I have no intention of making that mistake.'

'Have you already begun your work again here in Carlsbruck?' Kleve wanted to know.

'The foundations have been laid.' Frankenstein smiled.

Kleve sat forward excitedly.

'The ideal would be to transplant a living brain into an already living body,' Frankenstein went on. 'The host body must be alive when the brain is introduced or there is too much trauma caused by the amount of reanimation needed. The body must be viewed as a separate entity. It is merely a vessel for the brain that it will carry.'

'So the brain is the most important part of your work?'

Frankenstein smiled.

'Finish your drink, Hans,' he said, getting to his feet. 'There is something I want you to see.'

Twenty-One

C arl Lang sat naked on the edge of his bed, his head cradled in his hands.

In his small attic room he could hear very little from the hospital below, especially at such a late hour. His duties for the day were over now, his time was his own. It was in the darkness, in the dead of night that Carl's loneliness weighed in on him most heavily. During the day when he was busy and moving around the hospital he didn't have time to think about his isolation but now, alone in his room, he felt surrounded and suffocated by these thoughts.

Now, as he straightened up, he looked down at his body and the pain of his isolation seemed to intensify. It was as if the physical state of his body was exacerbating his feelings of detachment from those around him. Why would anyone want to be close to him, looking the way he did? He stood up falteringly and ran an appraising gaze over his own body. The stunted legs, the twisted hips, the jutting belly and the narrow chest – each one as a single impediment would have been dispiriting enough but combined they were appalling. And on his back the hump that made it look as if something had crawled up inside his skin and was hunkered there on his shoulder blade. From that same shoulder his withered arm extended, the fingers shorter and stubbier than on the other hand. He felt at his skin with his good hand, the flesh on his face puckered and holed as if he'd survived smallpox. The flesh on the right side of his face was like gnarled wood. The lids of his eye appeared too large and they hung like fleshy flaps over and beneath the orb which was bloodshot and constantly watering.

No wonder none of the girls across the street in the brothel had wanted him near them.

You don't know that, you didn't wait to find out.

Who would want a man like him? he thought. What kind of woman would want some misshapen creature crawling over her and pawing her? And if women who accepted payment for their services didn't want him then how would any normal woman ever entertain his advances?

They wouldn't. They would shun you. Treat you with contempt and disgust just as they always have.

Carl crossed to his coat that was hanging on the back of the bedroom door. He slid his hand into one of the pockets.

The blade of the knife that he pulled out was only three inches long but it was viciously sharp.

Carl held it in his good hand, studying every inch of the gleaming metal, his eyes drawn to the razor-sharp cutting edge.

He pressed it gently against his throat.

Go on. Cut. Drive it deep into the flesh and hack through the veins and arteries until the blood spurts and you lose consciousness and die. What's the point in living when your life is so empty?

He hesitated, the metal cold against his skin.

Rid yourself of so much suffering.

Carl swallowed hard, his Adam's apple brushing against the knife as he did so.

There'd be no pain. Just release. Do it. Free yourself. Death would be quick.

Carl closed his eyes, tears beginning to trickle down his cheeks.

One second of courage and all your suffering will be over for ever.

Carl let out a gasp of despair and kept the blade at his throat.

Do it.

He grunted and lowered the blade, his whole body shaking now as he sobbed helplessly.

Frankenstein had promised to help him. He had sworn that Carl would have a new body, not this abomination that he had inhabited all his life.

And what if he's lying? What if he fooled you? Used your trust just to escape the guillotine?

Carl shook his head. He moaned, hurled the blade away and sank down on his haunches in the middle of the room.

Frankenstein had promised his help but Carl knew that he could wait no longer for that aid. The time had come. He lay on the floor, curled into a foetal position, his sobbing muffled as he pressed his head against his chest.

He lay like that for almost an hour.

Twenty-Two

For long seconds Hans Kleve was unable to speak. He stood in the centre of Frankenstein's huge underground laboratory, his gaze darting in all directions, drawn towards the dizzying array of equipment and apparatus jammed into the subterranean room. Frankenstein watched the expression on his face change from one of awe to one of incredible excitement. When the younger man finally turned to face him, the Baron himself was grinning.

'This is incredible,' Kleve said breathlessly.

'It's taken me three years to assemble the equipment here,' Frankenstein told him. 'Three years to get to the stage of my work that I have now reached.' Kleve crossed to a microscope and peered through it at the slide below. As he straightened up he glanced at the tank that held the severed hands.

Frankenstein watched him closely but the expression on his face never changed.

'How did you come by these?' the younger man asked, pointing towards the hands.

'The hospital has many uses,' Frankenstein said flatly.

'These hands were taken from one of your patients?' Kleve asked.

'Yes. Does that shock you?'

Kleve shook his head.

'So were many of the internal organs that I've used in my work,' Frankenstein went on. 'I told you that there were problems I encountered at the beginning with reanimation. I don't have those problems here. If I need a body part I take it from one of the patients in the hospital – providing that it is in good condition.'

Kleve nodded.

'Assembling a body from dead parts was my downfall last time,' Frankenstein admitted.

'And the damage to the brain,' Kleve added.

'Quite,' the Baron said. 'But not this time. My research has been painstaking, my attention to detail faultless.' He began walking towards the rear area of the cellar and Kleve followed, seeing the array of monkey cages ahead of him.

'The first time you tried – where did the body parts come from?' Kleve enquired, walking along just behind the Baron in an almost reverential manner.

'From the gallows, the charnel house, the graveyard,' Frankenstein told him. 'Dead flesh that had to be stitched together and then reanimated. I'm sure you heard the stories, Hans.'

'There were many stories about you, doctor.'

'I imagine there were. Told by the ignorant and stupid, trotted out by superstitious fools afraid of their own shadows.' The Baron turned and looked at Kleve. 'No one knew what actually went on except myself and the man I worked with.'

'What became of him?'

Frankenstein allowed his gaze to drift past Kleve for a moment, his mind conjuring mental pictures. Kleve saw the knot of muscles at the side of his jaw pulsing angrily.

'He is still in Innsbruck,' Frankenstein said. 'He helped to condemn me and then left me to rot. But I will find him again one day when my work is complete and when it is celebrated by all true seekers of knowledge. I will visit that man again. I will have my revenge. The world will never be rid of me.'

Kleve could see the fury in the Baron's eyes as he spoke.

'And the brain?' the younger man asked quietly. 'Where did that come from?'

Frankenstein glanced at Kleve briefly, his anger subsiding noticeably as he spoke again.

'From a man who had been a genius in life,' the Baron said. 'My old teacher.' His expression darkened slightly. 'But the time between his death and the insertion of his brain into the skull of my creation was too great. Speed is of the essence, Hans,' Frankenstein went on excitedly. 'To prevent tissue damage, removal of the brain from its original body and its transfer into the new host must be completed with the minimum of delay.'

'Is that what caused the damage to the brain you selected?' Kleve wanted to know.

'No. It was the meddling of someone else. Someone not as dedicated to the final outcome of my work as I was. I would have worked alone if I could have, but some aspects of the process required two people if they were to be completed to a satisfactory standard.'

'And what about them?' Kleve said, pointing at the monkeys and smiling. 'Are they going to help you?'

'The brain of a primate is the closest thing to a human brain and my work on these creatures has been of immense help to me. If the next step in my work is successful then I will be ready to continue with a living human brain.'

'What do you intend to do?'

'With your help, I will transplant the brain of that orang-utan into that chimpanzee.' Frankenstein pointed at each animal in turn as he spoke.

The animals looked back with indifference at the watching men.

'With my help?' Kleve said slowly.

'You wanted to learn from me, Hans, you wanted to assist,' Frankenstein stated. 'I am offering you that chance.'

Twenty-Three

Frankenstein poured two more glasses of red wine and pushed one across the desk towards Hans Kleve.

'The greatest handicap to the advancement of medical science is ignorance,' the Baron said, sitting back in his seat, the wine glass cradled in his hand. 'And that ignorance is as ingrained within the scientific and medical community as it is within the general population.'

'Not everyone has your desire to explore the boundaries of medicine and science, doctor,' Kleve suggested, taking a sip of his wine.

'But isn't that our duty, Hans?' Frankenstein said, sitting forward in his seat. 'To break down barriers, to cross the frontiers of ignorance? How can mankind hope to progress if he is paralysed by fear of what he might discover?'

'It isn't always fear that holds men back but the ignorance you speak of.'

'And there is no better example than the Medical Council here in Carlsbruck.'

Kleve raised his eyebrows. 'They are somewhat set in their ways, I'll admit that,' he conceded.

'They are blinkered fools,' Frankenstein snapped.

'But they have power here in Carlsbruck.'

'Only among those similarly short-sighted and lacking in ambition. You at least had the good sense to seek knowledge away from their stagnant and outdated views.'

Kleve sipped more of his wine, then cleared his throat peremptorily. 'How much did Professor Brandt know about your work?' he asked.

'Brandt was a good man,' Frankenstein said slowly. 'But he had no part in my work. Not the work that you will aid me in.'

'Why not?'

'Because for all his intellect he lacked one very necessary character trait, Hans.'

'Which is?'

'Ruthlessness.' Frankenstein sipped from his glass. 'The work I chose to embark upon calls for more than a touch of that and Brandt, for all his gifts, did not possess it.'

'How do you know that I do?'

'Because you're young and determined and in some ways you remind me of myself when I was your age. Barriers and rules are of no concern to you, just as they weren't to me – and that is how it must be if you are to work with me. Lives are insignificant compared with the final goal. If sacrifices must be made then I expect you to make them, just as I have done over the years.'

Kleve looked intently at the Baron and nodded almost imperceptibly. 'I understand,' he said, quietly.

'I hope so, Hans,' Frankenstein replied. 'I hope you

realise how far you may have to go to work at my side. You may have to do things that you could never have imagined before.'

'There is nothing I wouldn't do.'

Frankenstein smiled thinly. 'You say that now,' he murmured.

'What must I do to prove myself?' Kleve snapped.

Frankenstein merely stared at him silently over the rim of his wine glass for a moment longer.

'You have no need to doubt me,' the younger man insisted.

'Do any members of the Medical Council know you were coming here?' Frankenstein enquired again.

'No. Why would I tell them?' Kleve said.

'Not much happens in this town that they don't know about. They have eyes and ears everywhere.' The Baron paused. 'I was thinking of the possible effect they could have on your career, Hans, not on mine. I am beyond their reach.'

'You seem very sure of that, doctor.'

'If they were in a position to do anything about my practice here they would have done it by now. I suspect that cowardice is as much a part of their distinguishing character as ignorance. They plot and scheme against me because they see me as an outsider and a threat, but none of them have the courage to confront me. None of them have even set foot inside this hospital since I opened it.'

'What do you think they would do if they knew who you really were?'

Frankenstein smiled.

'I can guess, Hans,' he said. 'But they will never know, will they?' He fixed the younger man with a withering stare.

Kleve shook his head.

'I would never betray you,' he said.

The Baron said nothing but merely sipped at his wine. After a moment he sat forward and raised his glass in salute.

'We begin work tomorrow, then,' he proclaimed. 'And we will not stop until we have succeeded.'

Kleve too raised his glass to echo the toast.

'Here's to a new world, Hans,' Frankenstein said. 'A world of knowledge and discovery that you and I will create together.'

Kleve nodded.

'And God help anyone who tries to stop us,' Frankenstein continued.

Twenty-Four

She was the most beautiful woman he had ever seen.

That was the first and only thought that entered Carl Lang's mind as he stood at the top of the stairway looking down at Margaret Conrad.

As he descended the stairs he was able to see more easily her flawless alabaster skin and her long dark hair, despite the fact that most of her flowing tresses were pinned up and hidden beneath the hat she wore. She was looking around helplessly and it was as Carl moved closer that she saw him. He froze, expecting the usual look of distaste or revulsion to cross her face.

She smiled at him.

Carl swallowed hard, his body quivering now.

This stunning woman was looking at him and smiling. She wasn't wrinkling her nose in disgust or turning away, she was actually smiling. He moved nearer, painfully aware of his disfigurement. He tucked his withered arm inside his jacket as if that simple act might hide it from her. He wished that he could do the same with his wrinkled and pockmarked skin and his face. Even more he wished there was some way he could hide the hump on his back from her gentle gaze. But she looked only into his eyes, seemingly unworried by his physical shortcomings.

'Hello,' she said brightly. 'I'm looking for Doctor Stein – I wonder if you could help me.'

Carl nodded and lowered his gaze almost guiltily.

'I can take you to him,' he said, aware of the smell of perfume wafting his way every time she moved.

'My name is Margaret Conrad,' she said. 'He is expecting me.'

'You don't look like one of his patients,' Carl said falteringly.

'I'm not.' Margaret laughed. 'I'm going to work here as a nurse.'

Carl turned and looked at her, his lips curling upwards into a smile.

'Do you work here too?' she asked.

'Yes,' he told her. 'I've been here for three years, ever since the doctor arrived in Carlsbruck.'

'What's your name?'

'Carl.'

He was shaking as they reached the door of Frankenstein's office, unable to believe that this woman was speaking to him not only without displaying any signs of repugnance but actually with warmth in her voice. She seemed unaware of his deformity, untroubled by his appearance and demeanour. Carl tried to swallow but his mouth and throat were dry and when he reached up to knock on the door of Frankenstein's office his hand was shaking noticeably. He sucked in a deep breath to try and steady himself and looked at Margaret. Again she smiled at him.

He knocked and waited.

'Come in,' Frankenstein called and Carl backed away as if he was in the presence of royalty.

'Thank you, Carl,' Margaret said. She reached out and touched his arm gently as she passed.

He felt as if an electric shock had been passed through his body. As she stepped across the threshold of the office and closed the door behind her Carl looked down at the part of his arm she had touched. He placed two fingers on that spot, gently feeling the material there. It was as if he could still feel the warmth of her touch and its gentleness. He hadn't known much tenderness in his life and such fleeting experiences were to be savoured, especially when administered by a woman as beautiful as she. Carl managed a smile and stood close to the door. He could hear the voices of Margaret and Frankenstein but he didn't really care what they were saying. Just the sound of her voice was enough. It was like a song to him, each word lilting and carried on the air like exquisite notes.

'What the hell are you doing lurking around outside the doctor's office?'

These new words shattered the stillness in the corridor and made Carl spin around to discover their source.

As he turned he saw an all too familiar figure ambling towards him.

It was Meyer, the janitor, his huge belly jutting out as if he was pregnant.

'Why are you still here?' Carl asked. 'I thought you go home at sunrise.'

'I'm supposed to but one of the patients died,' Meyer said, snorting loudly. 'The nurses asked me to help them move him down to the morgue. I'll ask His Highness Doctor Stein for more money.'

Carl raised his eyebrows contemptuously.

'That's your job,' Meyer rasped. 'You're supposed to help with the filthy tasks like that, not me. Where have you been? Hiding in your room?'

Carl looked the bigger man up and down scornfully. 'I've had other things to do,' he said dismissively. 'Not that it's any of your business.'

Meyer looked at him with something approaching disgust. 'You cripple,' he hissed.

Carl reached into his jacket pocket and pulled the knife free in one fluid movement. He pressed it against Meyer's bloated stomach.

'I should gut you like the fat pig you are,' Carl snapped. 'Why don't you leave me alone?'

Meyer looked down at the blade and then at Carl's face.

'You haven't got the nerve,' he sneered.

Carl kept the knife pressed against the big man's stomach for a moment longer, then pulled it away and slid it back into his pocket. He turned and walked away from Meyer who watched him go, the twisted grin still on his pockmarked face.

'Go on, little hunchback,' he called, mockingly. 'Run

away. Run to your room and hide. Hide that ugly face and that twisted body so no one can see it.'

Carl kept walking.

Meyer's laughter echoed loudly in the corridor.

Twenty-Five

The babble of voices that Doctor Hans Kleve had heard just before he and Frankenstein entered the ward stopped abruptly.

As the two doctors paused at one end of the long room all eyes turned in their direction. The vaulted ceiling usually seemed to amplify any noises but upon the appearance of Frankenstein and his younger companion nothing broke the stillness apart from the odd moan of discomfort or a cough.

Kleve glanced at his companion and saw that Frankenstein was gazing at the patients in the beds nearest to him. He crossed to the first of them, a wiry-looking man with black hair and bushy eyebrows.

'And how are you feeling today?' Frankenstein asked, glancing at the man who seemed to shrink back into his bed as the Baron approached him.

'My arm's still sore, doctor,' the man said.

'Let me see it,' Frankenstein said sharply, watching as the man pulled his arm free of the bed sheets.

There were bandages wrapped tightly around the limb from the bicep to the wrist.

'Have a look and see what you think,' Frankenstein

said to Kleve as if he was asking him to inspect a price-less jewel.

The younger man slowly removed the bandages, recoiling slightly when he detected a particularly rancid odour.

'Gangrene,' he said, wrinkling his nose. 'I can tell without even looking.' He started to wrap the bandages around the limb once again.

Frankenstein nodded. 'Our friend here broke his arm,' he explained. 'And he didn't come here quickly enough for help.' The Baron looked almost accusingly at the man. 'Did you?'

The patient shook his head.

'The compound fracture became infected,' Frankenstein went on. 'We'll probably have to remove the arm at least from below the elbow.'

'But if you do that, doctor, I won't be able to work,' the man protested.

'Would you rather keep the arm and die of blood poisoning?' Frankenstein asked coldly.

The man shook his head, watching as the two doctors moved across the ward to another man who was coughing loudly, one pudgy-fingered hand held against his chest.

'A bronchial infection?' Kleve said, pulling his stetho-scope from around his neck and pressing it to the man's chest.

Frankenstein nodded. 'He works in one of the facto-ries on the outskirts of the town,' he said as Kleve moved the end of the stethoscope around on the man's chest, pressing it against the flesh here and there to listen.

'There's a lot of phlegm in the lungs by the sound of it,' Kleve observed. 'They could be drained.'

The patient looked concerned.

'It's a simple operation,' Frankenstein told him. 'You'll be out of here in two weeks.'

Before the man could reply Frankenstein made his way to the next bed, with Kleve hurrying to keep up.

The man in this bed had his leg in plaster and he nodded amiably at the two physicians as they approached him.

'How did you break your leg?' Kleve wanted to know.

'I'm a coach driver,' the man told him. 'I fell from the coach and the damned horses trampled me.'

Frankenstein leaned closer to the man and pointed at the tattoo on his powerful right arm.

'That's a wonderful piece of workmanship,' the Baron said.

'Thank you, doctor, I had it done in Danzig when I—' the man began.

'Unfortunately you'll have to lose the arm,' Frankenstein said, cutting him short.

The colour drained from the man's face and he looked imploringly first at Frankenstein and then at Kleve who turned in surprise to his fellow physician.

'Blood poisoning,' Frankenstein said.

'But there's nothing wrong with my arm,' the coach driver said frantically.

'Are you a doctor?' Frankenstein asked calmly.

'No, but I—' the man protested before he was cut short again.

'Then allow *me* to make the medical decisions,' Frankenstein interrupted. 'I wouldn't presume to tell you how to drive a coach. The arm will be removed tomorrow.'

'Please don't take my arm,' the man said breathlessly, tears forming in his eyes.

'This matter isn't open for discussion,' the Baron told him with an air of finality. 'I will amputate tomorrow.'

The man opened his mouth to protest once more but Frankenstein merely turned and walked away.

'Is it really necessary?' Kleve asked, lowering his voice. 'There didn't seem to be any evidence of infection in that man's arm.'

'The arm is in perfect condition, Hans,' Frankenstein said flatly. 'And it will be much more use to me than it is to that man. Besides, he will have paid no money for his treatment here; he should think himself lucky that the prolonged good health we have granted him is costing him only his arm.'

Kleve suddenly understood. He nodded slowly.

'Many of the internal organs belonging to these patients and others before them are worthless to me, naturally,' Frankenstein went on. 'Livers ruined by the effects of too much drinking, lungs filled with the filth from factories, hearts strained by too much menial work. But the poor usually display reasonable qualities when it comes to external physical attributes.'

'But not when it comes to their brains?' Kleve grinned.

Frankenstein laughed. 'No,' he said. 'Not brains.' The

smile slipped from his face. 'I have other sources for those.'

As the two doctors made their way towards the far end of the ward Frankenstein looked up and saw that another figure had joined them to attend to the sick and infirm residents. Margaret Conrad was bustling efficiently around the beds at the other end.

Kleve too saw her and Frankenstein noticed his interest.

'I want you to meet our new nurse,' the Baron said, motioning Margaret towards him. She left the woman she'd been tending and joined him, smiling at Kleve as Frankenstein performed the introductions.

'Hans, I'd like you to meet Margaret Conrad,' he began. 'Margaret, this is Doctor Hans Kleve, my new assistant.'

They shook hands and Kleve smiled approvingly.

'You live with Countess Namarov, don't you?' Kleve asked.

'I'm her niece,' Margaret explained.

At the other end of the ward a cluster of patients, two of them on crutches, were standing around the bed of the man with the tattooed arm, staring at the little group with narrowed and resentful eyes.

'Bloody butcher,' snarled the man with the tattoo.

'They're all as bad,' another man added.

'Still, if it wasn't for this hospital some of us would be dead by now,' a man with a bandaged head said.

'And if it wasn't for Stein I'd be leaving here with both my arms,' the tattooed man snapped. 'We're like the rats they experiment on in their laboratory.'

'They're no better than the doctors who look after the rich bastards that run this town,' another insisted. His arm was in a sling.

'I wouldn't mind that new nurse looking after me,' the man with the bandaged head observed, grinning crookedly.

The other men laughed and nodded their approval.

'We'll have to keep our eye on her, boys,' one of them added.

'It's not my eyes I want to use on her,' the man with the broken arm grunted. His remark was greeted with more coarse laughter.

Even from the far end of the ward Frankenstein heard the noise. He turned and glared at the group of men. They fell silent instantly.

'Scum,' the Baron murmured under his breath. 'Nothing but scum.'

'What did you say, doctor?' Margaret asked, uncertain of what Frankenstein had said.

'Nothing, my dear.' The Baron smiled. 'Now, you continue with your work. Doctor Kleve and I must inspect the patients in the other ward.'

As the two doctors left, from the far end of the ward angry stares followed them.

Twenty-Six

As Carl emerged from Frankenstein's office he saw Margaret Conrad heading away from him down the corridor towards one of the wards. Carl drew a deep breath and wiped the sweat from his face with the grubby handkerchief he kept in his trouser pocket.

He had been working in the basement laboratory for over an hour, moving equipment around and dragging several large specimen cases into the places that Frankenstein had indicated. It had been tough and gruelling work and Carl was exhausted and sweating like a pig as he stood in the corridor. But he forgot his weariness when he saw Margaret.

Instantly he was aware of his dishevelled and filthy appearance and he hesitated a moment before walking along the corridor after her, keeping a reasonable distance and always ensuring that there was a doorway for him to duck into should she turn around. He didn't want her to think he was following her. Carl preferred to think of it as observing her movements. He smiled to himself and watched as she walked into the room used by the nurses, only to come out a moment later carrying what looked like a bottle of medicine in one hand as she continued on her way to the ward. Carl wiped his face once again, aware that perspiration had soaked into his shirt and trousers, such had been the extent of his exertions.

He stuck one hand beneath his armpit and then sniffed his fingers, relieved to find that he didn't smell. He muttered irritably to himself as more sweat ran down his face but he continued after Margaret nonetheless.

She walked into the ward and Carl saw her approach a large man who had a bushy moustache and was lying propped up against several pillows, his bare chest covered with thick hair. There were three other men gathered around the bed and none of them moved as Margaret approached them. 'You should be resting in your own beds,' she said gently.

'We just want to be near you,' one of them said, smiling.

Margaret smiled back and began to unscrew the cap of the medicine bottle.

'Doctor Stein won't be very happy if he finds you all out of bed,' she said.

'We don't care what he thinks,' another of the men snapped.

Margaret looked warily at the man who had spoken.

'You should be grateful that he helps you,' she insisted.

'Grateful to him?' the man said. 'That's like saying a horse should be grateful to the vet that gelds him.'

Even the man in the bed was looking at Margaret now, his hooded eyes fixing her with a piercing stare.

She poured some of the medicine into a spoon that

she slid from the front of her apron. She pushed the remedy towards the man's mouth.

'You have to take this,' she said to the man, who shook his head. 'It'll help you get better.'

The man hesitated and then opened his mouth as Margaret bent over him. Carl saw one of his pudgy hands reaching around behind her and he could see the other men watching intently.

As Margaret pushed the spoon into his mouth the man in the bed squeezed her backside. He and the others laughed.

Margaret jumped back and looked reproachfully at the man in the bed.

'You remind me of my daughter,' the man told her, grinning lecherously.

'Well, you wouldn't do that to your daughter, would you?' Margaret scolded him.

'He would,' one of the other men chuckled. A chorus of ribald laughter rose around the bed.

Carl gritted his teeth as he watched and saw Margaret's cheeks colour.

How dare these men treat her this way? Carl thought. His hand fell to his pocket, his fingers closing over the knife that he kept there. He gripped the small handle and squeezed it tightly, his body shaking with rage.

He watched as Margaret regained her composure and moved further along the ward, the men's laughter ringing in her ears.

Carl waited a moment longer. Then he shuffled to the ward entrance and stood watching as Margaret administered to the other patients before disappearing through the exit at the far end. Then he moved into the ward himself.

The men gathered around the bed looked at him in bewilderment as he approached, his face twisted into a look of pure fury.

'I saw what you did to her,' he snarled, his hand again slipping into his pocket.

The man in the bed looked at him in confusion.

'You animal,' Carl rasped. 'How dare you put your hands on her?'

'Shut up,' another man sneered. 'What does it matter to you?'

'I bet *you*'d like to put your hands on her, wouldn't you, Carl?' the man in the bed snarled, his lips sliding back to reveal a set of rotten discoloured teeth.

The other men laughed.

Carl slid the knife from his pocket and held it against the neck of the man lying in bed.

'You ever touch her again and I'll cut your throat,' Carl hissed.

The man looked at him warily and tried to swallow but the knife blade pressing against his Adam's apple made that difficult. He raised both hands in a pleading gesture but Carl kept the steel edge where it was.

'Do you understand?' Carl went on. 'If you ever touch her or harm her in any way you're a dead man.'

'All right,' the man gasped, his chest heaving.

Very slowly Carl removed the blade, his gaze still fixed on the man in the bed who finally managed to swallow.

'Don't tell Doctor Stein about this, will you?' the man asked feebly.

It was Carl's turn to smile.

'You know what he'd do if I did,' he hissed.

'Please,' the man begged.

Carl merely turned away and headed out of the ward.

It was another thirty minutes or more before he spotted Margaret again, alone in the corridor outside the other ward of the hospital. Carl watched her unseen for a moment, then shuffled towards her. She heard him coming and looked around, smiling happily when she saw it was him.

'Hello, Carl,' she said brightly.

He managed an awkward smile and lowered his gaze as if to look upon her for too long was somehow harmful.

'Do you like it here?' he asked, his heart beating faster. 'Here in the hospital?'

'I think Doctor Stein has done a wonderful job for the poor of Carlsbruck, don't you?' she asked.

'I don't think they all appreciate it,' Carl said, keeping his stare fixed on the floor close to her feet.

'I'm sure they do, Carl. Without this hospital they would have nowhere else to go for medical care.'

'I don't think some of them appreciate you,' Carl mumbled, his voice trailing away.

Margaret smiled but looked a little puzzled. 'What do you mean?' she asked.

'I saw what happened earlier,' Carl told her. 'I saw that man touch you. He shouldn't have done that.'

'Nurses have to expect things like that, Carl—'

'He shouldn't have touched you,' Carl repeated, interrupting her, his tone angry. He looked straight into her face, his own features contorted with rage. 'I told him what would happen if he ever did it again.'

Margaret nodded, not sure whether she should be grateful or not.

Carl looked down once more. 'Men like that have no respect,' he said, his voice losing some of its furious edge. 'I've seen them all my life. I saw plenty like that before I came here.'

'Where were you before, Carl? You've always been with Doctor Stein, haven't you?'

'I worked in a prison in Innsbruck. I met Doctor Stein there. He was the only man who ever showed me any respect or kindness. People pretend to care but they don't.'

'Some people do, Carl.'

Margaret reached out and touched his arm gently.

Carl looked at the delicate hand she had laid on him and then at her face. It was as if he was looking into the face of an angel. Some heavenly entity that had appeared to him here in this hospital. When she withdrew her hand he stared at where she had laid it, as if he expected to see some kind of imprint on his clothes.

'You can't trust these people,' Carl told her falteringly. 'They don't care about you. They don't care about anyone except themselves.'

'I'll be careful, I promise. And thank you, Carl.'

He could only nod.

Again she smiled at him. Then she turned to walk away.

Carl thought about trying to say something but he simply watched as she headed off along the corridor.

And he wasn't the only one who watched.

Twenty-Seven

'Three years we've allowed him to practise in this town and yet he still hasn't the good manners to speak to us.'

A chorus of approval greeted this remark from Oscar Kiesel. He nodded to himself as he looked around the room at his colleagues, all of whom seemed to be in agreement with what he'd just said.

Kiesel was a tall man with jet-black hair and piercing blue eyes that were set on either side of a nose that made him look more like a huge bird of prey than the Head of Carlsbruck Medical Council. He was in his mid-forties but looked older. When he walked it was with a slight limp, due to the gout caused by the large amounts of alcohol he imbibed frequently. He was a heavy drinker but never got drunk – even when he was fatigued his eyes never seemed to lose their almost malevolent sparkle. Now he poured himself another glass of port and looked at his colleagues seated at either side of the long table at whose head he sat.

Molke and Hauser were both older than him. Bergman was in his early sixties, a large, almost over-weight man who looked as if he'd been dropped on his chair from a great height. He drew on his cigar and watched as the smoke rose in great clouds around him, much to the irritation of Molke who coughed theatrically and moved his chair further away from the fumes.

The room in which they sat was large. The ceiling was high and vaulted and from it were suspended two large chandeliers. The walls were lined with portraits of men who had occupied their positions over the years, doctors who had lived and worked in Carlsbruck and cared for its community (or at least parts of it) to the best of their abilities. Admittedly, it was the rich who saw the most care from the Medical Council but that was the way it had always been. Only in the last three years had those at the other end of the economic scale been able to enjoy the kind of care they now did in the hospital near the centre of the town.

It was the plans of this hospital that Kiesel had spread out before him on the large oak table.

'Were any of us consulted before he began his work here?' he muttered.

'No,' Molke said.

'Were any of us invited to join him?' Kiesel went on.

'No,' Hauser said.

'And yet he comes here and expects to work within our community without even acknowledging our presence or our standing here,' Kiesel stated. 'It isn't right, gentlemen. It never has been and I think the time has come to do something about this interloper.'

'But if we take action against the Hospital for the Poor and against Doctor Stein won't it make us look as if we are victimising the needy?' Bergman asked. 'After all, the hospital does a lot of good – there are many in the town who approve of it.'

'The only ones who approve of it are the poor,' Molke said dismissively. Kiesel nodded in agreement.

'But it doesn't affect our practices or our patients,' Bergman suggested. 'None of us have suffered financially from the building and operation of this hospital.'

'But we *have* suffered financially with Stein taking away some of our patients,' Molke snapped.

'That isn't the point,' Kiesel reminded him. 'The fact is that this Doctor Stein chooses to ignore our organisation and our reputations and yet he expects to continue working here in Carlsbruck. He must be made to understand that he cannot just pretend this council does not exist. He owes us his respect if nothing else.'

'And even now, all this time since his arrival here, what do we actually know about the man?' Molke wanted to know. 'He came here three years ago and set himself up in practice. Before that no one had even heard of him. Where did he study? Where did he take his degree? Do any of us know? He could be a charlatan for all we know. And yet here he is, well established, the most popular doctor in Carlsbruck by all accounts. Perhaps that is why he chooses not to meet with us. He's afraid we will expose him for the fraud that he is.'

There were murmurs of approval from around the table.

Kiesel poured himself more port and sipped from the crystal glass. 'And now, to add insult to injury,' he went on, 'he has enticed one of our own to work for him.'

'Doctor Kleve was always headstrong,' Hauser suggested. 'As are most men of his age. He thought he could find something within the walls of Stein's hospital that he could not find with a practice here in the town.'

'Like what?' Molke enquired.

'Perhaps we should ask him,' Kiesel mused.

'Kleve is still a member of this council – perhaps he will see how it could benefit him to help us,' Hauser said.

'How?' Bergman asked.

'He works in the hospital with Stein. He could tell us what goes on there,' Hauser stated.

'You mean you want Kleve to spy for us?' Bergman exclaimed.

'I wouldn't put it like that,' Molke said dismissively. 'He would simply be relaying information for us so that we were aware of Doctor Stein's work. He may need our help at some time even if he doesn't know it yet.'

The other men laughed.

'And if he refuses?' Bergman asked. The question hung in the air as heavily as the cigar smoke.

Kiesel looked at each of his companions in turn and then nodded. Hauser got to his feet and crossed to the large double doors that opened into a smaller room. He beckoned to the occupant of that room and Doctor Hans Kleve followed him into the larger chamber where all eyes turned in his direction.

'Doctor Kleve, good of you to come,' Kiesel said,

motioning to a chair set at the far end of the large oak table around which the other men sat.

Kleve nodded and seated himself.

'I trust you didn't have any trouble getting away from the hospital,' Kiesel went on. 'Doctor Stein didn't object to you coming here to see us?'

'Why should he?' Kleve said good-naturedly.

'Perhaps he feels your services cannot be spared,' Kiesel said. 'After all, you are his assistant at the hospital now, aren't you?'

'I do assist him, yes, but he has other staff there too,' Kleve replied.

'But you're the only doctor other than Doctor Stein?' Molke asked.

'There are nurses and some other staff but, yes, I'm the only other doctor,' Kleve explained.

'And what exactly are your duties at the hospital?' Molke enquired.

'I assist Doctor Stein in his work,' Kleve said.

'Which is?' Kiesel enquired.

'He cares for the poor, gives them the kind of treatment they could not normally expect,' Kleve said.

'And all for nothing?' Kiesel asked. 'He seeks no payment for this work?'

'The people he treats in his hospital have no money,' Kleve told the watching men. 'He does what he does to help them, not for financial reward.'

'He has enough rich patients to finance his work there, then?' Molke snorted.

'He should have – he took enough away from us when he came here,' Hauser added.

'And you, Doctor Kleve, why do you work at the hospital?' Kiesel demanded.

'I want to learn from Doctor Stein,' the younger man said.

'And what can you learn from him that you couldn't learn anywhere else?' Kiesel asked. 'What makes him so skilled and the rest of us so insignificant?'

'I didn't say that,' Kleve answered.

'Perhaps you should remember that you are still a member of this council, Doctor Kleve,' Kiesel said darkly. 'Your loyalty lies with this organisation first, not with some newcomer.'

'My loyalty lies with the sick of this town and I would suggest, gentlemen, that yours should too,' Kleve said irritably. 'Are people only entitled to the best treatment if they can pay for it?' He looked challengingly at the other members of the council. 'The poor would die if it was down to you because they haven't the money to help themselves or to pay for your services.'

'Doctor Kleve, you go too far,' Molke hissed.

'When we took our oaths wasn't it to help all men and women?' Kleve went on. 'Not just the rich?'

'Are they your words or those of Doctor Stein?' Molke asked.

'I share his sentiments regarding the treatment of all, not just the well-off,' Kleve said.

'We understand that the niece of the Countess Namarov now also works at Doctor Stein's hospital,' Kiesel said.

'That's true, she's a nurse,' Kleve told him.

'And the other staff?' Bergman wanted to know.

'They were appointed by Doctor Stein. They were already there when I went to work for him,' explained Kleve.

'But who are they?' Molke persisted.

'If you want information about Doctor Stein's hospital I suggest you ask him,' Kleve said. 'Better still, go to the hospital and see what wonderful work he is doing there. I'm sure he'd be happy to enlighten you.'

'Doctor Stein sees fit to ignore this body and has done so since he arrived here in Carlsbruck,' Kiesel stated. 'Otherwise we would ask him. We have invited him to address one of our meetings but he's seen fit to ignore that invitation too.'

'He's a very busy man,' Kleve said, smiling as warmly as he could.

'Or he thinks himself somehow above us,' snapped Molke. 'Perhaps your new employer would do well to learn some humility to go with what appears to be his considerable skill as a physician.'

'I have no idea what Doctor Stein thinks of the Medical Council,' Kleve insisted. 'He never speaks of it.'

'Because it is beneath him and what he considers to be his necessary work,' Kiesel said. He steepled his fingers and peered at Kleve over the top of them. 'It might be in your best interests to find out his views and intentions, Doctor Kleve. After all – as I have already stated – you are still a member of the Medical Council. It is because of us that you have a practice here in Carlsbruck to begin with. Without us you would have had no patients to tend. It would be just as easy to remove those patients from your list. Without them how would you earn a living here?'

'Are you threatening me, doctor?' Kleve enquired.

Kiesel snorted dismissively. 'My dear boy,' he said quietly. 'I am merely pointing out that every doctor who has a practice in this town needs the help and support of the Medical Council and that to ignore that help and support may be detrimental to a man's career. After all, Doctor Stein may not remain in this town for ever and when he's gone you may need the kind of backing offered by us.'

Kleve got to his feet. 'I didn't come here to be threatened,' he said. 'And I certainly didn't come here to discuss the work of a colleague behind his back. If you want to know what Stein does in his hospital then go and see for yourselves.' He turned and headed towards the doors behind him. 'Good day, gentlemen.'

Kiesel allowed the younger man to reach the doors before he spoke again. 'Just remember what was said here today, Doctor Kleve,' he called. 'You would do well to consider it.'

'And perhaps you would do well to consider the words of the Hippocratic oath you took,' Kleve said without turning around.

'I beg your pardon?' Kiesel snapped.

'I think you heard me, doctor,' Kleve said softly. He hesitated a moment longer before pulling open the doors and stepping through them.

'Impudent young pup,' Molke rasped.

'I suppose you have to admire his determination,'

Bergman said. But he lowered his gaze when Molke glared malevolently at him.

'He is insolent,' Molke went on.

'Because he is backed by Stein and he thinks he doesn't need us any more,' Kiesel murmured. 'At least, not yet. Perhaps he's right, though. Perhaps it *is* time we paid Doctor Stein a visit.'

Twenty-Eight

Frankenstein held the bone saw in front of him for a moment, its blade glinting.

Hans Kleve watched him as he steadied the implement against the skull of the orang-utan, resting the serrated edge on the exposed cranium of the animal. Then he began to cut.

Tiny fragments of skull flew up around the blade as Frankenstein worked, using a combination of strength and care to make the initial incision. The blade made a high-pitched sound as it carved through the bone. Kleve watched intently, one hand resting on the gurney beside him that bore the body of the chimpanzee.

The smaller primate's skull was already open, gaping wide to expose the empty cavity within. Its own brain, already removed by Kleve, floated lazily in a tank of preservative fluid on one of the worktops nearby.

On the other side of the gurney stood Carl, his gaze fixed on the Baron's movements as he cut carefully through the ape's skull, pausing occasionally to wipe away the blood that trickled from the widening gash. Finally he put down the saw and reached for a long metal probe, which he inserted with infinite care into the cut that he'd already made. Working slowly and diligently, Frankenstein prised the probe upwards a fraction, then repeated the action again and again all around the shaven skull. As he made the last movement there was a low sucking sound. The Baron nodded, dropped the probe next to the bone saw and several other glinting implements, and picked up a scalpel.

Using the very tip of the blade he loosened the cap of the skull some more. Carl saw more blood dribbling from the large cut around the animal's cranium and almost by reflex he touched his own temple with one finger, tracing the route of the cut that had been inflicted on the orang-utan.

Frankenstein pulled the top of the skull free to reveal the primate's brain.

It was greyish-white in appearance, criss-crossed in all directions by thick swollen blood vessels, slicked with blood and covered with a gelatinous membrane that Frankenstein now began to cut through with the scalpel.

Both Carl and Kleve watched with awestruck fascination as the Baron worked, the skill of his movements matched by their speed. Time, he had told Kleve, was of the essence. There should be no delay in transplanting the brain into the body of the host. Deterioration of brain matter could occur almost immediately upon removal from the host. Both men watched as the Baron cut around the inside of the skull, slicing through veins and tissue to free the brain from its position. He wiped some perspiration from his cheek and left a streak of blood there but he paid it no attention, concerned only with completing the transplant now as quickly as he could.

He slid his fingers into the cranial cavity of the orang-utan skull, the brain contracting slightly as he grasped its spongy bulk. Kleve turned the gurney so that the head of the chimpanzee was only inches away, its own empty cranium waiting to be filled.

Frankenstein pulled the brain free and held it before him for a second, marvelling at its weight and texture. Several thick droplets of blood and other fluid dripped to the floor as he transferred it the short distance to the skull of the chimp.

Carl watched as if hypnotised.

That will be your brain soon. Transferred into a perfect new body.

He stroked his withered arm almost unconsciously, desperate for the time when he would no longer have to feel the wrinkled, mottled flesh there. His mouth was dry with excitement as he watched, his heart thudding hard against his ribs.

When the brain was in place, Frankenstein pushed the top of the chimpanzee's skull back into position and held it there as Kleve reached for the first of a series of small metal clips. He pushed each end into the skull above and below the cut that had opened the cranium, sealing it again. Carl watched as at least a dozen of these steel clips were inserted to secure the top of the skull. Frankenstein hastily wrapped bandages around the head when Kleve was finished and Carl saw the smile flickering on his lips.

'Now we wait,' the Baron said.

'For how long?' Kleve asked.

'It should take about twelve hours for the anaesthetic

to wear off,' Frankenstein told him. 'After that we'll have some idea of how successful the operation was and if everything is in order. Then you, Carl, will be next.'

Kleve reached out and squeezed Carl's arm.

The hunchback nodded, barely able to contain his excitement now.

'How soon, doctor?' he asked.

'We'll keep the chimpanzee under observation for a couple of days and then proceed,' Frankenstein told him. 'You can look forward to a new life, Carl.' He looked down at the body of the orang-utan, its skull still gaping open to reveal the empty space within. 'Get that out of here. Put it in the furnace.'

Carl nodded.

Frankenstein began to pull off his bloodstained apron, finally tossing it aside.

'As for you and I, my friend,' he went on, 'I think we deserve a glass of wine.'

Hans Kleve nodded.

It was early in the morning as Frankenstein and Kleve sat in the Baron's office, both of them sipping from glasses of red wine.

Frankenstein was gazing ahead of him, his attention apparently on something not inside the room. He looks distant, his thoughts anywhere but here, Kleve thought.

'Is something wrong, doctor?' the younger man asked, seeing the distracted demeanour of his companion.

'I was just thinking,' Frankenstein told him. 'I wonder

what the members of the Medical Council would say if they could see what we have done tonight. How will they react when they see what we will accomplish using Carl's brain?'

Kleve regarded his companion silently for a moment. 'They wanted to know what kind of work you were doing here,' he said finally. 'When they interviewed me, they seemed obsessed with you and this hospital.'

'And what did you tell them, Hans?'

'I told them nothing. Certainly not about the kind of work we're engaged in. I hope you trust me.'

'I learned a long time ago, Hans, it is best to trust no one when it comes to my work.'

'What about Carl?'

'Carl thinks that he will be the one to benefit from our work once all of this is over,' Frankenstein said. 'His brain in a new body. An end to the life of misery he has known. I suppose it's the least I owe him. But that isn't the end for Carl; it's just the beginning – as it will be for us, Hans.' The Baron sat forward in his seat, his eyes glinting excitedly. 'He will become a testament to my genius and ideas, a monument to a new age of science and medicine that none can imagine now.'

'What are you going to do with him?'

'I will exhibit him, Hans. I will show him around the world at medical conferences and exhibitions. The entire medical world will witness just how far I have pushed the boundaries of science and surgery and Carl will be the crowning glory, the pinnacle of my work.'

'Does he know of your plans?'

'Not yet. But what does it matter? People have stared

at him all his life for the wrong reasons, now they will gaze at him for different reasons.'

'And how do I figure in these plans, doctor?'

'You will stand beside me, Hans, and the dry old men who think themselves knowledgeable will see that you and I together have shown them the way forward.'

Kleve smiled broadly and accepted the refilled glass that the Baron pushed towards him.

'By the end of the week,' Frankenstein said, 'we should be ready to take the final step.'

Twenty-Nine

No one heard the sounds from the laboratory.

Hidden deep below ground as it was, the subterranean room was effectively soundproofed from the rest of the hospital and also from the outside world. What went on inside it was hidden from all but the most privileged eyes and any noises coming from it were masked by the thick stone walls and heavy ceiling.

Even if anyone had heard the cacophony of shrieks and wails coming from within the laboratory it was unlikely that they would have investigated. Staff at the hospital knew that, with a few exceptions, the cellar was off limits to them and now, at such an ungodly hour of the morning, few were either present or awake anyway to track down the source of the frightful sounds emanating from below.

Meyer, the janitor, had completed his nightly rounds and he now sat in the small office he occupied at one end of a corridor on the first floor. He could hear nothing from where he was. Furthermore, he had little interest in anything going on outside the small room at present. What did occupy his mind was the figure of the girl standing before him.

She was barely out of her teens. A skinny

malnourished girl with greasy blonde hair and wide eyes that stared at the janitor with a combination of weariness and disgust. She watched silently as he slowly undid his trousers, lifting his bloated backside off the chair to ease them down, beckoning her towards him with one dirty-nailed finger. He smiled crookedly and licked his lips. The girl sighed and advanced towards him. She gritted her teeth, knowing what she must do. The only comfort she could gain was that her task would at least, if it was like every other time, be over quickly.

In the wards of the hospital no one heard the sounds from the cellar either. The usual chorus of coughs, snores and grunts filled the high-ceilinged rooms as those who could tried to snatch some fitful sleep surrounded by their sickly companions. The nurses didn't do their rounds after midnight; anyone suffering would have to wait until they returned at six the next morning. Those unwilling to drag themselves to the lavatories emptied their bladders or bowels where they lay and remained in their own filth, some even managing to sleep in sheets spattered with their own excreta.

For those that did there was punishment, of course. Usually they were denied their morning meal while the nurses changed their filthy linen but those who performed such desperate and revolting actions cared little. Some genuinely couldn't help themselves. They too were punished when the time came.

*

In his attic room Carl Lang sat at one end of his small wooden bed, gazing out of his window at the other buildings nearby.

He wondered what the people inside those buildings were doing. He pondered on what kind of lives they led. Who they loved and who loved them. And when he thought of that his mind turned inevitably to Margaret Conrad.

Carl wasn't sure exactly what it felt like to be in love. He didn't know if it changed a man mentally and made him act in different ways but he was sure that he was in love. He was hopelessly infatuated with Margaret. Lost in his desire for this perfect creature. Even the thought of her caused his twisted features to curl into a smile and once he started thinking about her he found it difficult to stop.

And soon, when the operation that Frankenstein had promised him for so long was complete, he would be able to approach her as a real man. Not the disfigured, twisted specimen he was now but a man who could look her in the eye and speak to her as an equal. The smile on Carl Lang's face grew wider.

From his position high in the attic of the hospital, even if he'd been listening he would never have heard the sounds coming from the cellar.

The sounds continued for almost ten minutes. Strident caterwauls that sometimes sounded like screams of rage or pain. When they finally subsided the silence that descended was even more disconcerting. It seemed to close conspiratorially around the laboratory and the hospital itself.

Dawn was still two hours away.

Thirty

The large glass case that Frankenstein rolled into view was about seven feet long and half that in width.

Covered from top to bottom with a thick tarpaulin, the contents were hidden completely from the watchful eyes of Hans Kleve and Carl Lang who both stood in the laboratory.

Frankenstein looked at his two companions and smiled, aware of their fascination with what lay beneath the material. Finally, with something of a flourish, he pulled the tarpaulin away.

The contents of the glass case were now fully exposed.

Revealed was the naked body of a man, over six feet tall. His head was topped by a mane of black hair that fell almost as far as his broad shoulders. His chest was thick and muscular, as were his arms. In life he had obviously been a strong man because the muscles in his legs were also large.

Carl moved a step closer and inspected the face, noting how expressionless it seemed to be. And yet there was a serenity to the features and the hunchback was sure that the lips were curled slightly in the shape of a smile. Perhaps the motionless body somehow knew that life was close to being restored to it, he mused. He reached out and gently touched the glass above the face.

'The next time you see this body, Carl, will be from the inside,' Frankenstein said.

'It certainly is a fine specimen,' Kleve observed. 'Who is he?'

'No one – he hasn't been born yet,' Frankenstein said quietly. 'It is who he will become that matters. No misshapen monster but a perfect man.'

Kleve looked at Carl and smiled. 'That will be you, Carl,' he said, watching as the hunchback continued to gaze raptly at the body in front of them.

'It is *already* you, Carl,' Frankenstein said. 'And once the operation is completed it will be just a matter of time before you can begin to live the kind of life you have only dreamed of previously.'

'How will the body itself be reanimated?' Kleve asked.

'It is alive now,' Frankenstein said. 'By keeping it in temperatures below freezing the cells remain dormant but they don't deteriorate. This body is waiting for the spark that will allow it once again to walk and talk and when it does it will be with Carl's will and his voice.'

'It's incredible,' Kleve said.

'No, my dear Hans, not incredible,' Frankenstein said, smiling. 'It is the pinnacle of my work and it will be a living monument to my genius.'

Carl was still gazing at the body. He touched his own withered arm as he shuffled slowly around the glass case, his stare never leaving the motionless occupant.

Frankenstein watched him, the smile fading from his lips.

'It won't look like me,' Carl said quietly, sliding his fingers over the top of the case.

'You should be grateful for that, Carl,' Frankenstein said curtly. 'All that matters is that the brain inside that body will be yours. Once the operation is completed you will have no use for that body you now inhabit. It will be a relic. An unwanted reminder of a past that you once had and a life you hated. Imagine what your life will become.'

Kleve caught Frankenstein's eye for a second before the Baron also gazed down raptly at the face of the body inside the case.

'I'll be like every other normal man,' Carl said.

Frankenstein nodded. 'But you won't be just a normal man, Carl,' he said. 'You'll be better than the others. A new kind of man. The first of a new and more superior breed. Nothing will be beyond you.'

A tear formed at the corner of Carl's eye and rolled gently down his cheek. Kleve reached out and put one hand comfortingly on the other man's shoulder.

'Don't weep, Carl,' Frankenstein said. 'You are the one who will have the strength. It is the world that will weep when they see you. The men who doubted *me* will shed tears.'

There was a loud howl from the far end of the laboratory and all three men turned towards the noise.

It took them only a second to realise that the sound had come from the chimpanzee cage. Kleve headed for it immediately, Frankenstein following him. Carl lingered beside the body. The body that would be his.

When Kleve reached the cage he could see that the chimpanzee was sitting in one corner, idly scratching itself.

In a nearby cage a female chimp was hanging from the bars, looking at her companion, occasionally extending a long arm in his direction.

Kleve smiled when he saw the gesture.

'The chimp looks fine,' Frankenstein said. 'The brain transplant was obviously successful, as I expected.'

'It looks as if the female wants her mate back,' Kleve said.

'We'll put them in the same cage tomorrow,' Frankenstein stated.

'Shouldn't we keep the male under observation for a little longer?'

'No need. He's fine.'

Frankenstein turned away from the cage.

Kleve waited a moment, then followed him.

The female chimp continued to reach out to her mate but the male remained, motionless now, in the corner of his own cage. He watched her silently for a moment longer, then turned away.

Thirty-One

To the rear of the hospital, surrounded by a high wall and hidden from prying eyes, there was a small but well-kept garden where patients were allowed to walk if they felt strong enough and if they had been given permission by one of the doctors or nurses.

It was in this garden that Doctor Hans Kleve now sat, enjoying the scent of the flowers, massaging the back of his neck to try and alleviate a headache that he'd had for most of the afternoon.

He looked up when he heard footsteps on the path nearby.

'I didn't mean to disturb you, doctor,' Margaret Conrad said apologetically.

'You're not,' Kleve told her, getting to his feet. 'I should be back inside the hospital, anyway; I just stepped out to get some fresh air.'

'It can get a little overpowering sometimes, can't it?' Margaret said.

'I've been in surgery all day so far,' he replied. 'The workload here is unrelenting, shall we say.' He managed a tired smile.

'I'd noticed,' Margaret agreed, smiling herself.

'You seem to have settled in here very well since you arrived,' Kleve observed.

Margaret nodded. 'Doctor Stein has been very helpful,' she said.

'He's a marvellous man, isn't he? I've never worked for anyone like him. I feel I've learned more from him during the last month or so than I have in my whole career. I find his enthusiasm and ideas so fascinating.' Kleve held up his hands. 'Excuse me but I get carried away when I talk about work.'

'It's good to see a man so dedicated. Where were you working before you came here?'

'I had my own practice here in Carlsbruck.'

'Is that where you're from?'

'No, I was born and brought up in Innsbruck. I went to medical school in Vienna. What about you? Were you born here?'

'No, in Carlsbad. I moved here when my parents died.'

'I'm sorry,' Kleve said quietly.

'I live with my aunt,' Margaret told him. 'I have done since it happened.'

'The Countess Namarov, I heard.'

'Have people been gossiping about me, Doctor Kleve?' Margaret smiled.

'Hans,' he corrected her. 'Please call me Hans.'

'So, Hans, have people been talking about me?'

'It's a small town – word gets around very easily.'

'Someone once told me that small towns make small minds.'

Kleve smiled. 'I fear that can be true as well,' he said.

'They obviously make jealous minds too, from some of the things I've been hearing about Doctor Stein,' Margaret went on.

'From who?'

'My aunt, for one. She knows several members of the Carlsbruck Medical Council and she says they don't want Doctor Stein here.'

'No, they don't. They don't like him because they can't frighten him. He doesn't care about them and what they do here. All he cares about is his own work.'

'The work with the patients here?'

'And his research.'

'Into what, Hans?'

Kleve hesitated for a moment. Then he moved a little closer to her and lowered his voice almost conspiratorially.

'Things that the Medical Council could never dream of,' he explained. 'Ideas that their blinkered members couldn't even begin to comprehend. He has opened my eyes to scientific and medical procedures that I had never encountered before.'

'Like what?'

Kleve drew a deep breath, wondering if he'd already gone too far. He looked at Margaret and held her gaze for a moment before continuing, unable to restrain himself such was his fervour and enthusiasm.

'The transplantation of organs, the reanimation of cells,' he said, his eyes blazing.

Margaret looked a little shocked and Kleve caught the flicker of distaste (of actual revulsion, perhaps) on her features.

'And this work takes place in his laboratory in the basement?' she enquired.

Kleve nodded. 'And when it's complete it will bring the rest of the scientific world to its knees,' he went on excitedly. 'The advances Doctor Stein is making are unimaginable.'

'And you're helping him?'

'Learning from him.' He smiled. 'And struggling to keep up, sometimes.'

They both laughed.

Carl Lang heard the laughter as he observed them from the first-floor window of the hospital. He had been watching them since they first began speaking, a feeling growing inside him that he recognised as anger. He glared at Kleve, his jaw clenched and his fist banging almost unconsciously against his thigh.

Keep away from her, Doctor Kleve. She's mine.

That was the only thought in his head now as he looked at Margaret, sickened by the fact that she was looking so raptly at Kleve.

And inside his head he screamed the words furiously.

SHE'S MINE.

Thirty-Two

Frankenstein looked from one body to the other and nodded almost imperceptibly.

On one trolley lay the unblemished body that he and Kleve had removed from the specimen case. Next to it was the twisted humpbacked form of Carl Lang.

The heads of both figures were gaping open, the skulls empty and the tops of each cranium hanging free like the lids of opened cans. It had already taken three hours to prepare the two of them for the next stage of the procedure. Both Frankenstein and Kleve were sweating from their exertions and both men were spattered with blood.

Frankenstein looked at Kleve who advanced towards the larger body carrying Carl's brain in his expert hands.

The Baron watched as Kleve placed it inside the open cavity of the other man's skull.

'A living brain into a living body,' Frankenstein said, smiling.

Kleve wiped one bloodstained hand on his apron, then set about sealing the skull.

'No wonder he hated that body,' Frankenstein said, looking disdainfully at Carl's hunchbacked corpse, the left arm and leg dangling as uselessly as those of a puppet with its strings cut.

Kleve didn't reply but continued with his task, checking that the fissure in the skull was properly sealed. He wiped some sticky fluid from the gash with one gloved hand, occasionally glancing at the cadaver's face as if expecting it to look back at him. Naturally it remained expressionless and Kleve thought that it could as easily have been fashioned from flesh-coloured clay, such was the flawless nature of its skin and features. For fleeting seconds he wondered who the man had been in life – but that wasn't important. Who he had been didn't matter any more, while who he would *become* was of the utmost and sole importance. Lying before him like the bodies of Carl and the anonymous man was his own future too, he mused. Once this experiment was completed and enough time had passed to ensure that success had been achieved then the next stage would come. Showing the medical and scientific world what he and Frankenstein had accomplished. The thought sent a shiver through Kleve and he had to steady himself slightly as he continued with his work, forcing himself to concentrate on the task before him and not what lay ahead. However, his excitement was almost uncontainable.

Frankenstein moved closer and inspected his work, nodding silently, a slight smile on his lips. It was sign enough for Kleve that what he was doing was right and satisfactory. He looked at the Baron as if for confirmation. Frankenstein inspected the raw cut around the skull carefully to ensure that it was sealed. Satisfied, he himself began to bandage it, wrapping the linen carefully around the head as Kleve stepped back, the perspiration beading and then running down his face as a result of such sustained concentration.

Frankenstein looked at his younger companion and saw the determination in his eyes. 'Do you think this is what God felt like, Hans?' he asked. 'Standing over beings He had created, waiting to give life?'

Kleve could only shrug. 'I thought you didn't believe in God,' he said.

'It's difficult to believe when you have the kind of power that you and I have.'

Kleve nodded. 'How long before we'll know if the operation has been successful?' he asked.

'A day or two,' Frankenstein told him. 'Carl needs to be kept somewhere alone where he can be cared for constantly if necessary. He must rest and have no sudden movement. It may be best to keep him strapped down. I was going to ask Margaret to undertake his care.'

Kleve looked concerned. 'But what will we tell her?' he wanted to know.

'We will tell her nothing,' Frankenstein snapped.

'But she knows Carl,' Kleve persisted. 'She knows what he looks like. Once the surgery is done she's going to see the difference, isn't she?'

'So what do you suggest we do? Tell her the intricacies of the operation? Inform her that we've transplanted Carl's brain from his old body into a new one? Do you think she will actually be able to comprehend the enormity of such work, Hans?'

Kleve took a deep breath. 'She'll notice the difference in him,' he said. 'She'll wonder where Carl has gone. She's not stupid.'

'As far as she'll be concerned Carl will have gone away,' Frankenstein said. 'The patient she'll be asked to care for will also be called Carl – it isn't such a stretch of probability that two men should share the same common name, is it?'

'It sounds a little convenient.'

'That's as may be. But I don't want her hearing any details about what has been done. Especially not from you.'

'What's that supposed to mean?'

'I've seen the way you are around her, Hans, and I can understand your interest. She's a beautiful girl but you must be careful. She is never to know what has gone on here tonight.'

'So what do we say to her?'

'Carl will be taken back to his room and treated as a new patient. She will be charged with his care twenty-four hours a day. Only when we're sure that the procedure has been a one hundred per cent success will she need to know the truth. Carl himself will be instructed to say nothing to her about his situation or what has been done to him. Do you understand?'

'I too am aware of the importance of this work, you know, doctor.'

'Did I ever say anything to the contrary, Hans? I merely mentioned that I had noticed your interest in Margaret. It wouldn't be the first time that a pretty face has caused a distraction when it comes to work.'

'You need have no fear on that count, doctor. I am as committed to this work as you.'

'What an unfortunate choice of words, Hans. Because I suspect that if any members of the Medical Council could see us now that is precisely what they would seek to do with us: commit us.'

'Or burn us at the stake as wizards,' Kleve said.

'Quite so.'

Frankenstein stepped back from the body and looked down at it with pride. 'Tomorrow he begins a new life,' he said quietly.

'What about Carl's old body?' Kleve wanted to know.

'It will be kept and preserved so that when we begin visiting universities and medical colleges with our work they can see how we helped Carl become a better man instead of the worthless cripple he was before.'

'How do you think he will feel about that?'

'To be honest, I really don't care. Carl's only emotion from now on should be gratitude.'

Thirty-Three

C arl Lang opened his eyes with difficulty.

It seemed as if the lids were sewn shut and weighed down with lead. His head felt as if someone had inflated it with air and pain was gnawing at him like a hungry dog. It was inside his skull, in every muscle of his body, and it was dreadful.

He groaned softly and this time succeeded in opening his eyes fully. Immediately he winced as the sunshine pouring through the window to his left seemed to set the optic orbs ablaze. Carl let out another low breath and blinked myopically. He tried to raise one arm to cover his eyes and that limb too felt leaden and unresponsive. The pain, however, diminished slightly.

'Don't try to move.'

The voice floated around him as if from a dream but he thought he recognised it.

With his eyes closed he felt something cool pressing gently against his forehead and he realised that a damp cloth had been placed there. The sensation against his flesh was pleasing and he relaxed a little more, the pain that seemed to be flowing through his veins like liquid now receding somewhat.

'You must stay still if you can,' the voice told him softly.

Carl opened his eyes again, this time more easily, and he saw a blurred shape beside him.

'Go back to sleep,' the voice encouraged him.

Carl moved his lips and tried to say something. He wanted to tell the owner of the voice that he was in pain. He wanted to ask for something to help it stop but no words would come forth.

He closed his eyes once more and felt darkness closing in all around him. He didn't fight it this time.

When Carl woke again he had no idea how long he'd been unconscious. All he knew was that the pain which had gripped him so severely was still present but was nowhere near as crippling as before. For that at least he was grateful.

Again he tried to open his eyes and once more he felt as if the lids had been sewn shut.

Perhaps they have been. Perhaps you're dead and in the ground, put there by Frankenstein after the experiment failed.

He let out a long breath, then coughed, and that action sent sharp pain once again lancing into his head and the back of his neck.

The experiment. Frankenstein.

Carl began to wonder where he was. When he moved his fingers he could feel something soft beneath their tips. After a moment or two he realised that it was linen of some sort. He tried to clench his fists and it took an almost superhuman effort to accomplish that small task. But he managed it and when he finally relaxed his fingers they were shaking. He allowed his hands to drop back down and decided he would try to open his eyes once again.

When he did so he found himself in darkness. Carl blinked hard, trying to see around him, desperate to learn where he was.

He saw only blackness.

Are you inside a coffin? Buried and discarded as a failure?

He took a sharp breath and raised his head slightly, fearing for one second that it might connect with the wooden lid of a coffin. But it didn't. Pain enveloped him once more and he lay still.

As his eyes slowly became accustomed to the gloom he grew aware that he was in a small room, lying on a bed. *His* bed. Carl realised that he was lying in his room at the hospital. A sudden surge of relief coursed through him and it seemed to drive the pain from his system as surely as an anaesthetic. He let out a small murmur of relief.

'Can you hear me?'

The voice floated to him once again through the gloom and through his consciousness. He realised that it wasn't the fragment of a dream but was here in the room beside him. Its source was the same blurred shape he'd seen when he'd woken before.

He felt a gentle touch on his right hand and looked down. Carl tried to speak but found that words still would not form properly on his trembling lips. His mouth was dry and it felt as if his tongue was sticking to its roof. He made a guttural sound in his throat.

'Would you like some water?'

The voice was close to him now and Carl turned his

head towards it, squinting to make out the source through the darkness and his own blurred vision. He tried to reach up to rub his eyes but found that he couldn't move his arms. He sucked in an anxious breath and then realised that his arms were held fast by thick leather straps. There were more straps across his chest and stomach, fastened tightly and holding him against the mattress.

He recognised the young woman who was smiling down at him.

Margaret Conrad was holding a glass of water in one hand, pushing it gently towards him.

As Carl raised himself up as far as he could, she slipped her other hand beneath the back of his head, trying to help him. Then she pressed the glass to his lips. He felt cool water spill into his mouth and down his throat and he gulped thirstily. Some of the liquid trickled down his chin onto his neck and chest but he kept swallowing, trying to get as much of the welcome fluid down as he could.

'Not too much,' Margaret said quietly, taking the glass away and allowing him to lie down once more.

Carl tried to speak again but it was as if the effort of drinking the water had somehow tired him out. He felt an uncontrollable exhaustion envelop him. Try as he might he could not keep his eyes open. He knew that he was drifting off again but this time he fought against that feeling. He didn't want to sleep; he wanted to speak, to look at Margaret. He wanted to tell her that his pain was leaving him. He wanted to shout from the rooftops that he felt good. In that split second he realised that the operation had been successful and even though he couldn't speak his lips curled upwards in a smile. He flexed his fingers and curled them into fists once again.

'I'm going to stay with you,' Margaret said softly.

Carl smiled again.

He was still smiling when he blacked out.

Thirty-Four

'**M**ove your right hand.'

Carl Lang heard the words and turned his head slightly in the direction from which they had come.

Inside the small attic room Baron Frankenstein stood beside the bed, peering down at him.

Carl stretched the fingers of his right hand, then clenched them into a fist.

'Good,' Frankenstein said, nodding. He moved a little closer, then reached into his pocket and withdrew something that Carl couldn't see. Carl hissed loudly a second later when the Baron jabbed a pin into the ball of his thumb. 'Nothing wrong with the reflexes.' Frankenstein smiled. 'Now move the left hand.'

Carl looked at his left hand and arm. All his life the limb had been withered and useless, the skin puckered and dry, but now it looked strong – and he could *feel* the strength in it. There was no loose flesh there now. He flexed the fingers and curled them into a fist, smiling slightly when he felt the muscles in his forearm and bicep contract. He lifted the arm into the air, then lowered it slowly while Frankenstein watched.

Carl was lying on his bed, his body naked except for the short pantaloons that he was wearing.

On one side Frankenstein stood looking down at him and on the other Doctor Kleve too was running an appraising gaze over Carl's new form. Carl himself had been staring down at his torso for most of the time the two men had been with him, as if unable to believe that the body he could see was his own. The scars around the wrists and the forehead had healed cleanly and he felt no pain now apart from a little stiffness in his lower back from lying immobile for so long.

'I want you to stand up,' Frankenstein told him.

Carl nodded and carefully hauled his legs from the side of the bed, putting his weight on them as he struggled to stand up. He swayed uncertainly for a moment, then steadied himself and managed to remain upright.

Frankenstein smiled.

'It's incredible,' Kleve whispered in awe.

'Yes, it is, Hans,' the Baron murmured. 'Incredible what we have done.'

Carl stood where he was for a moment, awaiting further instructions.

Frankenstein wasn't slow to supply one. 'Walk across the room and back again,' he ordered.

Carl put one foot falteringly before the other, then set off slowly and shakily like a child taking its first steps. He stumbled and almost fell. Kleve stepped forward to help him but Frankenstein shot out a hand to prevent him reaching Carl.

'Keep going,' he snapped.

Carl looked down at his left leg and saw the muscles in the thigh bulging. No longer was the leg twisted and withered and when he walked now it was with a powerful stride. He took several more steps, then turned and walked back towards the bed where Frankenstein motioned for him to sit down.

'You need a little more rest,' the Baron observed. 'But I can see no problems so far. You've made better progress than even I dared hope.'

'Doctor,' Carl croaked, clearing his throat. 'There is one thing.'

'What is it?' the Baron asked.

'My face,' Carl said, touching the smooth skin beneath his left eye. 'I don't know what I look like.'

Frankenstein nodded and slipped his hand inside his jacket. He pulled out a small mirror and held it in front of Carl who looked towards the glass with a mixture of trepidation and excitement.

The image he saw was of a man in his thirties with high cheekbones and thin lips. It took him a moment to realise that it was his own image that stared back at him. He drew a breath and used both hands to touch his face, tracing his fingertips over his skin, particularly on the left side of his countenance, the side that had formerly been disfigured. He smiled, his eyes filling with tears. This was no misshapen freak that stared back at him but a normal man.

'Get used to that sight, Carl,' Frankenstein said.

Carl nodded, tears now coursing down his cheeks. 'Thank you, doctor,' he said breathlessly.

Frankenstein laid one hand comfortingly on his left shoulder and set the mirror down on the bedside table.

'You'll need this from now on, Carl,' he said. 'There's no need to hide from your reflection any more.'

Carl couldn't answer. He merely continued to cry tears of joy, something he had never done before in his life.

It was a good feeling.

Thirty-Five

The body had been torn to pieces.

One of the arms had been wrenched from its socket and lay discarded on one side of the cage, the jagged ends of a bone sticking through the mess of bloodied muscle that formed the stump. There were several large lumps of flesh and crimson-encrusted matter spread around like reeking confetti. But there seemed to be a lack of internal organs.

As Doctor Hans Kleve surveyed the carnage inside the chimpanzees' cage he realised that not only had the female chimp been gutted, the stomach cavity and chest wrenched open, but most of the viscera contained within her body were gone.

The male sat in one corner. He stared blankly at Kleve, then at the corpse of his mate.

There was blood around the male's mouth, on its long sinewy fingers and also splashed on its face and chest. It took Kleve only a moment to realise the full horror of what he was looking at.

The lack of internal organs. The riven torso of the female and the gouges and wounds on her lifeless body indicated only one thing. She had been attacked, killed – and parts of her had been eaten by the male.

The eyes were missing from the sockets of her skull, torn wildly from their rightful place in the frenzied assault that had killed her. Predators usually ate the soft parts of their victims first, Kleve reminded himself, and it looked as if the male chimp had done just that.

As Kleve stood transfixed by the sight the male suddenly hurled himself at the bars, gripping them with his long powerful fingers and slamming his face against the metal struts. Kleve stepped back involuntarily, aware of the fury burning in the eyes of the chimp as it shook the cage, its teeth bared. He noted, with some disgust, that there were still lumps of flesh stuck between them. The show of aggression lasted only a moment and then the chimp slumped back into a corner of the cage, tracing one finger through a pool of blood and innards close to it.

Kleve stood for a moment longer, gazing at the scene of slaughter. Then he turned and hurried through the laboratory, making his way up the stone steps and into the office beyond. He found Frankenstein seated behind his desk, scanning several sheets of handwritten notes. The Baron looked up as Kleve walked in.

'You look troubled, Hans,' he said, matter-of-factly returning his attention to his paperwork.

'I think we may have a problem,' Kleve told him.

'With what?'

'The chimpanzee that we did the brain transplant on has attacked and killed its mate.'

'That may have nothing to do with the operation.'

'It's eaten parts of the female.'

'And what makes you think that has anything to do with the procedure we performed?'

'Because chimpanzees aren't cannibalistic. I know they occasionally eat meat in the wild but they don't usually devour each other.'

'That still doesn't mean that it was anything to do with the transplant. Those tendencies may have been dormant in that individual even before we experimented on it.'

'And what if they weren't?'

Frankenstein looked up from his paperwork, dropped his pen and regarded Kleve quizzically across his desk.

'What are you getting at, Hans?' the Baron asked.

'If it happened with the ape what's to stop it happening again?'

'You mean to Carl?'

Kleve nodded.

'The chimp became agitated after the operation and he damaged some of the cells of his brain,' Frankenstein said. 'He wasn't kept restrained for long enough. Unlike Carl. Why do you think I have been at such great pains to ensure that Carl remains rested and immobile? His brain must be allowed to heal properly.'

'Then isn't there more to worry about? There are more problems that could occur with the brain of a human.'

'The chimp was wild. You cannot attach the same criteria to it that you would to a human brain. Besides, if there had been an adverse effect of that kind with Carl we would have seen it by now.'

'You're very sure of that?'

'Trust me, Hans, there is no need to be concerned. The transplant we performed on Carl was a great success. You know that, you've seen him; you've seen the progress he's made in such a short time. Also, we transplanted the brain of an orang-utan into that chimp. The fact that we were using two different species could be relevant. That wasn't the case with Carl and I've never experienced that kind of reaction at any time before.'

'But for it to turn cannibalistic . . .' Kleve muttered, his brow furrowing.

Frankenstein merely shrugged. 'You're worrying for no reason,' he said dismissively.

'What do we do with it now?' Kleve enquired.

'We'll keep it under observation if that will make you feel happier,' Frankenstein said. 'But it's served its purpose. It's no use to us any more.' He smiled. 'Besides, we have a much more interesting subject to occupy us now, don't we?'

Kleve smiled too, his concern seemingly evaporating for the time being.

'Have you seen him today?' Frankenstein asked.

'Not yet. I was going to check on him after my rounds.'

'He is getting stronger with each passing day. His powers of recovery have been remarkable and the scars on the head seem to be healing even faster than usual.'

'Could that be a result of the transplant?'

'It's possible. But the brain was in excellent condition and so was the host body – there was no damage to either. The combination seems to be working to Carl's advantage.' Frankenstein sat back in his seat, his gaze directed past Kleve as if he was focused on something that only he was capable of seeing. 'There have been no mistakes this time, Hans,' he went on, his voice low. 'The things I did wrong previously I have rectified. I have learned from my mistakes and soon I will show the world what I have achieved.'

Kleve nodded.

'Now, if there's nothing else,' Frankenstein said, looking at his younger companion, 'I have work to get on with. Carl is fine. There's no cause for concern. Trust me.'

Thirty-Six

Doctor Hans Kleve tapped lightly on the attic-room door before stepping inside.

As he walked in he glanced at the bed and saw Carl lying motionless there, the thick leather straps around his chest and stomach holding him tight against the mattress.

Next to him Margaret Conrad was gently mopping his brow with a damp cloth.

'Is everything all right?' Kleve asked, moving towards the bed.

'His temperature was up,' Margaret explained. 'And he says he's feeling some pain.'

Kleve looked down at Carl, then reached for his arm and checked the pulse.

'The pain is to be expected, Carl,' Kleve said. 'It'll pass but I can give you something for it if you'd like.'

'I'll be fine, doctor. I think I just want to get out of here and walk around,' Carl said.

'I know that,' Kleve told him. 'Doctor Stein advised strapping you down again in case you hurt yourself. He knows how impatient you are to be mobile again.'

Margaret smiled and continued mopping Carl's head.

Kleve nodded towards the clothes that were hanging

up behind the door. 'You'll soon be able to wear those, Carl,' he said. Then he turned towards Margaret. 'You can leave us for now. I'll tend to Carl – there are some tests that Doctor Stein wants done on him and I'm sure you can find plenty to do down in the hospital.'

Margaret nodded and touched Carl's cheek gently. 'I'll come back later,' she said.

Carl smiled broadly as she walked out of the room.

'Now,' Kleve said, perching on one side of the bed and leaning over Carl. 'Let's have a look at you.'

Carl relaxed as the doctor gently pulled down his lower eyelids and looked into his eyes. Kleve checked the pupillary dilation and nodded in satisfaction. He was similarly impressed with Carl's reflexive responses and when he stood up he looked down on the other man with an expression of combined warmth and pride.

'Doctor Kleve,' Carl said, clearing his throat, 'what is to happen to me?'

'What do you mean, Carl?'

'When all this is over – what will happen to me?'

'There are great plans for you, Carl,' the doctor said, beaming. 'Doctors and scientists will come from all over the world to see you and to talk to you. You're a very important person now.'

Carl listened warily. When he tried to swallow he felt as if his throat was filled with chalk.

'People coming here to see me?' he said quietly.

'Yes, doctors, surgeons, students. All kinds of people.'

'But why?'

'Because you're a very remarkable man, Carl, and what has happened to you is unlike anything that has ever been seen before. You should be happy about it. You'll be famous.'

'People will stare at me.'

'They'll speak to you. Ask you questions.'

'People will stare, just as they've stared at me all my life.'

'No, this will be different, Carl.'

'No, it won't,' Carl said.

'They'll see you, a normal man with a normal body, side by side with your old body.'

An expression of despair crossed Carl's face and he allowed his head to sink deeper into the pillow as he let out a deep breath. 'I'll be like an animal in a zoo, to be stared at and pointed at by anyone who wants to look at me,' he sighed.

'No, Carl, you're going to be a wonderful example. You'll be able to play a great part in the advancement of medical science.'

Carl shook his head gently and Kleve was sure he could see tears welling up in the other man's eyes.

'I thought once this operation was done I would be as other men,' Carl muttered. 'Able to live a normal life. I didn't expect to become some kind of laboratory rat for anyone who feels like it to stare at and poke and prod.'

'It won't be like that, Carl. Doctor Stein has your best interests at heart.'

'He only cares about his work, I know that.'

'You shouldn't be ungrateful, Carl. Never forget that it was Doctor Stein's genius that turned you into the man you are now. The man you will become.'

'The sideshow freak, the circus attraction?'

Kleve looked down at the man, then reached out and placed one hand on his forehead. 'I think your temperature is falling,' he remarked, attempting to sound detached and professional. 'I can give you something for the pain if you like.'

Carl shook his head.

'Then you must rest,' Kleve insisted.

'Send Miss Conrad back up, please, doctor,' Carl asked quietly as the other man turned towards the door. 'I don't want to be alone.'

Kleve hesitated, thought about saying that Margaret had work to do. But then he nodded. 'I will,' he murmured, opening the attic-room door and stepping past it. He pulled it shut gently and stood against it for a moment before making his way towards the stairs.

Inside the small room, Carl heard the doctor's footsteps receding.

Thirty-Seven

Frankenstein must be in the laboratory beneath him. That was Kleve's first thought when he entered the office and found it to be empty.

A kettle was bubbling on a stove in one corner of the room. Kleve poured some hot water into a mug before adding some brandy and sipping the mixture slowly.

He was about to sit down when the door opened and the bulky form of Meyer ambled in, pausing at the threshold where he looked towards Kleve. The fat man coughed theatrically and rubbed his chest, his stare fixed on the mug that the doctor held.

'All right, come in,' Kleve said reluctantly. 'And by the way – next time you come in here knock first.'

'Yes, doctor, sorry, doctor,' Meyer said, closing the door behind him. 'I was looking for Doctor Stein, you see, and thought he might be in here.'

The fat man coughed again and drummed on the shaft of his broom with his fingers.

'Here,' Kleve said, handing him a mug and tipping some brandy into it.

Meyer smiled crookedly and slurped at the contents. 'Well, doctor, if you insist,' he grunted, wiping his mouth with the back of one pudgy hand. 'Just the stuff for a cold day, eh?' He snorted loudly.

Odious man, Kleve thought.

'If you used that broom a bit more you wouldn't be cold,' the doctor said, sipping at his own drink.

Meyer nodded and sat down on the edge of the desk, his heavy bulk causing the wood to creak menacingly for a moment. Kleve regarded him coldly.

'My old bones are aching,' Meyer said.

'Try losing some weight. They won't ache if they haven't got so much to support and it'll be better for your health.'

'Otherwise I might end up in here, I suppose.' Meyer laughed throatily.

'You just might.'

Meyer took another slurp of his drink. 'How's the special patient, then, doctor?' he asked. 'The one in that room in the attic.'

'What do you know about him?'

'Nothing except that he's special. What's so different about him? Hasn't he got fleas?' Meyer laughed that throaty and mucoid laugh again.

'If you washed yourself you wouldn't have fleas,' Kleve said, wiping some tweezers with a piece of cloth.

'Me, wash? I'd get pneumonia,' Meyer protested. 'No, thanks. I'll keep my fleas and have my health and strength, thank you very much.'

The two men regarded each other silently for a moment. Then Meyer spoke again.

'Now, take the animals in the jungle,' he said. 'They

don't wash and yet you don't hear of them getting sick. Why? Because they're good and dirty.'

'What do you know about the animals in the jungle?' Kleve said, transferring his attention to a small pair of scissors. He cleaned those with the same diligence as he had the tweezers.

'You'd be surprised. I'm a big animal fancier. I know all about their habits.'

'Because you practise them yourself?'

'And what's wrong with that? They were here before we were and they'll be here a long time after we've gone. They know how to look after themselves.' He seemed to be warming to his subject. 'Take the monkeys, for instance; they've got a good layer of dirt to keep them warm.' He scratched his chest through his dirty shirt. 'Plenty to eat and plenty to drink. I bet they laugh at us sometimes.'

Kleve raised one eyebrow. He was beginning to tire of this man and his musings.

'If you get hungry you have to cook yourself some meat and potatoes,' Meyer went on. 'Not them. They just reach out and get a banana. They don't have to worry about cooking. They don't even eat meat.'

'No,' Kleve murmured, looking up, his brow furrowed. 'They don't, do they?'

He put down the scalpel he'd been cleaning and turned towards the door that led down to the underground laboratory. 'You get back to work,' he called to Meyer.

Thirty-Eight

He wasn't sure how long he'd slept.

Carl Lang didn't even remember falling asleep. He opened his eyes slowly at first, then jerked them open as he realised that he was not alone.

Carl turned his head.

'I'm sorry; I didn't mean to wake you.'

Margaret Conrad was standing beside the bed, smiling down at him. Carl smiled back at her. He moved as if to sit up but the straps that restrained him prevented that simple movement. He sank back onto the mattress and lay still. Carl was filled with an overwhelming desire simply to reach out and touch Margaret's hand but even that motion was denied to him by the straps. He wondered if her skin felt as soft as he had imagined. He swallowed hard and kept his gaze fixed on her for a moment longer.

'You didn't wake me,' he lied. 'I'm pleased to see you.'

'Are you feeling better now?'

'A little,' he croaked. 'Did Doctor Stein send you to see me?'

'No,' Margaret told him. 'I came back to check on you, see if there was anything you wanted.' She pulled the wooden chair near the bed closer and sat down. 'Is there anything?'

'Just to be out of this room,' Carl said.

'I don't blame you for that. You've been recovering in here for days now. It must have been a very complicated operation that you went through.'

Carl nodded.

'Doctor Stein is a marvellous surgeon, though, isn't he?' Margaret said. 'He does such wonderful work here. You must be so grateful to him.'

'Yes,' Carl told her, his voice emotionless. 'Yes, I am.'

She leaned closer and he could smell the scent of her hair. He turned his head to look at her and she smiled warmly.

'And when you feel better you can return to work,' she said.

'I have no work.'

'You'll soon find some when you leave here and when you do you'll forget all about your illness.'

Carl gritted his teeth, fighting the urge to tell Margaret what he was doing here in this room, strapped to this bed. But how could he begin to explain? How could he possibly ever tell anyone about the circumstances he had found himself in?

'I'll help you when you're better,' Margaret went on. 'You should come and see me.'

Carl swallowed hard.

'I'll write down my address for you, shall I?'

He nodded. 'I've never met anyone like you before,' Carl told her. 'No one so kind and no one so beautiful.'

Margaret squeezed his arm. 'That's very kind of you to say but you'll embarrass me,' she said, smiling.

'I'm sorry, I didn't mean to . . .'

'I'm joking. It's a lovely compliment.'

'Do you live near the hospital?'

'I live with my aunt outside the town on the Namarov estate. Do you know it?'

'I've heard of it.'

'Well, when you're better you must come out to my aunt's house. We could go riding together.'

'I've never done that before.'

'It's wonderful. It makes you feel so free.'

Carl's expression darkened. 'I sometimes wonder if I'll ever be free of this place,' he murmured, glancing towards the small window on the other side of the room. 'Sometimes I wonder if Doctor Stein wants to keep me here for ever.'

'Why would he do that?'

'If he doesn't, then why does he keep me strapped down like some kind of wild animal?'

'The straps are to stop you hurting yourself.'

'Well, they're too tight.' Carl clenched his fists and raised his arms as high as he could with the leather bindings around his wrists.

Margaret hesitated a moment, then carefully loosened them. She did the same with those on his chest and stomach.

'You have to rest and remain as still as you can,' she said. 'Those are Doctor Stein's instructions. You wouldn't want to get me into trouble with him, would you?'

Carl shook his head and eased one hand almost free

of the strap around his left wrist. 'Thank you,' he whispered. 'You can leave me if you need to. I'm going to sleep, as Doctor Stein recommended.'

'If you're sure,' Margaret said.

'Yes, I'm sure.'

She stood up. 'Just rest,' she told him.

'I will,' Carl said. 'I'm more comfortable now that the straps are looser.'

'I'll be back in a little while,' Margaret said, turning towards the door.

Carl smiled.

Thirty-Nine

'Does Carl know what happened to the chimpanzee?'

Kleve followed Frankenstein as he moved through the basement laboratory towards the cages at the rear where the primate he spoke of sat. The chimp seemed uninterested in the presence of the two men – indeed, it only looked at them when Frankenstein tapped the bars gently.

'Does he know that it killed and ate its mate?' Kleve persisted.

'Does it matter?' the Baron answered. 'If we told him it might worry him.'

'And with good reason,' Kleve said.

'I told you before, Hans, the chimpanzee turned cannibalistic because there was damage to the brain shortly after the operation we performed. Had it been kept in restraints the way Carl has been then the problem might very well never have occurred.'

Kleve sighed and looked worried.

'I don't want you to mention it to Carl,' Frankenstein said, placing one hand on the younger man's forearm. 'He's recovering well. I don't want any undue stress put upon him.' The Baron smiled. 'Although if we did tell him then he'd have even less reason to take any unnecessary risks.'

Kleve looked concerned for a moment, then saw the smile on Frankenstein's face and nodded.

'As long as you're sure,' the younger man said.

'I'm sure,' Frankenstein told him, the smile fading from his lips. 'I finished something today, Hans; I'd like to show it to you.' He guided Kleve towards a curtained-off recess deep in the rear of the laboratory. Behind the curtain which the Baron pulled aside was a gurney. There was something covered by a white sheet on it and the familiar shape beneath the material looked to Kleve as if it could be just one thing. Frankenstein looked at him, then pulled the sheet back.

There was a body on the gurney, the head, except for the face, wrapped in bandages.

Kleve leaned closer, his eyes widening in surprise.

The figure lying there bore a striking resemblance to Frankenstein himself.

The Baron was gazing down at the cadaver in the same way a man would look fondly at his offspring.

'I thought you'd be interested,' Frankenstein said quietly.

'How long have you been working on this?' Kleve wanted to know.

'For some time. Since before you joined me, which was why I didn't mention it to you.'

Kleve moved closer, inspecting the body's features, touching one cheek with his index finger.

'Call it a labour of love,' Frankenstein said quietly.

'It's remarkable. Was it assembled using body parts taken from the hospital?'

'Some parts were indeed donated by the patients.' Frankenstein smiled again and indicated the left arm.

'The arm you took from the man we spoke to the other day,' Kleve exclaimed, gazing raptly at the brightly coloured tattoo on the forearm.

'There are more scars because I grafted skin from different parts of the body to cover blemishes or imperfections,' the Baron went on. 'But once those have healed the features will be perfect.'

Kleve stood transfixed for a moment longer, noticing also that the eyes of the body were the same piercing blue as Frankenstein's own. The resemblance was both uncanny and unsettling. Kleve couldn't help but think that the similarity was deliberate but he couldn't begin to imagine why.

'It . . . it looks like you,' the younger man said falteringly.

'Before you go back to work I want you to help me get him into the tank,' Frankenstein said, laying one hand gently on the head of the body before pulling the sheet back into place.

As the two men moved the trolley across the lab they passed another sheet-covered shape and Kleve paused beside that too.

He looked quizzically at Frankenstein.

'Carl's old body,' the Baron told him. 'I injected it with embalming fluid to preserve it but it needs to be stored in a better environment to prevent it deteriorating – there's been more cell corruption than I expected.

When we show it off next to his new one it won't look so convincing.'

'Have you spoken to Carl about your plans for his future?'

'Carl has enough to concern him at the moment. Besides, he has what he always wanted now. He'll go along with my plans. And to be honest, Hans, what choice does he have?'

Forty

It was almost dark when Carl Lang woke.

Time seemed to have lost all meaning for him during the last few days. Here inside the small attic room and without access to a timepiece he could only judge the passing hours by looking at the strength of the light flooding through the window opposite him.

The colour of that light as he now looked was a golden-red and he realised that the sun was setting, bleeding its brightness into the heavens as night approached swiftly. Carl smiled to himself and gently eased one hand free of the straps that, until Margaret Conrad had loosened them, had bound him so tightly to the bed for what had felt like an eternity. He raised one arm and flexed the fingers, then did the same with his other hand. Once that was free too he swiftly unbuckled the thicker straps across his chest and stomach and swung himself upright on the bed, sitting motionless for a moment or two.

He crossed to the clothes hanging behind the door and pulled on the trousers, fastening them at the waist before slipping on the shirt, stopping every now and then to look at his left hand. The fingers were long and slender, unlike the twisted digits he had possessed before. He felt slowly along the entire limb as if he still couldn't believe that there was any feeling in it. Carl rubbed one hand across his shoulder and his smile widened. No hump there any more, no disfiguring mound of flesh and bone to weigh him down, he thought. He walked slowly across the room, pressing his left foot hard against the wooden floor, putting weight on it as he'd never been able to do before.

And as he turned he caught sight of his reflection in the mirror.

The upright figure that he saw stared back at him blankly.

Carl moved closer to the mirror, reaching up again to touch his left shoulder. It was as if he expected the hump to have materialised there once more. He feared it might have somehow returned to disfigure and twist his body, like some kind of huge tumour that had been growing while he slept. He turned slightly and inspected the area, his heart pounding hard against his ribs.

There was no hump.

His body was as perfect as Frankenstein had promised him it would be.

And now that body was to be paraded in front of anyone who wanted to look at it, Carl remembered. He had thought the years of being stared at were over but he'd been wrong. Life would become even more intolerable now. He swallowed hard, the realisation unbearable. He wasn't going to be allowed to enjoy a new life; he would merely exist in an equally restricted way. The only thing that would make his life different would be the body that people focused their attention on. He couldn't stand that.

Carl pulled on the jacket that hung on the door and slid into it. Then he crossed the room towards the window.

He turned its handle slowly, fearing that it might be locked. But he was delighted to find that it opened easily.

Without hesitating he peered out and down, noting that there was a ledge just below and densely planted trees that would aid his descent and also keep him hidden from the view of anyone who happened to be passing.

Carl lifted himself up on to the sill and swung his legs out, holding the frame of the window with both hands, gripping it strongly as he eased the lower part of his body free.

The cool breeze swept over him as he hauled himself out on to the ledge. It brought with it the smell of flowers.

For Carl it was like the smell of freedom itself.

But, as the darkness grew deeper, he knew that must wait. Before he left this place there was something he had to do.

Forty-One

The girl was barely more than eighteen.

A slight, pale and underweight creature who shook a little as she dressed, her fingers trembling.

She stepped into her shoes and pulled her shawl tightly around her shoulders, not looking at the desk behind which sat Meyer. He rubbed his mountainous belly and belched loudly. The girl closed her eyes, fighting back the tears of pain and humiliation.

'Now then, darling,' Meyer grunted. 'You'll come back and see me again tomorrow night, won't you?'

The girl didn't answer him. She kept her back to the big man as she fastened the buttons of her blouse.

'I always treat you well when you come to see me, don't I?' Meyer went on.

The girl didn't answer. Meyer rose to his feet now and moved towards her, knocking over a chair in the process. The sound of the toppling furniture finally made the girl look round.

'Come here,' Meyer said, beckoning her with one fat finger.

She moved a little closer and he took another step towards her.

She could smell the garlic on his breath now and she

recoiled slightly. But he shot out a pudgy hand and gripped her by the arm.

'Give me a kiss before you go,' he growled, licking his thick lips and coating them with spittle.

She shied away, repulsed by him.

Meyer grabbed her and pulled her close to him, one hand slipping between her legs, pushing up the flimsy material of her skirt.

'Do I have to pay again just for a kiss?' he sneered.

He pushed his face towards the girl who winced as she felt his bloated and slippery lips press against her cheek. He left a large slick of saliva there as he pulled his head away, laughing. He left his hand between her legs, his fingers pressing against the smooth, soft skin of her thighs.

'You know how much I care about you, don't you?' he breathed thickly. 'I always make sure that it's you who comes here. I don't care about any of the other girls, only you.' He pushed his fingers hard against the material of her panties, pulling the gusset aside in an attempt to reach the warmth beneath. 'You know that, don't you?'

The girl was rigid in his arms, shaking slightly and more intent, it seemed, on not breathing in too much of Meyer's noxious breath rather than preventing his fingers from penetrating her.

He licked her face again, then laughed loudly, pushing her away.

'Go on, then,' he rasped. 'If you have to go then go to the next man – but you'll be back here again tomorrow night. You'll be back here as long as I put two gold crowns in your hand, won't you?' He dug in his pocket and pulled out the coins. He held them at arm's length for a moment, then dropped them on to the floor of the office. The girl dropped to her knees and scooped them up. Meyer advanced a couple of steps towards her, his eyes fixed on her raised buttocks as she crawled on all fours.

'You're teasing me now,' he said, leering.

She remained in that position for a moment, then hauled herself upright as he advanced once more.

'Will you do that for the next man?' he rasped. 'And the next?'

She didn't answer but instead moved towards the office door, reaching out blindly for the handle as she kept her gaze fixed on Meyer.

He was rubbing one hand across the front of his trousers now and she noted with disgust the outline of an erection beneath the material there.

'You're not going to leave me like this, are you?' he said, grinning and rubbing his crotch harder.

The girl reached the door and pulled it open.

'See you tomorrow night,' Meyer called as she slipped out of the room, slamming the door behind her. He laughed loudly, the raucous sound echoing in the corridor beyond. He stood in the centre of the room for a moment longer. Then the smile dropped from his face and his features crumpled like crushed paper. 'Bitch,' he hissed under his breath before belching loudly. He wiped his mouth with the back of his hand and returned to the desk where he'd been sitting. There was a bottle of wine on it that he noted with irritation was almost empty. He downed the last of it and dropped the bottle into a nearby waste bin. He snorted and picked up the wooden stick he'd laid on the desk, winding the leather thong around his wrist. It was time, he reminded himself, to take a stroll around the hospital and its grounds.

He was about to leave the office when he heard a sound from below.

Meyer spun around as the noise came again.

It had come from the underground laboratory, he was sure of that. Doctor Stein and Doctor Kleve had left hours ago, he recalled. Whoever was down there shouldn't be.

'Right, you bastard,' he growled under his breath, heading towards the door that led down into the cellar.

He hefted the stick in front of him, his knuckles turning white as he gripped it hard and reached for the door handle.

From beneath him he heard more sounds of movement.

'I'm coming, you bastard,' Meyer hissed quietly. 'Whoever you are, you're going to be sorry.'

Forty-Two

As he made his way through the underground laboratory, Carl Lang occasionally paused beside some of the many fluid-filled vessels, peering at the differently coloured contents and wondering what they held.

He could smell the many assorted chemicals in the air as he moved furtively around the subterranean room. There were other smells that reached his nostrils that he also recognised, such as the aroma of burning oil coming from several lamps that were still lit inside the gloomy chamber. It mingled with the stronger scent of smoke coming from the furnace at the far end of the huge room.

Frankenstein must have been disposing of something in those flames, he told himself, because he could hear the roaring sound of the furnace occasionally as he continued his exploration.

Medical instruments were laid out on one of the worktops and Carl ran appraising eyes over the gleaming metal implements, even reaching out to touch a scalpel. Was it one such as that which had cut through the skull of his old body? he wondered. How had his brain been removed and replaced in this new form that he now strode about in? He stopped and glanced around. It was as if he was seeing the laboratory for the first time through these new eyes. Its sights seemed more vivid and almost confusing to him now.

The specimen tanks that stood on the workbenches were still present but were empty now – the organs that had been floating inside them were gone.

Carl wondered if they were being used in some new experiment that Frankenstein was conducting.

Just as he himself had been an experiment, he reasoned, looking down at his hands. What was he now but the result of Frankenstein's work? A living monument to what that man had striven for.

Carl's musings were interrupted by a rattling sound from behind him and he spun around to find the source of the noise.

In the cage at the far end of the laboratory the chimpanzee was pulling lazily at the bars. Carl looked at the creature for a moment, then continued with his search of the laboratory, desperate to find what he sought. He wanted to be away from this place for ever once he'd done what he'd broken in to do. He never wanted to see the inside of this laboratory again. Would this, he wondered, be where Frankenstein had planned to show him off to the world? Would he be chained here like some freak-show exhibit while anyone who wanted to could inspect him or prod and probe him? Carl shuddered involuntarily and moved on through an archway towards the dull orange glow that indicated he was nearing the furnace.

There was a body lying on a table nearby.

It was covered with a sheet and Carl could see

spatters of yellowish liquid on the material in several places. There was a strong acrid smell coming from the figure, too, one that intensified when he lifted the sheet.

He gasped as he looked down at the figure before him.

Carl was looking down at his old body.

He felt a momentary twinge of emotion but it was quickly replaced by a rapidly growing feeling of revulsion. This was the creature he *had* been, not who he was now. Slowly, he touched the face, recoiling as he felt the mottled and dried-up skin on the left side of the skull. It was the same with the withered left arm and leg. Carl shook his head. This empty husk was a reminder of the misery he had endured ever since he'd been born: it had no place in his world any more and he was determined to ensure that it played no part there.

The thought of standing beside this twisted form while others stared and pointed out the differences between it and his present body made him feel nauseous. He clenched both fists, anger welling up within him. He turned and strode towards the furnace, reaching for the metal handles on its doors. He hissed angrily as he burned himself on the hot metal and he looked around for a rag, snatching one up from the floor. He wound it around his hand and pulled the doors open.

A great blast of heat enveloped him and he raised a hand to shield his face as he gazed into the roaring flames. The furnace had been stoked recently and the coals at its centre were white-hot. They would consume anything placed on them in a matter of moments.

Carl turned back towards his old body.

He stared at it with utter disgust for a second, then slipped his arms beneath the shoulders and dragged it from the table with one powerful movement. The lifeless legs smacked against the floor and the arms lolled uselessly like those of a puppet with its strings cut. Carl dragged the body across the room towards the gaping doors of the furnace. No one was ever going to know that he used to inhabit this broken and perverted parody of a man, he thought angrily. No one was ever again going to gaze upon this excuse for a human being. He hauled the corpse closer to the flames, their intense warmth bathing him now.

Sweat was beading on his forehead, both from his exertions and from the fierce heat that was filling the room as the furnace yawned open. It was like looking into the mouth of hell itself, Carl thought as he lifted his old body up slightly, glaring at the head and face, staring at every detail of the disfigurement there. One of the eyes was slightly open and it gazed back blindly at him.

Carl manoeuvred the corpse so that it was resting against the furnace's gaping entrance; the skin soon began to redden in the incredible heat. Then, using all his strength, he pushed the recalcitrant form into the flames, wincing when he burned himself again on the metal of the doors. But the pain didn't stop him as he continued to push and shove his former body into the fire. One foot became hooked on the edge of the furnace portal but Carl kicked at it angrily, dislodging it and ensuring that it too would be consumed.

An acrid stench of scorching flesh began to fill the air but he stood as close to the fire as he could, staring into it and watching as the body blazed, devoured easily by the raging inferno. Carl watched as the hair and then the rest of the face and skull ignited, rapidly followed by the remainder of the twisted shape. Noxious black and grey smoke began to fill the air and Carl coughed as it filled his lungs. But there was a smile on his face as he watched the destruction of his old body and when he finally backed away from the furnace he could feel tears of joy running down his cheeks.

Behind him, the chimpanzee was shaking the bars of its cage, chattering and shrieking loudly as the reek of the burning human meat began to fill its nostrils too.

Only as Carl turned did he hear the words.

'Who's down here?' bellowed Meyer.

Carl recognised the voice immediately and looked around frantically for somewhere to hide.

'If you're down here, I'm going to find you,' Meyer yelled. 'And then you'll be sorry.'

Carl was shaking now, desperate to get away but knowing that there was no way he could reach the door without having to pass the burly janitor.

And the next time the voice came it seemed to be only a few feet away. Carl ducked back into a recess and held his breath.

Forty-Three

'Where are you, you heathen?'
Meyer's voice reverberated around the underground laboratory, echoing off the walls. Carl tried to push himself further back against the wall, wondering if he could possibly slip past the vile janitor somehow and reach the steps that led out of the subterranean room.

'I know you're down here somewhere,' Meyer roared and, to add weight to his words, he whacked his stick against one of the tables as he passed.

Several test tubes and glass specimen jars rattled from the impact.

The chimpanzee screamed and began shaking its cage bars again as Meyer drew near.

'Shut up,' he grunted at the animal but the chimp continued to agitate the bars violently.

'I said shut up,' Meyer shouted, banging the cage with his stick.

The chimp stuck a hand through the bars and tried to grab at Meyer but he moved back and struck at its outstretched limb with the baton. Hurt by the impact, the ape withdrew to a corner of the cage and hissed at Meyer.

'I told you to shut up,' he growled at the ape.

Carl edged out of his hiding place slightly, ducking back when Meyer turned.

He moved a fraction too slowly.

'There you are,' Meyer snarled, fixing him with a furious glare. As the bulky janitor advanced he hefted the staff ahead of him, swinging it hard so that it made a high-pitched whooshing sound as it parted the air. 'Trying to hide from me, you bastard?'

Carl backed off, shaking, his stare fixed on the heavy stick that Meyer held.

He bumped into a table, causing the beakers and flasks there to shake. Some of the brightly coloured contents spilled and one or two of the receptacles fell to the stone floor where they shattered, glass spraying in all directions.

'See, now you've gone and damaged things,' Meyer snarled. 'You shouldn't be down here anyway and now you've broken valuable equipment, you bastard.'

Carl snatched up one of the beakers and brandished it like a weapon. He had no idea what the green liquid inside it was but wondered briefly if it might be some kind of acid. If he could use it as a weapon he would. He clutched it for a second, then flung it at Meyer. But it missed and shattered against the wall behind him.

'Afraid I'm going to bust your skull in, are you?' the big man chided as he avoided the flying beaker and took several more steps towards Carl. 'Well, you're right – I am.'

He swung the stick and it caught Carl across the shoulder.

Pain lanced through Carl and he raised his arm to block the next powerful blow that was aimed at him. The staff slammed into his forearm and he grunted in pain, trying to avoid the big man's frenzied attack. But Meyer moved a lot faster than his bulk might have suggested and he struck out again, catching Carl first in the stomach and then the ribs.

The blows doubled him up and as he staggered in front of the janitor Meyer hit him across the back of the head. A blow that sent him crashing to the stone floor, blood oozing now from a cut on the back of his skull.

Carl dragged himself upright and held up one hand. 'Please don't hit me,' he begged.

Meyer drove a fist into his face, the impact sending him hurtling backwards. He slammed into another table and it overturned, receptacles and their contents all crashing to the ground. Many of the glass vessels shattered and Carl found himself growing dizzy. His face was wet and he wasn't sure whether it was from the spilled fluid or whether the damp warmth he felt was his own blood.

'Bastard,' Meyer growled and hit him hard in the stomach.

Carl grunted at this new pain and tried feebly to strike out at his attacker. But the punch he landed did little to stop Meyer's onslaught.

The big man grabbed Carl by the collar, steadied him and then drove another powerful punch into his face. The impact split his lip and loosened two teeth but Meyer continued the onslaught driving his fist upwards this time, slamming it up under Carl's chin as he released him, watching as he toppled backwards into yet more equipment. Carl hit the ground hard and rolled over, his back to the advancing janitor.

'Now I'll have to hit you again because of all the damage you've just caused,' Meyer rasped.

Carl's hand closed around the neck of a broken flask, its bottom jagged and sharp where it had shattered. As he turned to look at Meyer, he gripped it in his bloodied hand.

The expression that Meyer saw on Carl's face now wasn't that of a snivelling victim – it was one of pure fury. His features were twisted into a grimace of anger. As the big man watched, Carl hauled himself upright again, the flask held out in front of him, the jagged edges glinting like razor-sharp teeth.

'So, going to fight back, are you?' Meyer chuckled. 'Good.'

Meyer swung the baton and caught Carl across his face, opening a cut on his chin. But the impact seemed to have no effect this time and with one furious lunge Carl was upon him.

Forty-Four

Roaring with rage, Carl thrust the improvised weapon forward, aiming the jagged glass at Meyer's face.

The big man managed to deflect the blow but he yelped in pain as the glass cut into his thick forearm. Blood burst from the wound, some of it spattering Carl who drew the broken flask back again and struck at his opponent even more savagely.

The second blow caught Meyer on the palm of his right hand and tore the flesh open, slicing through nerves and tendons so that Meyer's thumb flopped down limply as blood erupted from the deep cut.

'Bastard,' the big man grunted, striking out with his other hand and catching Carl across the face. But the impact wasn't hard enough to prevent another attack.

Carl hurled himself at the janitor again, wrapping one arm around his neck as he stabbed furiously with the flask. He snaked his legs around Meyer's huge bulk and clung on, stabbing constantly into his larger opponent's face and neck, each movement accompanied by a grunt of rage. Meyer tried to push him off but it was useless. Carl clung on like a terrier that had caught a rat in its jaws.

The sharp glass sliced easily through the skin of Meyer's cheek, cutting so deeply that it exposed the bone. Blood spurted into the air and Carl seemed to be spurred on by the sight of the crimson fluid. He drove the flask at Meyer's neck again, carving away a portion of flesh just below the left ear lobe before hacking into the ear itself with a blow so ferocious that the fleshy appendage was simply torn away. Meyer shouted in pain and fear as his ear dropped to the stone floor and now, weak from loss of blood and confused by the savagery of the unrelenting attack, he began to sway drunkenly.

Carl slammed the broken flask full into his face, gouging into his nose and one of his eyes. The eyeball simply burst, blood and vitreous liquid spilling down Meyer's face, and now at last he toppled backwards, landing with a bone-jarring thud on the stone floor, his head slamming against it with a sickening crack. Fresh blood began pouring from the latest gash. Carl rolled to one side, dropping the flask. As Meyer lay there bleeding, he threw himself back onto the big man, fastening his hands around the janitor's throat, digging his thumbs into his windpipe as hard as he could.

Dazed by the outflow of his blood and the blow to his skull, Meyer was helpless to fight back and could only raise his hands weakly as Carl drove his thumbs deeper into his trachea.

Meyer looked up at the contorted face that glared down at him and saw the veins on Carl's temple bulging with the effort he was applying to throttling him. The janitor felt as if his head was filling with air – he was finding it difficult to breathe. His tongue protruded from one side of his mouth, spittle dripping from it.

Carl gritted his teeth and squeezed even harder, straddling the big man now, determined not to let him get up. He saw Meyer's eyes roll upwards in their sockets and in a final surge of rage he lifted the larger man's head up from the stone floor and then slammed it back down as hard as he could. The crack of splintering bone reverberated around the subterranean room.

Breathing heavily, Carl stood up, looking down at Meyer's body. Perspiration was running down Carl's face and he was shaking, compulsively flexing his fingers. He kicked at the motionless form of the janitor, then stooped low over it to check that life had indeed left the fat man. For good measure, he picked up the flask and ground it into Meyer's face.

Behind him, the chimp was rattling the bars of its cage and yelping as if to signal its approval of what it had just seen.

Carl glanced at the howling ape, then looked at Meyer's body again. He started to shudder.

He was salivating uncontrollably, sputum dribbling over his lips and chin as he looked down at the corpse. It was as if thousands of volts of electricity were being pumped through his body. His stomach was convulsing and he was overcome by a feeling that he recognised as hunger. Again he looked down at the body of the fallen janitor and the feeling seemed to intensify.

Behind him the chimp was howling madly now.

Carl bent low over Meyer's body, reaching for the broken flask that he had jammed into the dead man's face.

As if urging him on, the chimp rattled the bars of its cage and continued to shriek wildly.

Carl was breathing heavily now, clutching the flask so tightly that it seemed the glass neck would shatter in his grip. He used the jagged implement like a knife and slowly and expertly flayed off a large piece of flesh from Meyer's face, pulling it back to expose the muscles and blood vessels beneath. He held the piece of hacked-off skin inches from his own face, his mouth now full of saliva.

Carl opened his mouth.

The ape screamed even more loudly.

Carl suddenly roared something unintelligible and tossed the piece of bloodied skin away before scrambling backwards, his stare still fixed on Meyer's bloated body. Shaking his head, he wiped his hands on his jacket. Then he turned and ran towards the stairs that would lead him out of the underground laboratory.

Deep within Carl the dreadful feeling of hunger still gnawed.

The chimp continued to howl.

Forty-Five

Frankenstein took down the heavy metal key from the top of the door frame and inserted it into the lock. He turned it and the attic-room door opened easily.

The Baron stepped across the threshold, glaring around the small room, an expression that darkened rapidly on his face.

'Where is he?' he hissed. 'Where is Carl?'

Both Frankenstein and Kleve could see that the room was empty, the straps that had held Carl to his bed undone and hanging free. And, on the far side of the room, the single window was open.

'Where is he?' Frankenstein repeated angrily, crossing to the window and peering out.

Kleve could only look on in bewilderment.

'Did you let him out?' the Baron snapped, glaring at the younger man.

'Of course not,' Kleve countered. 'Why would I?'

'Then it must have been Margaret. She must have released him from the straps.'

'But why would she do that?'

'How do I know? All that matters is that he's gone. We can only guess at how long it's been since he escaped.'

'You make him sound like a prisoner.'

Frankenstein held the gaze of his younger companion. 'The fool,' he snarled. 'He knew the dangers. God alone knows what kind of damage he may have caused.'

The Baron crossed to the clothes hooks behind the door as if a closer inspection of them would still reveal the garments that had been hanging there before. He banged angrily on the door with one fist.

Kleve stood gazing at the bed and the straps. 'But how?' he murmured, picking up one of the crumpled sheets that lay on the bed. 'He was falling asleep when I left him, I think. How could he have undone the straps?'

'Why, not how. Why? There's always a reason why,' Frankenstein snapped. 'What happened before you left him?'

'What do you mean?'

'What happened? It's not a difficult question! What happened before you left him?'

'I don't remember.'

Frankenstein crossed to the younger man and stared angrily into his face. 'Think, man, think,' he rasped.

'I talked to him,' Kleve stuttered.

'About what?'

'About your plans for his future . . .'

'You fool,' Frankenstein snarled. 'You told him that? You stupid fool.' He lashed out and caught Kleve across the cheek with a stinging blow of his hand. The younger man reeled for a moment but Frankenstein gripped him by the shoulders and held him upright, glaring into his eyes. 'I gave you more credit, Hans. Do you know nothing of human reactions?' The Baron's voice was loud now. 'It isn't just Carl's physical well-being that we had to attend to, it was his psychological frame of mind as well.' He released his grip on the younger man. 'Do you know what damage you could have done to him? The entire experiment might fail because of what you told him.'

'He would have had to know eventually.'

'When he was fully recovered and able to adjust to information like that, not in the vulnerable state he's in now,' Frankenstein shouted. He drew a hand across his forehead and seemed to recover his composure a little. The tone of his voice softened somewhat when he spoke again. 'You told him everything?'

'I told him you were going to allow people from the medical and scientific community to ask him questions and examine him,' Kleve said, his voice cracking. He touched his cheek where the Baron had struck him.

Frankenstein shook his head.

'I told him that he should be proud of his new body,' the younger man went on. 'That people would envy him for his situation now, that his old life was over and he had only good things to look forward to.'

'And as you can see,' the Baron sneered, indicating the vacated bed, 'your kind words obviously had an effect, didn't they?'

Kleve swallowed hard.

'Where would he go?' the Baron murmured, glancing around the room. 'Where would he go?'

'Where *could* he go? Surely in his condition . . .'

'He was well enough to walk, wasn't he? Well

enough to escape from this room. There's no telling where he might be now. It all depends how long ago he left here.'

'But he's got no money, no way of leaving Carlsbruck – and why would he want to run away?'

'Because you told him that he was going to spend the rest of his life being stared at like some kind of exhibit in a circus,' Frankenstein snapped.

'I told him the truth.'

'Sometimes the truth is best left alone, Hans. As you can see.' The Baron crossed to the window and peered out, gazing down into the courtyard of the hospital. He spun around suddenly. 'The laboratory,' he said.

'But how could he have got in there without us knowing?' Kleve protested.

'We haven't been in there all night, have we?' Frankenstein reminded him as he headed for the door. 'Come on.'

Kleve hurried after him and both men dashed headlong down the stairs to the lower levels of the hospital and then onwards into the office and through the door that led to the laboratory. Kleve was having trouble keeping up with Frankenstein but eventually the Baron slowed his pace slightly, his nostrils twitching as he detected the smell of chemicals and also an overpowering stench that he recognised.

'This way,' he said, urging Kleve to follow him towards the rear of the room.

The acrid stench was almost unbearable now and Kleve too recognised it. It was coming from the furnace, one door of which was slightly open. There was thick black smoke rising from it, tiny particles of soot twisting and turning in the air around it.

As the two men drew closer they could see the devastation and destruction. Shattered implements and equipment were scattered all over the stone floor like bizarre confetti and in the middle of it all they saw the body of Meyer.

But Frankenstein was more concerned with the furnace and its reeking contents. He wrapped a rag around one hand, crossed to the doors and prepared to pull them open, shielding his face against the heat and the foul smell. However, just before he did he glanced down at something lying close on the floor.

'Look,' he grunted, indicating the object.

It was a shoe. The leather was scuffed and dirty and it had been scorched in two or three places.

'He burned his old body,' Frankenstein said flatly, finally opening the furnace doors.

As he did so the stench of burning flesh enveloped him and Kleve and, peering into the roaring flames, they could see the remains of Carl's old body just about visible within the inferno. Flesh, hair and clothes had all been consumed and even bone had begun to turn to ash in the incredible temperature at the heart of the furnace. Frankenstein put a hand to his mouth and coughed as he tried to suck in air through the choking odour. He pushed the furnace doors shut, then moved away into the centre of the room where he looked down at the bloodied corpse of Meyer surrounded by broken glass, spilled chemicals and other paraphernalia.

'The janitor must have disturbed him,' the Baron mused.

'But what if Carl's brain was damaged in the fight?' Kleve asked breathlessly.

'You'd better hope it wasn't, Hans. After all, this is your fault.'

'I'm not to blame for what happened here.'

'You told Carl what was to become of him. He was frightened, that's why he ran away. If you hadn't told him those things then he'd still be safe in his room now.'

'You can't blame me for this.'

'And who else should I blame, Hans? You – and that stupid nurse.'

'Margaret isn't to blame, either. You're being unfair.'

'Am I? Who released Carl from the straps?'

'We're only assuming it was her.'

'No one else had access to that room except you and I. She was the only other one who could have got inside. Don't try to protect her, Hans. She's as much to blame as you are.'

Kleve opened his mouth to say something but the Baron continued, his gaze fixed on the mutilated body of the janitor.

'I can only imagine what kind of damage you've both done with your misguided concepts of truth and compassion,' he sneered.

'If I'd known, I never would have spoken to him about his future.'

'But you did, Hans, and there's nothing we can do about that now, is there?'

'I meant no harm.'

Frankenstein merely nodded.

'What do we do?' Kleve said.

'Sooner or later he'll need my help, he knows that. We'll carry on with our normal routine. He'll have to come back here eventually – he has no choice.'

'But shouldn't we search for him?'

'And where would we start, Hans? There are a million places he could be hiding. No. Do as I tell you. We'll wait. There's nothing else we can do.'

'And what about him?' Kleve asked, nodding towards the body of Meyer.

'The furnace,' Frankenstein said flatly.

Forty-Six

The horse made the jump effortlessly and Margaret Conrad patted its neck as it landed on the other side of the hedge.

The bay was a big animal but she had no trouble handling it, gripping the reins tightly and digging her knees into its flanks as she rode, the early-morning breeze whipping her long dark hair around her face. She loved this time of day more than any other, the hour just after dawn, and as she rode she felt the exhilaration pour through her as if someone had injected her with some kind of stimulant. If only this feeling could be bottled and sold, she thought. She wanted everyone to know what it felt like.

She sent the bay hurtling towards another hedge and it cleared the obstacle as easily as it had the others.

Again Margaret patted its neck and the animal tossed its head as if to acknowledge her affectionate gesture but also to express its own pleasure at the freedom it now felt. To be allowed to run at such speed across open fields and grassland was a joy indeed.

In the woods off to her left Margaret spotted a fox peering out at her – probably heading back to its lair for the day after a night of hunting, she thought. Its work was over for now while hers would be beginning soon. She would travel into Carlsbruck in her aunt's coach and begin her daily duties in the Hospital for the Poor. But that was all to come: for the time being she was alone out here with just the horse and the other creatures that were around at this hour. High above her, birds were black arrowheads against the orange sky as they returned to their nests. The air was crisp and she sucked in deep lungfuls of it as she rode. She had been taught to savour this time of the day by her father who had also been the one who'd instructed her in the art of riding. She rode like a man. Not side-saddle but with legs either side of the horse's flanks. Her father had told her that she'd be better able to control the animal that way and he'd been right. Not for her the courtly stance that most women riders adopted. Margaret Conrad rode because of the thrill it brought her and every time she mounted a horse she thought with pride of her father.

He'd been a major in the Austrian army, respected by his fellow officers, and loved by his men for his brilliance in the field but also for his compassion. Whatever he did he used kindness instead of threat and everyone had responded to his approach. He had told her of a Greek general called Xenophon who, many years before, had trained horses and men using gentleness rather than regimentation and he had sought to mirror that method. The memory of him still brought great sadness to Margaret even now, so long after his death. She still missed him deeply.

Death in battle would have been hard enough to cope

with but she and her mother might have expected that. After all, the threat of death was one of the things that those who lived with soldiers learned to accept. But the way he'd died had been even more unbearable. During a review he had been thrown from his horse and killed. Not the glorious death that a soldier wishes for but an ignominious and unjust end. A stupid way to die, someone had called it, and Margaret agreed wholeheartedly with that sentiment.

She could still remember the men who had come to their house bearing the terrible news. Two cavalrymen dressed in full uniform had brought the information and Margaret could remember watching them as her mother let them into the house, listening to them speak in hushed reverential tones while she marvelled at their superb uniforms. Then she had seen her mother burst into tears and she had run to her and she too had heard the news. She and her mother had clung to each other as they'd wept, united in a grief that she didn't think she'd ever be able to cope with or understand.

When her mother died Margaret had been forced to face that grief all over again, this time alone. It had been an intolerable burden and one she had feared she could not bear. But she had summoned the reserves of strength that her father had always told her she had and somehow she had survived. At first the world had been a lonelier and darker place without her parents but she had learned to cope and in the first hour of new light at the start of each day she found now that remembering her parents brought her more joy than pain. Her recollections were of the good things about them. Her father's patience, her mother's compassion. These were the things she remembered and savoured when she was out riding. This was the time of day when she could sift through her thoughts and discard those that caused her discomfort or distress.

Now, as Margaret guided the bay along the dirt track that led towards the stables at the rear of her aunt's house, she dug her heels into the animal's flanks, coaxing one last breakneck spurt of speed from it. She and the horse seemed to become one for fleeting seconds, each feeling the other's joy and pleasure as they hurtled along seemingly oblivious to whatever was around them.

As she neared the courtyard with its high wall she pulled on the reins to slow the galloping animal and it whinnied as if aggrieved at not being able to continue with its charge. Again Margaret patted its neck, which was lathered from the ride. She murmured words of encouragement in its ear as she guided it beneath the stone archway and into the yard.

As she swung herself out of the saddle a groom approached. He took the reins from her.

'A good ride, miss?' he asked.

'Very good, thank you, Joseph,' Margaret told him. She ran a hand through her long dark hair and watched as the groom led the bay towards one of the water troughs that dotted the yard. It drank gratefully.

'I'm just going in to see the ponies,' she called as she headed across the yard towards the entrance of the nearest stable.

'All right, miss,' the groom called back, pulling the saddle and blanket from the bay's back.

Margaret wandered into the stable and across to the first stall where she found a small piebald pony nuzzling the bars that topped the wooden gate there. She reached into her pocket and took out some sugar, laying it on the flat of her hand so the little horse could take it. She stroked the animal's neck, then moved on to the next stall where a sleek black pony waited. It tossed its head excitedly as Margaret approached and it too received some sugar from her. She remained in the stable for a moment longer, enjoying the scent of hay and straw and also the aroma that the animals themselves gave off. But she knew she had to prepare herself for the day's work so, with one last pat for each of the ponies, she turned to leave.

From the far end of the stable came a loud crash.

Margaret spun round to see what had caused it.

She could hear a low guttural sound as well but it didn't sound like any noise a horse would make, she told herself. She moved slowly towards the source of the disturbance, her eyes darting this way and that in the stable. There was an empty stall towards the back of the building and it was from there that the sound had come. There was a rustling through the straw and Margaret wondered if a rat might have got in. She reached for a nearby pitchfork that one of the grooms had left propped against a wall, determined to skewer the invading rodent if she had to.

She pushed open the stall door with the end of the pitchfork and peered in.

No rats. But the guttural sound was louder now. It was coming from behind a trough and some bales of hay at the end of the stall.

Margaret lowered the pitchfork slightly and advanced a couple of steps, the twin prongs of the implement gleaming as she held it at hip height.

Her eyes widened as she saw the figure rise into view behind the trough.

'Oh, my God,' she whispered.

Forty-Seven

'What are you doing here?' Margaret gasped as Carl Lang hauled himself upright.

She gazed at him as if mesmerised.

His face was beaded with sweat and spattered with dried blood, his hair unkempt. There was more dry blood on his clothes and hands. Pieces of hay and straw were sticking out of his clothes.

'What happened to you?' Margaret went on, lowering the pitchfork and placing it on the stable floor.

'I had an accident,' Carl told her, clearing his throat and trying to smile. But the expression on his face faded quickly and he looked at her imploringly. 'I had to get away from the hospital. You said you'd help me.'

'Does Doctor Stein know you've left the hospital?'

The look that crossed Carl's face was one of pure undiluted terror. 'No, don't tell him,' he gasped. 'Please, please don't tell him.'

'But he'll know you're gone when—'

'Don't let him know I'm here, I'm begging you,' Carl interrupted frantically.

'He'll have to know sooner or later,' she said, moving nearer to him.

Carl shook his head.

'You need looking after,' Margaret insisted.

'Let me stay here,' he gasped.

'Doctor Stein will be able to help you – I must tell him.'

'No,' Carl snapped, rising to his feet and towering over Margaret. His teeth were clenched and she could see something blazing behind his eyes. It looked like rage.

Margaret backed off slightly, her heart thudding more urgently against her ribs. 'You can't stay here,' she said softly. 'Not like this.'

'And what do you think he'll do when he finds me?'

'He'll help you, just as he helped you to begin with.'

Carl grinned crookedly. 'Help?' he groaned. 'He didn't help me. He turned me into one of his experiments.'

Margaret looked puzzled, taken aback by the tone of his voice and the expression on his face.

'He lied to me,' Carl went on. 'He said he'd make me like normal men and I trusted him.'

Margaret put out a hand and placed it comfortingly on Carl's left shoulder but he shook himself free, stepping away from her angrily. She withdrew her hand hurriedly.

'I wanted to live like others do,' Carl went on wearily. 'I wanted a life different from the one I'd had before but he knew that things wouldn't change. Not for me. Things will never change for me.'

'I just want to help you,' she said gently.

'You've been kind to me,' Carl told her. 'Let me stay here, please. Just don't tell Doctor Stein.'

'If I promise not to tell him will you stay here until I get back?'

Carl nodded.

'I mean it,' Margaret stressed. 'You must stay here.'

'I will,' he assured her.

'I won't be long. I'll tell Joseph to look after you while I'm gone.'

She hesitated a moment longer, then turned and hurried from the stable. Carl watched her all the way, his expression darkening. She was out of the building when he snatched up the pitchfork she'd put down earlier. He gripped the shaft tightly for a moment, the sharp prongs glinting in the sunlight that was flooding into the stable. One of the ponies whickered and Carl spun around, the implement levelled, his hands gripping it so tightly now that the knuckles turned white.

Can you trust her? How do you know she won't come back with Doctor Stein?

He shook his head.

You can't trust her – you can't trust anyone.

With a wail of despair Carl drove the pitchfork into the nearest bale of hay.

Forty-Eight

Hans Kleve inspected the cutting edge of the scalpel, peering closely at its razor-sharp edge for a moment as if reassuring himself that it was adequate for the task.

Apparently satisfied, he pressed the blade against the shoulder joint of the body that lay before him. The sharpness of the scalpel meant that it sliced easily through the flesh and muscle and Kleve put a little more weight behind it, cutting more deeply until he had exposed the joint itself. Known in anatomy as the glenohumeral joint, it comprised the ball-shaped ending of the humerus which fitted neatly into the socket formed by the glenoid fossa.

Kleve cut away more flesh so that he could reach the joint more easily and he pushed skin and muscle back with his fingertips, exposing the tip of the scapula and part of the clavicle too.

Satisfied that the joint was adequately exposed, he reached for the bone saw that lay on the trolley beside him. It was a heavy-bladed implement, much larger and with a thicker blade than those they had used to carry out the brain transplant on Carl. But, as Kleve reasoned, the bones of the shoulder and the lower parts of the body were much thicker than those of the cranium. Also, when they were being severed more force could be used than when one was working on something as fragile as the skull – and more particularly on its contents.

The saw which he now selected was fully twelve inches long, the cutting edge serrated to allow the necessary grip and friction when actually cutting the bone. It had an ivory handle and bore the inscription *Fischer* (denoting the maker) just above the groove at the top of the blade.

Most amputation saws were of similar length but varied in thickness, dependent on which limbs or appendages they were to be used to cut. Thus, a finger saw was narrow and light, as was a metacarpal blade, whereas those like the one Kleve now held and those used for the amputation of legs were much sturdier.

Many doctors, Kleve remembered, also used implements known as chain saws. These comprised several lengths of very thin serrated metal hinged in more than a dozen places to allow flexibility and attached to two ebony or ivory handles, one of which was detachable to allow the chain to be slipped around the bone to be cut or resected. The two ends of the chain would be attached to their handles once the device was in place and the surgeon would work them back and forth quickly to sever any more recalcitrant bones. These instruments were not greatly favoured by military surgeons because they took too much time to use but surgeons like Kleve found them invaluable when faced with more intricate work.

Now he wiped some perspiration from his forehead with the back of one hand and set to work cutting through the shoulder joint he was faced with.

The primary consideration in amputations was usually speed. A good surgeon could remove an arm in less than twelve seconds. This was vital to prevent undue pain and shock to the unfortunate who was losing the limb. A leg might take a little longer due to the thickness of the bones involved but, overall, a leg or an arm should be severed and cauterised in a total of less than fifteen seconds. This speed also prevented too much blood loss, which was the main cause of shock. Anaesthetic, usually ether applied to a gauze face mask held over the patient's nose and mouth, had also helped to reduce the cases of shock in day-to-day surgery. But this use of painkillers was limited to civil surgeons – those working in the army and navy had no access to them.

Kleve had considered at least one military position once he had graduated from medical school but had decided that he felt more at home in civilian life and besides, the pay was better. The work of military surgeons, especially in times of war, had a production-line quality where each casualty that was brought needed attention to be dispensed in the shortest time possible. If he was honest with himself, Kleve had also not relished the idea of working in a field hospital where death from enemy shells was as likely for a surgeon as it was for any of the battlefield casualties.

He drew a deep breath, reminding himself that he should be concentrating on the task in hand, not musing on other possible career paths he might have taken before he came to Carlsbruck. He'd already been in the underground laboratory for more than two hours and he felt weary. The sooner he was finished the better.

He began to cut again, the saw making a high-pitched whining sound as it was driven through the bone. Tiny fragments came away from the humerus but Kleve didn't bother himself with those and continued, drawing the blade back and forth energetically.

The arm came free and he pulled it away from the severed joint, ignoring the blood and the marrow that trickled from the bone itself. As he held up the saw he could see that there were small fragments of bone and flesh sticking to the blade, caught in its serrations, but Kleve wasn't concerned with those – they would be cleaned off later, once his task was completed. He would be here for another thirty minutes, he guessed, no more. The bulk of the work was done; it was now just a matter of tidying up.

He puffed out his cheeks and looked down upon what remained of the body of Meyer, the janitor.

It had taken Kleve less than ninety minutes to strip and dismember the corpse. Once that had been done each piece had been fed carefully into the raging fires of the furnace where it had been consumed. Now the doctor was left with just this arm, the torso itself and the head – which he had severed first.

None of the body parts were to be kept. Frankenstein had specified that they were all substandard and could not be used in their work. Every last trace of the janitor was to be consigned to the flames of the furnace and Kleve was close to completing that task now.

He wiped more sweat from his brow, then gathered up the arm and shoved it unceremoniously into the gaping mouth of the furnace.

The stench of burning flesh was already strong in the underground laboratory and, as Kleve watched, the latest portion of Meyer's body was also engulfed by flames.

Another ten minutes and the big man would be nothing more than ash.

Forty-Nine

Inspector Gustav Schiller of the Carlsbruck police stepped from the carriage and brushed some flecks of imaginary dust from the sleeve of his dark blue uniform.

Schiller was a wiry little man in his late forties, made to look even slimmer by the cut and colour of his jacket and trousers. Satisfied that his uniform was as spotless as usual he now turned his attention to his moustache, twirling the ends slightly as he waited for his companion to clamber from the coach.

Sergeant Dietz was a much larger man, his uniform buttons straining visibly to hold in the considerable belly that he sported. He scrambled from the coach with difficulty, almost knocking off his cap in the process. Schiller shook his head as he watched the bigger man struggling, clucking his tongue in frustration when Dietz stepped in a pile of horse droppings left by another carriage that had just rattled past on the other side of the street.

'Look where you're going, man,' Schiller said irritably. 'What sort of image does that give of the police here in Carlsbruck?' He watched as Dietz set about scraping the dung from his boot, using the kerb edge as an aid to remove the mess.

'I couldn't help it, inspector,' Dietz said. 'If they cleaned the roads more often it wouldn't have happened.'

'If you looked where you were going it wouldn't have happened,' Schiller retorted, striding across the street towards their destination.

Dietz scuttled along behind him.

'How often do you clean your uniform?' Schiller asked as the two men walked along the pavement.

'My wife washes it once a week, I brush it every night, inspector,' said Dietz, glancing down at the jacket he wore as if seeking out the blemishes he felt sure that Schiller had spotted. He could see none but feared that his sharp-eyed superior had spotted something he had missed.

'An important part of being a policeman is keeping the uniform immaculate,' Schiller went on. 'It's the first thing that members of the public see when they are confronted by one of us. If the uniform is anything less than perfect then it reflects badly not just on that individual but also on the police force as a whole.'

'As I said, inspector, I brush mine every night. Is it dirty?'

Schiller raised one eyebrow and looked at his companion. 'If it were I would not have allowed you to accompany me, Dietz,' he said. 'We are calling on very respectable people today – we have to look our most efficient.'

Dietz nodded and followed his inspector towards the main entrance of the Carlsbruck Hospital for the Poor. He glanced at the plaque on the wall outside as he passed it, stepping through the gates behind Schiller who led the way into a long corridor. There were a number of people gathered there, waiting outside a room that had the word SURGERY stencilled on the door. Those waiting looked at the policemen with a combination of concern and mistrust. Schiller ran appraising eyes over them and finally tugged the arm of a woman who was waiting to go in.

'We're looking for Doctor Stein,' the inspector announced.

'You'll have to wait your turn,' the woman said, coughing.

'We're not patients,' Schiller sighed.

'You'll still have to wait your turn,' the woman insisted. 'We're all sick here, you know.' She gestured at the others in the line.

Schiller wrinkled his nose as she breathed on him.

'You're not sick,' he grunted. 'You're drunk. What is that – gin?'

The woman was about to say something else when Schiller knocked on the door of the office and walked in without waiting for an invitation. Dietz followed, closing the door behind him.

Doctor Hans Kleve looked up and saw them, his brow furrowing slightly.

The woman he was attending to also eyed the two policemen warily as Kleve finished tying a sling around her arm and shoulder.

'I'll be with you in a moment,' he said to the two newcomers. Then, to the woman, 'You'll have to try and rest this as much as you can.'

'I've got to work, doctor,' the woman protested.

'I realise that but try to rest it when you can,' Kleve insisted. 'Come and see me again in a few days' time.'

The woman nodded and got to her feet. 'Thank you, doctor,' she said as she headed for the door and let herself out.

'Now, how can I help you, gentlemen?' Kleve asked. 'You don't look ill.' He smiled.

'We're here on official business, Doctor Kleve,' Schiller announced, glancing around the office. 'I'm Inspector Schiller and this is my assistant, Sergeant Dietz.'

Dietz nodded, then wandered across to a nearby filing cabinet that had a human skull perched on top of it. He glanced at the skull and swallowed hard.

'We wanted to speak to Doctor Stein, if that was possible,' Schiller went on.

'Doctor Stein's not here at the moment,' Kleve told him. 'But I'm sure I can help you.'

'We need some information about someone who works here at the hospital,' Schiller said. 'A man called Meyer.'

Kleve raised his eyebrows. 'Yes, I know Meyer. He's the janitor here,' he said evenly. 'Why, is there a problem?'

'When was the last time you saw him, doctor?' Schiller enquired. 'His wife said he never came home last night.'

'His wife?' Kleve exclaimed. 'I didn't even know he was married.'

'Well, it takes all sorts, doesn't it?' the inspector went on. 'What exactly did he do here, doctor?'

'As I said, he is the janitor. He sweeps up, helps with

some of the heavy lifting, and he acts as a guard at night – there's some expensive equipment in the laboratory downstairs.'

'And when was the last time you saw him?' Schiller persisted.

'Last night, before I left here.'

'And what time was that?'

'About seven o'clock,' Kleve lied.

'He's probably drunk in an alley somewhere,' Schiller said, and smiled. 'The man's a notorious scoundrel but we have to investigate these reports.'

'He has a criminal record,' Dietz added. 'He has a more than passing interest in young girls. *Very* young girls.'

'I didn't know that,' Kleve said. 'He was already working here when I came to assist Doctor Stein.'

Schiller looked at Dietz and frowned. The sergeant nodded and returned to gazing around the room.

'Might Doctor Stein know where Meyer is?' Schiller enquired.

'I doubt it very much,' Kleve said. 'They are hardly what you'd call close.'

'No, of course not,' Schiller said. 'How long have you worked for Doctor Stein?'

'I thought you came here to ask questions about Meyer, not me,' Kleve responded guardedly.

Schiller regarded the young doctor blankly for a moment. Then he smiled thinly. 'Sergeant Dietz will come back later and see if Meyer has turned up for work,' he said. 'Or if you hear anything perhaps you'd be good enough to let us know so we don't waste time searching for him.'

Kleve nodded. He was beginning to feel uncomfortable with these two uniformed men in the office and he hoped that the discomfort didn't show in his expression.

'If that's all, gentlemen,' he said, trying to sound as unconcerned and efficient as he could, 'I do have other patients to see.'

'Of course, doctor,' Schiller said. 'Thank you for your time.' He clicked his fingers and signalled to Dietz who joined him. Both men headed for the door.

They had reached it when it opened from the other side, pushed by Margaret Conrad. She looked in surprise at the two uniformed men, both of whom nodded affably at her before making their way out. Margaret waited a moment, then looked at Kleve who could see the concern on her face.

'They're looking for Meyer,' he told her. 'He's missing.'

'Hans, I must speak to you – it's urgent,' she said breathlessly.

'What's wrong?' he wanted to know.

'I found Carl this morning when I got back from my ride. He was hiding in the stables at my aunt's house.'

'Carl? My God. I'll get Doctor Stein.'

'No,' Margaret said urgently. 'Please don't. Carl's terrified of him.'

'But why?'

'He wouldn't say.'

'I'm sorry, I must get him.' Kleve was already shrugging himself out of his long white coat and reaching for his jacket.

'Please, Hans. The poor man's nearly out of his mind. Anyway, I promised him I wouldn't bring Doctor Stein.'

Kleve hesitated for a moment. 'Then I'd better come,' he said, pulling on his jacket.

'Thank you, Hans. My aunt's carriage is waiting outside.'

Fifty

The pain in his left leg had begun as a dull ache but had grown into a throbbing that would not subside.

On the straw-covered floor of the stall Carl Lang looked down at the limb, stretching it in front of him and flexing the ankle back and forth. The pain persisted. It seemed as if every muscle in the leg was contracting and stiffening.

He decided that exercise might be the way to banish the pain and prepared to lift himself. He gripped the side of the trough with his right hand and with his left pushed himself up from the ground.

There was a stiffness in his left arm and hand that he hadn't felt for a long time.

Not since before the operation.

He swallowed hard and forced himself on up.

Carl flexed each of the fingers of his left hand in turn, then rubbed it hard with his right hand, concentrating on the palm and the base of the thumb. His heart was thudding faster in his chest now as he squeezed the tips of each finger in turn, gasping when he felt such little sensitivity in the digits.

Just the way it used to be.

He dug his thumbnail almost angrily first into the

pad of his index finger, then the middle finger and the others. Finally he did the same with his left hand. Carl swallowed hard as he felt only slight pressure each time.

It's beginning all over again.

He stood in the stall, swaying uncertainly for a moment. Then he took a faltering step.

His left foot scraped along the floor of the stall, pushing up a pile of straw.

You can't move it, can you?

Carl looked down frantically at his left leg. He reached out with both hands to massage the thigh, feeling the stiffened muscle there. It was the same with his calf. He let out a groan of despair and struck at the limb angrily as if that simple act would cause it to begin working properly again. He shook his head and looked down again at the recalcitrant leg.

Frankenstein promised to help you but what has he done? Did he tell you that the help would be only temporary? No, he didn't.

Carl took another step but there was no more movement in his left leg than before.

He tricked you.

Carl struck out angrily at the wooden side of the stall, slamming his fist against the slats. He hit it so hard that two of his knuckles split and blood dribbled from the wounds.

One of the ponies whinnied at the sound of the blow but Carl ignored it, more concerned with his own predicament.

Again he tried to walk, glaring at his left leg as if

that action would somehow release the tightened knots of muscle that seemed to be constricting the limb. To his horror he found that the leg was still stiff and once more lacking in feeling. When he tried to stamp down hard on the floor of the stall he could barely lift his foot up high enough to perform this relatively simple task. In desperation he clutched at the leg with his left hand but could not close his fingers tightly enough.

It was as if the entire left side of his body was shutting down, the muscles dying and refusing to obey the orders that his brain was giving them.

Just like before the operation.

Carl let out a gasp and stumbled backwards, clutching now at his head, pulling at his hair in impotent frustration. He closed his eyes as he felt tears of fear and frustration building.

Everything you've been through and you're just as you were before.

He dropped to his knees, tears rolling down his cheeks.

Frankenstein lied to you.

Carl allowed himself to fall back down to the floor of the stall, his face in the straw, his sobs muffled. His left leg and arm seemed to grow even tighter as he lay there, as if someone were gradually turning an invisible screw on both limbs and now, for the first time that day, he noticed something else, too. A gnawing in his belly that could not be ignored. The most overwhelming feeling of hunger he had ever experienced in his life. He sat up, his lips flecked with saliva, some of which had dribbled down his chin.

He put his right hand to his stomach and remembered when he had felt this raging hunger before. Images of Meyer's body lying before him swam through his mind and for a moment he forgot all about his arm and leg. He continued to salivate as he propped himself against the wall of the stall, his eyes bulging wide. Now the craving in his gut was becoming painful, it was so intense.

He knew this hunger had to be satisfied and he realised there was only one way to do it.

Fifty-One

Kleve was pulling at the handle on the carriage door even before the vehicle stopped.

As it bumped over the rutted track leading beneath the stone archway into the stable courtyard the doctor fumbled with the catch and freed it.

Next to him, Margaret Conrad also wore an expression of concern and she touched Kleve's arm gently as the carriage came to a halt.

'He was in pain – I thought I was helping him,' she said.

'Of course you did,' Kleve assured her. 'You did the right thing coming to the hospital. He needs help and only Doctor Stein and I can give it to him.'

Kleve scrambled out and helped Margaret down. Then both of them hurried towards the stable where she had left Carl.

'In there,' she said, pointing to the building just ahead. But as Kleve advanced hurriedly towards it she caught up with him and gripped his arm. 'He was very distressed, Hans – please help him.'

'I'll do everything I can for him,' he assured her.

Together they entered the building, both ponies tossing their heads and whickering as the newcomers barged in.

'The last stall,' Margaret said, pointing towards the far end of the stable. She moved past Kleve as they approached.

'Carl,' Kleve called.

Margaret echoed him, glancing agitatedly around the inside of the stable. 'I've brought Doctor Kleve,' she added.

There was no answer and Margaret advanced further, peering into the stall.

'Where is he?' Kleve asked.

'I left him here,' Margaret insisted. 'I left one of the grooms with him.'

Kleve took one more look around the stall and shook his head. 'Well, he's not here now,' he said. 'Margaret, what did he say to you about Doctor Stein?'

She looked puzzled. 'What do you mean?' she asked.

'You said that Carl insisted he didn't want Doctor Stein to come here, didn't want him to know – what exactly did he say?'

'I told him that I'd have to fetch Doctor Stein, that he needed his help. But Carl seemed terrified of him, he begged me not to fetch him. Why would he be that way about Doctor Stein?'

Kleve shook his head contemplatively.

'Has he hurt Carl in some way?' Margaret wanted to know.

'Not as far as I know. Doctor Stein isn't that kind of man. Why would he hurt Carl?'

'Well, there was *some* reason he was afraid of him.'

'That isn't our concern at the moment. What *is* our concern is where Carl has gone. He has to be found before he injures himself or someone else.'

Margaret shot Kleve a worried look. 'Injures someone else?' she gasped. 'Why would he do that?'

'The operation that he underwent was extremely delicate and complex. We have no way of knowing what the effects could be if he isn't treated properly and kept under observation.'

There was a movement at the door of the stable and both of them spun around to see a dark-coated groom wander in.

'Joseph,' Margaret called to the newcomer.

The man ambled across, becoming aware of the concerned expressions on the faces of the two people in front of him. He ran an appraising gaze over Kleve and then smiled at Margaret.

'Joseph, that man I left here for you to look after – where is he?' she asked.

The groom shrugged. 'I don't know, miss,' he confessed. 'I went to water the horses and when I came back he'd gone.'

'Did he seem agitated to you?' Kleve asked.

The groom looked blank.

'Was he aggressive or violent in any way?' Kleve went on.

'No, sir – he did seem a bit confused, though,' the groom said.

'And he didn't say anything to you?'

'No, sir. He can't have got too far, though.'

'Why?'

'Well, he wasn't moving about too well. It seemed as if he had a bad leg – he could hardly move it when he walked.'

Kleve's expression darkened.

'That's all, Joseph,' Margaret said.

'Doctor Stein will have to be told now,' Kleve exclaimed.

'Do you want me to come with you?' Margaret asked.

'No, stay here. Stay in the house. If Carl comes back tell him to wait here. Tell him we'll help him.'

'I hope he believes me.'

Kleve hesitated a moment. Then he headed off to the stable entrance, his face etched with concern.

Fifty-Two

'It's filthy in here.'

The man who spoke the words was in his sixties. A small white-haired man with one arm in plaster and bandages wound around his skinny chest. In places where the bandages didn't cover his pale flesh the outline of his ribs was clearly visible.

Frankenstein began bandaging the man's other arm as far as the wrist, covering the cuts and laceration there which he had already cleaned.

'By the look of you you're no stranger to filth,' the Baron murmured. 'Perhaps you should concentrate more on your condition rather than the state of the hospital.'

'It's cleaner than my house,' said a man in the bed opposite.

'I don't doubt that,' Frankenstein mused without looking at him.

'It's dirty because Meyer hasn't been around to sweep up in here,' a man with a bandaged head called.

'No, he hasn't, has he?' the man opposite added. 'Where is he?'

Frankenstein continued with his task, barely raising his head as the chatter went on around him. But he could hear every word clearly.

'Perhaps he's looking after the special patient,' someone else said.

Still the Baron didn't respond but merely continued dressing the wounds of the white-haired man.

'He must be special,' the man with the bandaged head added. 'He doesn't have to stay in the ward with the likes of us, does he? He gets his own room. His own private room.'

'And with someone special to look after him, too,' said another man, coughing as he spoke.

'I'd like her looking after me,' the man in the bed opposite said lecherously. 'She could give me a bed bath any time.'

He and the other men roared with laughter.

'Yes, with that lovely dark hair hanging down as she did it,' the man went on.

'And her nice soft hands all over you,' another one said, leering.

Only now did Frankenstein glance around at the men in the beds around him. 'I assume you're talking about Nurse Conrad?' he said flatly.

'Well, we wouldn't want to get a bed bath from Meyer, would we now, Doctor Stein?' the white-haired man grunted.

'You're disgusting,' the Baron said derisively. 'All of you. You're filthy physically and mentally too. Your bodies are diseased and your minds are like sewers.'

'Just because we like the look of a pretty face?' said a man nearby.

'And the touch of a soft hand?' another one called out.

'Does that make us wrong, doctor?' the old man in the bed in front of him asked.

'It makes you scum,' Frankenstein sneered.

'I bet you've felt her hands on you before now,' rasped a man behind him, whose arm was bandaged from shoulder to fingertips. He was in his thirties, a tall, well-built fellow whose imposing bulk hadn't been much diminished by years of poor nutrition. When he looked at Frankenstein it was with barely concealed distaste.

'What did you say?' the Baron hissed, turning towards him with anger in his eyes.

The tall man swallowed hard. 'It's well known, isn't it?' he said with a little less bravado. 'Doctors and nurses are always at it.'

'At it?' Frankenstein sneered. 'Is that the kind of gutter term you use?'

'I've heard about it before,' the man went on. 'Doctors and nurses getting friendly.' He smiled crookedly and nodded.

One of the other men grunted in agreement.

'And what exactly have you learned in your encyclopaedic knowledge of the medical profession?' Frankenstein challenged, holding the younger man's gaze. As he spoke he began rolling up the sleeves of his shirt a little further.

'What?' the man grunted.

'About doctors and nurses,' Frankenstein went on. 'What have you learned about them and what they get up to? Enlighten us all with your intellect.'

The man looked bewildered and he seemed to shrink

back into the pillows that were piled up behind him on the bed.

Frankenstein bent down and reached into the small leather bag that he always carried with him during his ward rounds. From inside he produced a pair of scissors.

'What are you doing?' the tall man asked, his voice cracking slightly.

'I'm going to have a look at your bad arm,' Frankenstein told him. 'See if the infection is healing.' As he spoke he began cutting through the bandages, starting at the shoulder and easing the twin blades down the length of the man's dressing with consummate ease and skill. 'We can't have it going unattended, can we?'

This time the man said nothing. The colour had drained from his face and he was gazing fixedly at the Baron who seemed to be staring at the gauze on the patient's arm. He finally looked into the tall man's face and then began to peel away the gauze. As the final piece of dressing came free the damage beneath was revealed.

The arm had been lacerated in several places in an industrial accident, as far as Frankenstein could remember. Only some exceptional work by him had managed to save the limb from amputation. There were two deep wounds on the bicep and inside the forearm and a less savage gash that ran from the wrist to halfway up the forearm. However, it was this one the Baron now turned his attention to. The flesh around the extremities of all three wounds was healing exceptionally well, the reddish tinge that the flesh had displayed finally having healed. There was even some scar tissue on the two deeper cuts, indicating that they were repairing themselves. Frankenstein ran his index finger slowly up and down the edges of the more shallow wound and nodded. Then he reached into his leather bag and produced a long thin metal probe.

The man in the bed was shaking slightly now.

'Just because the wound appears to be healing doesn't mean there isn't still infection,' Frankenstein said quietly. 'I'm just going to have a look.' He stared at the man unblinkingly. 'You don't mind, do you?'

The tall man didn't speak. His gaze was now fixed on the long metal probe, which Frankenstein was holding close to the wound. The doctor moved the implement closer to the cut, pressing lightly on the flesh at the extremities. With infinite slowness he moved higher and higher up the arm, exerting more pressure occasionally despite the gasps and whimpers of the tall man.

'It seems to be healing properly,' Frankenstein said without looking at the man. 'Perhaps I won't have to remove it after all.'

'You never said anything about having to cut off my arm,' the tall man blurted.

'Well, that depends on the condition deeper inside the muscle, doesn't it?' the Baron said. 'Or perhaps you'd prefer to let Nurse Conrad look at it.' He looked at the man and, as he did, he pushed the probe an inch into the wound.

The tall man shouted with the sudden pain and

looked down at the implement which was now sticking partly into his arm. Frankenstein withdrew it for a second, then moved it further up the cut, pressing it once more between the ragged edges of the wound.

'Do you think that Nurse Conrad could do a better job than this?' he said through clenched teeth, his face only inches away from that of the tall man. As he spoke he pushed the probe deeper, raking it against muscle and sinew and causing the man's fingers to curl.

'You bloody butcher,' one of the other men shouted.

Frankenstein ignored the comment, his stare fixed on the tall man's face that was now contorted in pain.

'Please don't hurt me again,' the tall man gasped.

'Perhaps it's your tongue I should remove, not your arm, then I wouldn't have to hear the filth you speak,' Frankenstein breathed, leaning close to his ear. 'It's bad enough that I have to smell you without having to hear you too.'

The tall man let out a loud shriek of pain and fear.

Frankenstein removed the probe and glared at him. 'The wound seems to be clean,' he said, flatly. 'But I'll examine it again tomorrow and decide whether or not to amputate the arm. One of the other nurses will be along shortly to rebandage it. It won't do it any harm to give it some air that will aid the healing process.'

The tall man didn't speak, he merely watched Frankenstein as the Baron turned and headed further down the ward, pausing beside a chubby woman who was sitting on the edge of her bed and coughing throatily.

'He's not taking my arm,' the tall man said under his breath.

'How are you going to stop him?' an older man asked.

The tall man continued glaring at Frankenstein but he kept his voice low. 'I'll kill him if I have to,' he murmured.

Fifty-Three

Banks of thick cloud drifted across the cold white moon, briefly blotting out the gleaming sphere and plunging the land beneath into blackness.

Far away there was a low rumbling that indicated a storm brewing and the breeze that had been blowing intermittently ever since darkness had descended was growing keener. It rattled hedges and caused trees to stir, their branches shuddering and waving when the wind became stronger.

Magda Klein pulled up the collar of her coat to shield herself against the gusts but it wasn't the weather conditions that were on her mind. She moved closer to the young man who accompanied her, smiling encouragingly at him. But the gesture seemed to have the opposite effect to that which she desired and he merely moved further away.

Frederick Keppler was almost nineteen, a year younger than Magda. He was a powerfully built lad who stood fully six feet tall and the jacket he wore could barely contain his broad chest. He'd always been tall but never gangly as was the way of some blessed with height. He worked in the gardens of the Namarov estate and had done since he was twelve. His family had been in service with the owners for as long as anyone could remember. Magda herself was a housemaid and had known Frederick for the last three years, ever since she had arrived from another wealthy household in Cologne. She had been struck instantly by his naive charm and his physical presence and she was sure that he had been similarly impressed by her slender shape and pretty face, framed as it was by long blonde hair that reached to the small of her back when it was allowed to hang loose.

However, she had found that his handsome appearance had not been matched by his wits and bravado, unlike many lads of his age whom she had known before. He was a solitary, reserved individual who seemed more at ease working alone or wandering the gardens and meadows of the estate once the working day was over. Magda herself would often take trips into Carlsbruck with some of the other maids when they had time off and there they would enjoy themselves as girls of that age tended to do, usually basking in the attention of the local men. But Magda had become determined that she would have some time alone with Frederick. She had often watched him working in the gardens of the house, stripped to the waist in the sunshine, displaying his enviable frame. Her attentions had been furtive, of course, as romance between workers was usually frowned upon in large households. At least, it always had been in those she had worked at before.

That had been the reason for her leaving her previous employment in Cologne. She had been involved first with one of the grooms at the stable and then with a butler inside the house itself. But what had finally forced her out was the attention paid to her by the eldest son of the house's owners. Magda had felt herself the wronged party, as it turned out. He had pursued her even though she had hardly put up a fight when the time finally came for them to consummate what had obviously been a mutual passion. But once he had enjoyed her he had wanted nothing else to do with her and she had found herself kicked out and without work. The post at the Namarov household had been very welcome and she had fitted in quickly, becoming popular among her co-workers.

Popular with everyone, it seemed, except Frederick.

For a while she had wondered if his sexual tastes were limited to other men, because not only did he never seem to look at her but the other girls of the household seemed either beneath or beyond his interest too. However, once she'd managed to speak to him she had learned that he was merely cripplingly shy. Magda had found this trait in his personality even more attractive and she became sure that he had never even slept with a woman. It was at that point she became determined to be his first.

However, as she sat on the grass now, gazing at him and tutting occasionally when he did not return her longing looks, she was beginning to wonder exactly what she was going to have to do to ignite his interest. The moon emerged from behind the clouds as she unbuttoned the top two buttons of her dress and moved closer to him once more.

Frederick merely reached behind him and pulled a

thin twig from the perfectly manicured hedge behind which they were sheltering. It was part of a topiary display and each end of the high hedge was cut into the shape of a horse's head. Frederick himself had helped the head gardener perfect the impressive privet sculptures and he certainly seemed more interested in those than he was in Magda.

She reached for his hand but he pulled away, his cheeks colouring. With the stick he had picked up he began stirring a patch of earth just in front of them. The movement of the dirt caused hundreds of ants to spill into view, each of them crawling and scrambling over each other as Frederick gently disturbed them, grinning at his discovery.

Magda looked less than impressed and moved back slightly, fearing that the ants would crawl in her direction.

Frederick peered down at them with a look of fascination on his face and wondered if this was what God felt like when He looked down at the Earth and saw humans scurrying about their business.

'Oh, stop that, can't you?' Magda said, wearily.

Frederick looked at her with surprise on his face, unable to comprehend why she should be so irritable.

'What are you getting annoyed about?' he asked.

'What do you *think* I'm getting annoyed about?'

He looked blankly at her.

'We've been here half an hour and all you can find to do is look at a lot of ants,' Magda said accusingly.

'Ants are interesting.'

'And I'm not?'

'I didn't say that, Magda. But you can learn a lot from ants.'

'Like what?'

Frederick shrugged. 'Well, you can learn all sorts of things about how they live and things like that,' he told her.

'Well, you haven't learned much.' Magda turned away slightly, hoping her display of petulance would spark his interest.

'What do you mean?' Frederick asked, still stirring the twig through the seething mass of ants in front of him. Some of the insects crawled onto the stick but most seemed intent on repairing the damage that had been caused to their nest.

'They've got more sense than to sit around all night,' Magda replied. 'They get on with it.'

'On with what?'

Magda let out a sigh of disbelief and then looked as intently into Frederick's eyes as he would allow. 'Have you ever been with a girl before, Frederick?' she asked.

He looked bewildered by the question for a moment, as if the very possibility was somehow alien. 'What do you mean?' he said falteringly.

'Have you ever been with a girl?' Magda repeated. 'I mean, you're a good-looking lad – there must have been others before me.'

Frederick still looked vague.

'Have you ever kissed a girl?' she persisted.

He shook his head.

'Have you ever touched one?' she went on, moving nearer to him yet again.

'What do you mean?' he asked.

'Oh, you know. You must have seen girls you like, girls you wanted to be with. You must have liked me or you wouldn't have agreed to meet me here, would you?'

'I like you, Magda, you're pretty and you're kind.'

'Then why don't you kiss me?'

Frederick swallowed hard and looked at her as if she'd just suggested that they should murder the entire Namarov family, all the residents of the house and stables and steal the contents of the buildings.

'I've never kissed a girl before,' he admitted shyly.

'I can show you how,' she said softly. 'You'll enjoy it, I know you will.'

As she spoke she reached out one hand and gently squeezed his knee. Frederick jerked as if a jolt of electricity had just been shot through him. Magda kept her hand in place and smiled at him.

'I'm not going to eat you, you know,' she purred. 'I just want to show you what to do. You don't have to be ashamed if you don't know – lots of men don't know how to do it properly.'

Frederick swallowed hard again but this time he moved a little closer, glancing first at Magda's insistent hand and then at her face. She licked her lips as seductively as she could and leaned closer to him.

As she did, something in the bushes behind her moved.

Fifty-Four

Magda twisted around towards the noise, her heart thudding hard against her ribs.

The sudden sound had certainly done more to get her blood pumping than Frederick had, she thought as she straightened up, squinting into the gloom.

'What's wrong?' Frederick asked, seemingly unaware of the noise that had startled Magda.

'Didn't you hear that?' she asked nervously.

'It's probably just a rat or something. Lots of animals come out at night, you know.'

'Just a rat? I'm not sitting here if there are rats around.'

'They won't hurt you. I see them all the time when I'm working in the gardens. They're probably more frightened of you than you are of them.'

'I doubt that.' Magda continued gazing at the hedge and bushes for a moment longer, then turned back towards Frederick. She smiled coyly. 'Are you going to protect me, then, Frederick?' she cooed. 'If it's a rat are you going to kill it for me?'

'Whatever it was it's gone now,' he said.

Magda moved her hand back to Frederick's knee, squeezing it gently.

'Now, what were we talking about before that nasty old rat interrupted us?' she breathed.

'It could have been a badger,' Frederick went on. 'They only come out at night too.'

'Well, like you said, it's gone now so we can forget about it, can't we?' she said tiredly. 'I was telling you that I could teach you how to kiss a girl if you'd like me to.'

Frederick looked a little bewildered but he moved a bit nearer to Magda, aware that her hand was gliding slowly further up his leg until it rested on his thigh. She squeezed and Frederick smiled, appreciating the sensations that were beginning to travel through his body. Magda stretched her legs out before her, pulling her dress up so that her calves and knees were exposed to Frederick's suddenly curious eyes. She took one of his large hands and placed it gently on her knee. He let it stay there, aware of how smooth the flesh was but unsure of what he was supposed to do next.

Magda slid her own hand higher up his thigh and Frederick decided this was his own best course of action. He trailed his fingers higher until they disappeared beneath the blue material of Magda's dress. He raised his eyebrows and closed his fingers around the soft firm flesh there, kneading it gently.

Magda smiled triumphantly and looked at him, licking her lips once more. 'Do you want to kiss me, Frederick?' she asked.

He nodded. 'I suppose so,' he said falteringly.

'You suppose so,' she said indignantly. 'Well, either

you do or you don't. There are lots of men who'd love to be in your position, you know.'

'Do you know lots of men, then, Magda?' he asked.

She looked curiously at him for a moment then frowned. 'What do you mean?' she asked.

'You asked me if I'd ever been with a girl before. Have you been with other men before?'

'Yes.'

'How many?'

'I don't know if I should tell you that,' Magda said coyly.

'Why? Have there been that many?'

'You're not supposed to ask a lady a question like that.'

Frederick chuckled. 'You're not a lady, Magda,' he said, grinning.

She looked at him furiously and pushed his hand away from her leg. 'What do you mean?' she snapped.

'People like Countess Namarov are ladies,' he said innocently. 'Not you.'

Magda struggled to her feet, brushing grass from her skirt as she straightened up. 'I'm not staying here to be insulted,' she said haughtily. 'I don't know who you think you are – insulting people like that isn't clever, you know.'

Frederick was on his feet now, looking anxiously at her, still not sure what he had said that was so wrong.

'If you've been with lots of men I don't care, Magda,' he said helplessly.

'I'm going home,' she snapped and shot him a furious glance.

Frederick watched as she headed off down a short path and disappeared between some tall hedges, her heels clicking on the paved walkway. He raised his hand as if to wave farewell. 'Goodnight, Magda,' he called, cheerfully, watching her as she disappeared into the night.

He wasn't the only one who watched.

Fifty-Five

M agda Klein couldn't remember when she'd been so angry before. As she stalked along the paved pathway that led away from Frederick she muttered to herself under her breath.

How dare he imply that she was anything less than a lady? In fact, he hadn't even had the courtesy to *imply* the fact, she told herself. He had come straight out and said it. And worse still, he hadn't even known that he was insulting her. The big oaf, he probably wouldn't have known what to do even if she'd shown him. She didn't need a man like him, she needed a proper man, one who knew how to treat her and touch her the way the others had.

Magda reached a small ornate wrought-iron gate and pushed it open, heading down the path that wound through one of the topiary-decorated areas of the grounds.

On both sides of her the heads of horses sculpted and shaped so lovingly and expertly from privet peered blindly at her as she passed. The shadows were thick here and tall trees also stood sentinel around the extremities of the carefully manicured lawn on either side of the path. Magda slowed her pace slightly, glancing around in the gloom, peering into the shadows as if to be sure that she was still alone.

For a second she thought she saw something move, away to her right.

Something low to the ground but something large that moved falteringly amid the concealing night.

She wondered if Frederick had followed her. Perhaps he'd realised his mistake and come after her, eager to rectify his error and to take back what he'd said.

No lady indeed, she thought indignantly. She was more of a lady than he'd ever have. Lumbering great fool – no wonder he'd never had a woman before. What kind of woman would put up with his pathetic attempts at wooing or his clumsy talk? From now on she would stick to the men of the town as she always had done before. And what did it matter how many of them there'd been? Who was he or anyone else to judge her? Wasn't she as entitled to seek pleasure where she found it as anyone else? The men were always willing and yet no one scorned them or called them names. Magda pulled her collar up against a particularly strong gust of wind and marched on.

Ahead of her was a flight of stone steps that led down to another part of the formal garden that they were in. More topiary animals and figures guarded the stone archway that had been built over the entrance to these steps. Faceless upright shapes stood on either side of the arch and when the wind blew they shuddered slightly like real people shivering from cold. Magda glanced at their featureless heads as she drew nearer to them, glancing behind her once more to see if Frederick was following.

She actually stood still for a moment and gazed back in the direction she'd come, waiting to see his large bulk come looming out of the darkness towards her, arms outstretched and asking for forgiveness.

There was no sign of him.

And yet she was sure that *something* was moving out here with her because once more she heard the snap of twigs and the rustle of leaves somewhere close by.

Magda spun round, her eyes open wide in an attempt to pick out anything there. She thought about calling Frederick's name, wondering if he was deliberately playing a trick on her. That was the kind of infantile joke that would appeal to his sense of humour. A real man wouldn't try to frighten her this way: he would have escorted her back to the Namarov house, walked her through the dark grounds, not let her storm off the way she had. But then again, she reasoned, if Frederick was a real man then she wouldn't be walking alone through the grounds now. She would be engaged in some more interesting and pleasurable activity.

Magda hesitated at the top of the stone steps then began to descend, moving slowly so she didn't trip in the dark. It seemed much gloomier here and she didn't want to risk falling. The heels of her shoes scraped on the stone and she almost overbalanced. Muttering to herself, she reached down and pulled off her shoes, knowing that she would be able to walk faster and more sure-footedly if she needed to.

If the need arose she could run well without shoes, she told herself.

Barefoot and with her shoes clutched in one hand she continued down the stairs.

Whatever she had heard moving in the bushes and shadows did so again as she reached the halfway point of the staircase.

It wasn't the wind blowing the trees and shaking the hedges, she was sure of it. There was an animal moving about nearby, she was certain of that now. What had Frederick said it could be? A rat? A badger? She swallowed hard and continued walking, the stone cold beneath her bare feet. She glanced behind her again, up towards the top of the steps, still harbouring some fading hope that Frederick would appear there and after much apologising would offer to walk her back to the house. She might, she told herself, even give him a second chance if he was apologetic enough. In fact, as she descended the stone steps, moving, it seemed, into even deeper darkness and shadow at their base, she began to hope more fervently that Frederick would appear. If there was an animal moving about close to her in the darkness then she didn't want to endure the long walk all the way back to the house with it sniffing and scratching about close by, watching her and possibly doing something worse.

Exactly what it was going to do to her Magda had no idea, but she felt very alone and more frightened than she should have been. The thought that it might be something bigger than a badger suddenly entered her mind. Were there wolves in this part of the country?

she wondered. There had been bears at one time. Magda swallowed hard and continued on down the steps, the gravel of the path at the bottom digging into her feet as she reached it.

She paused for a second, listening. Her ears attuned to the slightest sound, her eyes alert for even the smallest movement in the gloom.

There was one sound that she heard and recognised. It was the gentle trickling of a fountain as water sprayed into a large ornamental pond a little way ahead of her. The pond was surrounded by chest-high hedges and tall bushes and it was through these that Magda now had to pass in order to reach the main track that would lead her back to the house. High above her the moon floated through the night sky and she was bathed in its cold white light as she walked on, glad of the fitful illumination. In the brief moments of brightness she could see nothing moving or skulking in the bushes and that was a comfort to her. She looked up and saw that clouds were scudding once more across the face of the moon and she realised that they would soon once again blot it out completely. She wanted to be clear of the pond and these high hedges and bushes before that happened so she increased her pace, ignoring the gravel that stuck into her bare feet as she walked.

As she passed the pond she looked down to see several of the large fish in it rise to the surface and then quickly submerge again. The fountain sent out droplets of water like raindrops and the sound would have been comforting at any other time, Magda thought. But here, alone in the gloom, no sound seemed to bring her any comfort.

Especially not the rustling of branches close to her on the path around the pond.

She stopped and felt her heart banging hard against her ribs.

Perhaps it was Frederick playing some stupid joke. And yet, she reasoned, how could he have got in front of her? And for all his simple faults was he really the kind of man who would take pleasure from frightening her? She thought not.

The bushes rustled again and Magda shuddered, wondering if there was some other way she could get back to the house.

A shape emerged from the bushes, revealing itself on the path ahead.

It was a rabbit.

Magda smiled with relief as the little creature rose on its hind legs, its nose twitching as it looked up at her. Its long ears were upright as if it was listening for something.

Magda watched it for a moment, then saw the fur at the back of its neck bristle seconds before it darted away.

As if it had seen something behind her.

That thought stuck in her mind for a second.

It was the last she had before the hands that reached for her closed around her throat.

Fifty-Six

'How much longer?'

Frankenstein shifted impatiently in his seat, pulling the curtain aside to peer out of the carriage window.

The vehicle bumped and lurched over the rutted road, shaking the Baron and Kleve from side to side as it gathered speed. The two men could occasionally hear the crack of the driver's whip as he sought to coax extra speed from the four horses drawing the carriage.

'Why did you wait so long before you told me about Carl?' the Baron snapped.

'It wasn't my fault,' the younger man countered. 'You were visiting your other patients. I had no idea where you were or how to find you.'

'Then you should have tried harder. There's no telling where Carl could be by now.'

'Margaret's groom said that he wasn't moving too well. It sounds as if he'll have to stay pretty close to the house and grounds.'

'We should be concerning ourselves with why he's not moving very well.'

'Could it be a recurrence of what was wrong with him before we operated?'

'If his brain was damaged then it's a possibility.'

'And the other problem?'

'What other problem?'

'The chimp became cannibalistic after its brain transplant.'

'I told you, that isn't going to happen with Carl.'

'You sound very sure of that.'

Frankenstein held Kleve's gaze for a moment, then returned to looking out of the carriage window.

'I know you feel I'm to blame for this,' Kleve said at last. 'I know that if I'd come to you immediately then the situation might have been different but Margaret said Carl didn't want me to tell you. That was why I went myself and—'

'You should have told me immediately,' Frankenstein snapped, cutting across him. 'I don't care what Margaret wanted or what Carl wanted. You should have come to me.'

'Margaret felt that my presence—'

'I have no interest at all in what Margaret felt, Hans,' Frankenstein barked. 'I told you when she first came to work at the hospital that you should be careful.'

'What's that supposed to mean?'

'You wouldn't be the first man to have his head turned by a pretty face.'

Kleve was about to respond when the carriage came to an abrupt halt. Frankenstein looked even more furious by the interruption of their journey.

'What now?' he hissed.

As he looked out of the carriage window once again he could see lanterns being waved from side to side by figures that were moving in the road ahead. Two of those figures were now moving towards the coach and as they drew nearer Frankenstein could see that they were in uniform.

'Why have we stopped?' Kleve asked.

Frankenstein didn't answer – he was still watching the policemen who were moving towards the coach. The closest of them saluted sharply and Frankenstein recognised him immediately as Inspector Schiller.

The policeman touched the rim of his helmet deferentially when he saw the doctor.

'Doctor Stein, it's you,' he said. He peered past Frankenstein and saw Kleve within the vehicle. He nodded a greeting to the younger man too.

'Why have you stopped the carriage?' Frankenstein asked tetchily. 'What's going on?'

'I'm sorry to stop you, doctor, but we have to check on everyone passing this way,' Schiller told him.

'Why?'

'There's been a murder in the vicinity,' the policeman stated.

Frankenstein frowned as he stepped down from the carriage into the chilly night. 'Can I or Doctor Kleve be of assistance?' he asked as the younger man joined him.

'If you wouldn't mind having a look at the body, doctor,' the inspector said. 'It's not a pretty sight, though, I have to say.'

'When did it happen?' Frankenstein asked as he and Kleve followed the policeman across the verge next to the road. The Baron could see more uniformed men waiting close to a hedge a few yards further on. Kleve touched the Baron's arm and was about to say something but Frankenstein shook his head to cut short the kind of question he was sure Kleve was keen to ask.

Inspector Schiller led them through a gap in the hedge, nodding towards a constable who was standing there shivering in the increasingly chilly night air.

'Were there any witnesses?' Frankenstein asked as he and Kleve edged through the gap after the inspector who then guided them down a flight of stone steps.

'She'd been with a boy not long before she was attacked,' Schiller said.

'Did he see anything?' Kleve asked.

'It's hard to tell,' Schiller informed them. 'He's not said much.'

'Probably still in shock,' Kleve said.

The three men emerged into an ornamental garden dominated by a big pond and fountain. Sergeant Dietz was standing next to a large figure who was shaking, intermittently wiping tears from his face.

Frederick Keppler saw the two doctors but he said nothing.

'Did you see who attacked her?' Frankenstein said to him, seeing the distraught expression on his face.

Frederick merely shook his head. He looked as if he was trying to speak but when he opened his mouth whatever words he'd been trying to form merely dissolved in a fit of sobs. He turned his back on the others, aware of what lay beneath the blanket that they were now standing beside.

'All he could tell me was that when he heard the girl

scream he shouted,' Schiller said. 'And then the man rushed off—'

'Then he did see someone?' Frankenstein interjected, looking at the inspector and then at the cowering figure of Frederick.

'If it *was* a man,' Schiller said gravely.

'What do you mean?' the Baron grunted.

Schiller reached forward and pulled back the blanket.

Fifty-Seven

'My God,' Kleve murmured as the body of Magda Klein was exposed, visible to all now when the blanket was pulled away.

Her dress had been torn in several places, pieces of material ripped free, some of it lying close by. The garment had been split from neck to stomach and the flesh beneath was bare and clearly visible.

The skin on view was a patchwork of bruises and other contusions but it was the damage around the face and upper body that Frankenstein found particularly disturbing.

'Bite marks,' he said, glancing up at Kleve before returning his attention to the dead girl.

There were particularly deep and savage cuts and bruises around the neck and it was to these that the Baron turned his attention first. There was also blood around the girl's mouth and her tongue was protruding from her lips, blackened and swollen.

'By the look of it she was strangled,' Frankenstein noted, indicating the bruising around the throat.

'What about the bites?' Kleve asked, bending close to cast his own expert eye over the corpse.

The majority were on her face and neck but there were also some on her breasts, more on the belly.

'The boy did say that he thought she'd been attacked by an animal,' Schiller said. 'That would account for the bites, I suppose, but what kind of animal leaves marks like that?'

'No flesh has been taken,' Frankenstein said, outlining one of the bite marks with his index finger. 'None removed from the body.'

'It was no animal,' Sergeant Dietz offered. 'Animals eat what they attack – and besides, there are no wild animals here.'

'I agree with the sergeant, Doctor Stein,' Schiller said. 'I think this is more than just an ordinary murder.'

'Have you searched the park?' Frankenstein asked.

'Thoroughly, sir,' Schiller informed him. 'There's nothing untoward. No sign of any killer.'

'Whoever did this is probably miles away by now,' Kleve said.

'He must be a madman,' Dietz added.

'Have you any idea who the victim is?' Kleve asked.

'Her name was Magda Klein,' Dietz said. 'She worked for Countess Namarov. She was a maid. This boy works for the Countess too, for that matter.'

'It's a good job all the Countess's guests had arrived before this happened,' Schiller said. 'She's got some sort of party going on at her house tonight. Most of the members of the Carlsbruck Medical Council are there.'

'So I understand,' Frankenstein murmured, his gaze still fixed on the body of the dead girl.

'That's where we were going when you stopped us,' Kleve added.

'Of course, sir,' Schiller remarked, touching the rim of his helmet again. 'I'm sorry to have detained you.'

'I'm afraid there's nothing more I can do here, inspector,' the Baron said. 'If you're taking the body back to the mortuary I can inspect it more closely tomorrow and give you a proper report.'

'That would be most appreciated, Doctor Stein. Thank you,' Schiller said. He sighed and shook his head. 'Poor girl.'

Frankenstein turned and headed back towards the road and the carriage that was waiting. Kleve hurried along, struggling to keep pace with him. 'Those bite marks can mean only one thing,' he said anxiously. 'It's what we feared. The damage to Carl's brain has caused the same reaction as we saw in the chimpanzee.'

'We don't know that for sure,' Frankenstein insisted.

'How else do you explain those bites? His brain was damaged and he's become like the injured chimpanzee. He's displaying cannibalistic tendencies.'

'The bites were superficial.'

'My God, is that all you've got to say? If he'd had enough time there's no telling what he would have done. The damage to the body wasn't worse because he was interrupted by that boy before he could devour any of her flesh.'

'You think so?'

'It's obvious.'

'Is it?' the Baron snapped. 'Then the quicker we find Carl and do something to stop him the better.'

'Stop him?' Kleve said in puzzlement. 'I thought we were supposed to help him.'

'It might amount to the same thing. If his brain has been damaged to such an extent then there might not be much we can do for him.'

'And what then? Do we just abandon him?'

Frankenstein hauled himself into the waiting carriage and sat back in the seat as Kleve scrambled in.

'We cannot decide our course of action until we find him,' Frankenstein said. He banged on the roof of the carriage and it moved away as the driver cracked his whip. The four horses trotted off along the road, the coach bumping as it crossed each fresh rut.

'And what if we can't help him?' Kleve persisted.

Frankenstein didn't speak.

Fifty-Eight

His left hand was more like a claw now.

Carl Lang couldn't think of a better word to describe it. The fingers were curled round and fixed as if they had been clutching something that had been forcibly torn from their grasp. He shuddered when he saw small pieces of skin stuck beneath two of the nails. With his good right hand he pulled at the fleshy debris, picking it away and dropping it onto the ground beside him.

With that same hand he also wiped fresh tears from his cheeks.

The agony in his stomach was even more intense than it had been before he'd attacked the girl and he knew only too well what that pain meant. The cramping of muscles and what felt like the constriction of his insides was the most appallingly acute feeling of hunger he had ever experienced.

But, Carl reasoned, this wasn't the hunger of a man who hadn't eaten for a few hours – this was the raging, uncontrollable need of someone who hasn't had food in their belly for weeks. The feeling an animal gets when it must satisfy its appetite, no matter what.

It was an all-consuming urge and one that he'd barely

been able to control. He slumped against the stone pillar he was hiding behind and sobbed helplessly for a moment. He hadn't wanted to hurt the girl. He hadn't been able to help himself, though. If only she hadn't tried to scream then perhaps he might not have needed to choke her to silence her.

But you did more than just silence her, didn't you?

He closed his eyes tightly until white stars danced behind the lids.

You wanted to kill her.

Carl shook his head.

You wanted to kill her and much, much worse.

He slammed his head back against the stone pillar as if that would drive the voice away from inside his head. With his right hand he massaged his left leg, feeling how stiff and knotted the muscles were there. He could barely lift the limb and when he walked he dragged it uselessly. The entire left side of his body was beginning to tighten and spasm in the same way as his leg and arm. The tightness in the muscles of his neck was pulling his head to one side.

The way it used to be.

And again, into his mind's eye, the vision of the girl floated like the remnants of a nightmare – but, no matter how hard he tried, Carl could not banish the images this time. He sat shivering helplessly as he remembered looking down upon her lifeless body, tearing at her clothes to expose the soft, warm flesh beneath.

Even now he began to salivate and that action disgusted him. He shook his head again but the visions remained.

You wanted to taste her flesh, didn't you?

He could remember how warm it had felt against his tongue as he pressed his teeth into it. He could still recall how badly he had wanted to rip lumps of it from her and swallow them, to fill his belly with her. Anything to stop the terrible feeling of hunger – and yet somehow he had managed to stop himself, some part of his fevered and damaged brain had retained its grip on humanity and he had resisted that appalling urge, although he didn't know how much longer he could fight it.

Carl clamped both hands to his head, his eyes closed tightly.

When he opened them he saw above him a light flicker and he turned sharply to look up towards the soft warm glow.

A number of the rooms at the rear of the Namarov house had balconies and it was at one of these that Carl now looked.

He saw the figure emerge and walk to the wooden balustrade and he ducked down lower, seeking shelter amid the bushes in the garden beneath. From his vantage point he could clearly see the woman above him now.

Margaret Conrad stood in the cool night air, gazing out over the expansive gardens of her aunt's estate. She had heard a horse in the stables neighing and now she stood in the stillness, listening to the sound as it drifted on the wind.

Carl knew it was her even without seeing her face. He'd been watching her room for the last forty-five minutes, hidden in various places in the sheltered garden, and he had seen her emerge onto the balcony once before. This time, however, she was dressed in a beautiful gown, her long dark hair pinned up and held in place by a pearl-decorated band. Even from where he now crouched, Carl could smell the scent of her perfume as it was carried on the breeze. He wiped his face, brushing tears away.

She isn't going to want you now, is she?

He swallowed hard, fresh tears coursing down his face.

A murdering deformed animal like you. She'd hate you just like the rest of them. Just like they always used to.

Again Carl pressed both hands to his head. It felt as if his skull was swelling, ready to burst with the pressure inside. Under his breath he prayed to a God he didn't believe in to help him.

You know who has to help you: the man who made you like this.

The light in Margaret's room was just one of many burning inside the Namarov residence and Carl thought how warm and inviting it looked. He had seen people moving about inside, laughing and talking and enjoying each other's company. The sight had only served to reinforce his feelings of isolation. He felt more alone than he had ever done in his life.

Above him Carl heard a soft voice calling and he saw Margaret turn away from the balustrade.

He moved towards some bushes a short distance away so that he could still see her outline against the warm glow inside the room. But as he watched she closed her curtains and vanished from his sight. He raised one hand towards her balcony, the palm outstretched. It was a silent plea for the help he knew he needed but also knew he would never receive.

Carl moved back into the shadows, enveloped by them until he too, once again, was invisible.

Fifty-Nine

The hospitality of the Namarov family was famous in and around the town of Carlsbruck and had been for many years.

Even before the Count died the residence had been one of the centres for important social gatherings. All those prominent in Carlsbruck society were summoned almost every week to a dinner party or a ball or some other event.

After the death of her husband, the Countess had seen no reason to stop these soirées and if she was honest with herself the regular presence of people in her home was a comfort. The house was huge and even with the presence of the servants she sometimes felt lonely. The social gatherings were a way of staving off that loneliness, even if the relief was only temporary.

She still missed the Count and the passage of time had done little to soften the pain of his passing. Many had said to her that time was a great healer but she was beginning to think that was a lie.

She still woke some nights and expected to see him in the large bed beside her. Often, she would shed some tears when she realised once more that he would never again be with her. She had always been a God-fearing woman and religion had played a large part in her life but she was ashamed to admit to herself that her faith had wavered immediately before and after the passing of her husband.

She had nursed him through his illness, barely allowing the servants to go near him as he lay feverishly in his bed wasting away. It had been she who had mopped his brow and comforted him when the pain had become too great to bear. She who had given him laudanum, sometimes administering more than the prescribed amount when his pain became intolerable. She had watched him drift in and out of delirium, barely recognising her towards the final stages of his life but through all of that she had stayed at his side, ignoring her own needs. And all through that time she had prayed to God to deliver her husband from his suffering, either to make him well again or to show mercy and take him. Allow him to pass without the suffering and agony she had to witness every day. She didn't want that for the man she had loved since she'd been a teenager. No one should have to suffer the way he had. But God had chosen to ignore her prayers and she had found that hard to forgive.

The priest who had delivered the last rites and performed the burial service had told her that her husband was in a better place and having seen the way he had died she didn't doubt that. But what she did question was the need for him to be in that place. It was God's will, she had been told. God knew what He was doing. If that was the case, she had told the priest, then God was a sadist. The comment had not been well received but the Countess cared little for the feelings of a priest. She wanted her husband back but knew she couldn't have her wish. She didn't want to be with him in some promised afterlife – she wanted him with her now.

For weeks after his death she had remained alone in her rooms upstairs in the house, eating alone and barely emerging. But somehow she had found the strength to go on, as most do who lose those close to them, and painfully she had forced herself to accept life without the man she had loved so deeply and for so long.

Even now, as she sat in the drawing room of the house surrounded by guests and with the mellifluous tones of the string quartet before her filling her ears, she could not prevent thoughts of her dead husband from entering her head – and, indeed, she didn't try. She didn't want to forget him. She wanted to cling to those memories no matter how painful they might be. The piece that the quartet was playing had been a favourite of her husband's but she had encouraged them to play it. If he was listening and watching from a better place, she reasoned, then he too would appreciate the music they made.

The other guests sat around, appreciatively cradling their glasses of wine, port or brandy. A number of the men were smoking cigars and the pleasing aroma filled the air along with the music. The Countess sipped her own wine and shifted her position on the velvet-covered sofa. Beside her, Doctor Molke took another puff on his cigar and smiled at her. He wasn't the only member of the Carlsbruck Medical Council present that night.

Across the room sat Hauser and Kiesel, both of them accompanied by their wives. One of the other guests was a local magistrate. Another man, a professor of literature at the nearby university, was accompanied by a young woman who looked twenty years his junior. He had introduced her as his companion. Nothing more, just his companion. The Countess smiled to herself even now as she glanced across at them, wondering what the other guests at her gathering had made of the professor and his young friend. Tongues, she fancied, would be wagging.

And amidst this group sat her own niece, Margaret. The Countess felt such a swell of pride when she looked at the girl. She too knew what it was like to lose someone close and no one her age should have to suffer that way. The two of them had become wonderfully close since Margaret had arrived at the house and when she was present the huge building didn't seem anywhere near as empty. For that alone the Countess was grateful.

As the quartet finished their latest piece there was a polite but enthusiastic round of applause from the listening guests.

'I've nothing against the English composers,' the Countess said, leaning across to Molke. 'It's just that they won't let themselves go.'

Molke smiled.

'It's that English reserve, you see,' the Countess went on. 'I fear Napoleon was right when he called them a nation of shopkeepers but I've known more adventurous shopkeepers.'

Molke laughed and puffed on his cigar. 'What about

Handel?' the doctor enquired. 'Surely you wouldn't put him in the category of reserved?'

'Ah, but he was stolen from Germany,' the Countess reminded him.

Molke reached for his wine glass and sipped from it, nodding appreciatively. 'This really is most excellent claret, Countess,' he observed.

'It's from my very own cellar,' she told him. 'My husband was always a great wine lover and he stocked it comprehensively.'

'I salute his taste,' Molke said, raising his glass. 'The food also is excellent.'

'I've had the same chef working for me for the past twelve years,' the Countess said. 'I feel it's so important to retain the services of one so reliable. There are many fine cooks around, doctor, but there is a huge difference between a cook and a chef.'

Molke nodded in agreement.

'I was rather hoping that my other guests would have arrived by now,' the Countess said, glancing around the room.

'You seem to have a well-attended gathering as usual, Countess. May I ask who is missing?'

'I invited Doctor Stein and that young Doctor Kleve,' she said.

Molke's expression darkened. 'I wouldn't hold your breath awaiting Stein's arrival, Countess,' he said dismissively. 'He pleases himself in most things.'

'Well, we'll see,' said the Countess. 'There's still time. He's probably still at work in his hospital – he does such good work there.'

'So I hear,' Molke mumbled.

'My niece Margaret works there too, you know. She says he's a wonderful man. So caring.'

Molke was about to say something but decided instead to take a bite from one of the sandwiches arrayed on the plate in front of him.

'I admire Doctor Stein's attitude,' the Countess went on. 'I feel it's always important that those of us with more should give a little time and consideration to those who are not so well off. Don't you, doctor?'

'Whenever possible, Countess,' Molke said, crumbs dropping onto his waistcoat. 'Whenever possible.'

The conversation was interrupted by a sound from the rear of the room. A liveried servant coughed theatrically and waited until a number of the guests were facing him before announcing:

'Doctor Victor Stein and Doctor Hans Kleve.'

Sixty

The Countess rose immediately and walked towards the two newcomers. Molke and the other members of the Medical Council eyed the latest arrivals with something less than enthusiasm.

'Doctor Stein,' the Countess beamed. 'You came after all.'

Frankenstein took the old woman's hand and kissed it respectfully, his face still set in stern lines.

'Countess, I wish to speak with your niece,' he said. 'It's very urgent.'

'Always so efficient,' the Countess said, a little dismissively. 'The night is young, doctor – there is plenty of time for that.'

Frankenstein looked a little impatiently at the old woman, trying to force a convincing smile on to his face. He didn't quite manage it. 'It really is extremely important, Countess,' he persisted.

'Patience is a virtue, Doctor Stein,' she told him cheerfully.

'It may well be but I have no time for it now,' Frankenstein said sharply and turned, looking around the large room for the person he sought.

Margaret was standing with Doctor Kiesel and his

wife, engaged in some polite conversation, but Frankenstein had no time for that. He stalked off across the room towards her, with Kleve trailing in his wake.

'Ah, Doctor Stein,' Kiesel said. But Frankenstein merely nodded curtly, his gaze fixed on Margaret.

'May I introduce my wife?' Kiesel began, indicating the frosty-faced woman standing with him.

'Another time, perhaps,' Frankenstein snapped. 'I need to speak to Miss Conrad in private if you don't mind.'

Kiesel looked somewhat crestfallen and grunted, pulling his wife's arm to guide her away to another part of the room.

'Dreadful man,' the woman murmured as they walked off to find seats as the string quartet began to play again.

Frankenstein waited for a moment, aware that Margaret was looking at him with an expression of concern on her face. She looked to Kleve as if for some explanation of why the Baron was glaring at her so venomously but the younger man said nothing. She was still wondering what was wrong when Frankenstein reached out and grabbed her forearm a little too tightly.

'Doctor,' she said but he merely pushed her back towards an alcove beside one of the many huge bookshelves that dominated the room.

Margaret tried to shake loose, moving towards the French windows that overlooked a terrace beyond.

'When you found Carl in the stable,' the Baron began sharply, 'was he the same as when you saw him in the hospital?'

'What do you mean?' Margaret asked.

'Did he look the same?' Frankenstein snapped. 'Behave the same? Was his manner as it had been or would you say that he had changed? Do I have to spell it out for you?'

Margaret looked at him warily, then nodded. 'He was very distressed,' she said.

'Were there any physical changes that you could see?'

'Not really.'

'Was that the last you saw of him?'

'Yes. I left him with one of the grooms and told him I'd fetch help. That was when I went to get Doctor Kleve.'

'Are you certain he hasn't returned here?'

'Why would he?'

'Because he obviously looks upon you as some kind of guardian angel or else he wouldn't have come here in the first place.'

'He had nowhere else to go.'

Frankenstein continued to glare at her.

'He wouldn't go to you, doctor,' Margaret said defiantly. 'He seemed terrified of you. Why is that?'

Frankenstein turned away.

Kleve hesitated for a moment, then followed.

The Countess turned in her chair as she saw the two men moving towards the double doors that led out of the room. She rose, wondering why they were leaving in such haste. Frankenstein glanced back cursorily at her but continued on his way to join the liveried servant who prepared to open the doors for him. Kleve caught the Baron's arm and was about to say something to him but Frankenstein merely pulled free of the younger doctor's restraining grip.

Both men turned as they heard a deafening crash.

The French windows exploded inwards, pieces of glass and splintered wood spraying into the room, the curtains billowing as a strong breeze swept in and extinguished many of the candles. There were several screams.

Carl Lang stood silhouetted between the shattered windows, one hand gripping the frame, the other curled and twisted across his chest like a talon. His body was hunched over on the left side, his leg jutting stiffly before him. His face was contorted, its left side taut, the flesh there looking as if it had been stretched across the bone by some kind of muscular spasm. His face and clothes were spattered with blood and Frankenstein could see that there was thick spittle running down his chin. His unkempt hair was swept back from his forehead, revealing the angry red scar that ran from one temple to the other. His left eye was almost closed, sunken into its socket and surrounded by a yellowish discharge that was weeping down his cheek like discoloured tears. The right eye bulged with an insane fury. Carl looked around the room before taking a step further into it on legs that would barely support him.

A number of the guests moved back in terror as he stumbled into the centre of the room, stepping on pieces of glass that crunched loudly beneath his feet. All gazes were upon him now, fixed on this shambling mockery of a man. The people's expressions ranged from horror to revulsion and Carl could see that look as he swayed uncertainly. It was a look he had seen so many times before in his life. He stumbled forward, crashing into a small coffee table and spilling the contents over the carpet.

He saw Margaret and without thinking he lunged towards her.

She screamed and backed away, transfixed by the monstrous figure before her.

'Carl,' the Baron shouted.

Carl spun around and Frankenstein saw the fury and pain in that one bulging eye. Even he took a step backwards as Carl lurched towards him, his right arm outstretched.

'Frankenstein,' Carl screamed, the sound torn raw and bloody all the way from the base of his spine. It was a mixture of frenzy and despair.

The word cut through the air like a razor through flesh.

Carl staggered nearer to the Baron, his whole body shaking. 'Frankenstein,' he wailed again. 'Help me.'

He dropped to his knees, shuddering uncontrollably. Kleve reached for him in an attempt to break his fall as he pitched forward but it was too late. Carl slammed against the floor and lay still. Blood was running freely from his nose and ears, soaking into the expensive carpet beneath him. More of the crimson liquid had cascaded over his lips where the force of the seizure had caused him to bite through his own tongue.

Kleve pressed two fingers to Carl's throat and felt vainly for a pulse.

Frankenstein looked down impassively at the body, then at Kleve who shook his head.

'Frankenstein.'

The word was spoken by Molke who was glaring across the room at him. Others began to repeat it until the noise seemed to fill the space like some kind of chanted litany.

The Baron stood motionless, Carl's body at his feet, as the sound grew louder and louder until it almost deafened him.

'Frankenstein.'

Sixty-One

The air inside the room where the Carlsbruck Medical Council met was smoky with the fumes of cigars and pipes. Every member of the Council, it seemed, had decided to partake at once and it appeared to the man standing at the head of the table around which these smokers were gathered that he was the only one who did not indulge in this particular habit.

Doctor Molke waved a hand before his face to try and disperse some of the smoke before he spoke. He coughed theatrically, waiting until the attention of all the men in the room was upon him before he continued.

'"Frankenstein, help me",' he said, leaning on the table, his fists supporting him. 'Those were his very words.'

'And then what happened?' Bergman wanted to know.

'The poor fellow collapsed,' Molke went on. 'Dead.'

A babble of conversation rose at the mention of this latest detail.

'Stein and young Kleve carried him from the room,' Molke continued. 'I've never seen such a thing.'

'Did you recognise this man?' Bergman asked. 'The one who had called Frankenstein by name?'

'Poor chap,' Molke mused, shaking his head. 'He was in a frightful state. There seemed to be some kind of disfigurement to the left side of his body. Some kind of muscular seizure, caused by what I can't begin to imagine.'

'But you'd never seen him before?' Bergman pressed.

Molke shook his head. 'And none of us will ever see him again,' he added.

There was more mumbling.

'But that isn't the issue now,' Molke reminded them. 'What *is* at issue is what we witnessed, what we heard last night at Countess Namarov's house.'

'And you're sure the man said "Frankenstein"?' Bergman enquired.

'Absolutely certain,' Molke stated.

'You said there was something wrong with him, with this disfigured man,' Bergman went on. 'Could his problem have been a mental one?' He tapped his temple. 'If so, he might have mistaken Doctor Stein for someone else.'

'Rubbish,' Molke snapped. 'He knew who he was. There's no question of that.'

'You were right to call this meeting, Doctor Molke,' Hauser added.

'I agree,' Kiesel said. 'What we have to decide now, gentlemen, is whether this man is Frankenstein or not.'

'While I was waiting for the members to convene I spent my time going through the old records concerning this man Frankenstein,' Molke informed his colleagues.

'And?' Kiesel asked.

'And the description of him given in those records fits that of our Doctor Stein very closely,' Molke stated.

There was another babble of conversation, stilled when Kiesel raised his hand for silence. 'Assuming this man is who we think he is,' he said at last, 'what should our next step be?'

'If Doctor Stein is in reality Frankenstein then we should all be aware of how dangerous he is,' Hauser said. 'The stories about the man are horrific.'

'What exactly did he do?' Bergman asked.

'He contravened every law of God and nature during the course of his work,' Molke said.

'And what *was* his work?' Bergman persisted.

'It involved the reanimation of dead tissue,' Molke replied. 'He tried to bring life to the dead.'

'My God,' Bergman murmured. 'And this man is in our midst now?'

'There was talk of murders, of grave robbing and all manner of monstrous acts,' Molke continued. 'That is why we must prove his true identity once and for all.'

'And if he really is Frankenstein?' Kiesel asked. 'What then?'

The question hung on the air like the cigar smoke and the members of the Medical Council glanced at each other as if hoping that someone among them would have an answer.

No one did.

Sixty-Two

T he skull of the corpse was open, the cranial cavity empty.

The brain itself was in a receptacle on the desk in front of Frankenstein who was examining the gelatinous mass with some tweezers and a probe. Every now and then he would lean closer, frowning and muttering under his breath. Large portions of the brain were discoloured where veins and arteries had ruptured, staining the soft tissue around them. There were several much darker areas that looked like thick and congealed blood clots in the frontal lobe and Frankenstein used the probe to separate one of these, smearing it against the side of the container in which the brain rested.

'It's as I suspected,' he said, still poring over the mass of tissue before him. 'The greatest amount of damage was done to the frontal lobe of Carl's brain but there has also been considerable disruption here in the temporal lobe.'

The body of Carl Lang had been laid on a wooden operating table only feet away. The white sheet that covered it and hid it from view was stained with blood around the area of the head.

'The temporal lobe, as you know, controls emotion

and instinct,' Frankenstein went on. 'That could be why the changes that he suffered happened. Look, you can see that quite clearly just here.' He pointed to a particularly mangled portion of the organ.

Doctor Hans Kleve seemed unimpressed by Frankenstein's musings and he moved closer to the Baron's desk, an expression of deep concern on his face.

'Doctor Stein, I beg you to listen to me,' he said urgently. 'Get away from here, across the border. We can start again somewhere else.'

'There's no hurry,' Frankenstein said softly, his attention still riveted on the brain before him.

'Everyone heard Carl call you Frankenstein,' Kleve insisted. 'The Medical Council is bound to take action. You know the way they feel about you. This is the chance they've been waiting for.'

'There was always the risk that I might be identified,' the Baron said calmly. 'My plans were made accordingly.'

'And did your plans include being exposed before the leading lights of Carlsbruck society?'

'I care nothing for what those people think of me, Hans. The only thing that matters is my work.'

'After what happened last night you won't get the chance to continue with that work. Neither of us will.'

'If you're worried about your own part in this then I suggest that you make your own plans to leave. I shall not.'

'But you can't stay here.'

'And what is to stop me? I shall be at the surgery in the morning at my usual time.'

'Well, you'll be alone. The whole town knows who you are by now.'

'Do they?'

'You know how word gets around. I've even heard mutterings within the wards of the hospital. They know who you are. It's dangerous for you to stay here.'

Frankenstein shrugged.

'Even Margaret has refused to return here to work,' Kleve went on.

'That is her concern, not mine.'

'She won't come back here because she's afraid.'

'Of me?'

'Of what might happen to her if she continues working for you.'

'I fear your imagination is running away with you, Hans,' Frankenstein said. 'Even if anyone manages to prove my true identity what could they do about it? What would the police charge me with? Many people every year use assumed names in an attempt to build new lives for themselves. What is criminal about that?'

'But if they delve too deeply into your past—'

'What do you think they will find?' Frankenstein interrupted. 'All evidence of my previous work was destroyed – you know that.'

'But you're a fugitive from the law.'

'Baron Victor Frankenstein was executed three years ago: there's a grave in Innsbruck cemetery to prove that. How can a man who has been dead for three years be a fugitive? What are they going to do? Kill me again?'

Kleve was silent for a moment and Frankenstein returned his attention to the brain before him. 'Look at this, Hans,' he urged. 'The damage to the frontal and temporal lobes is doubtless what caused the problems for Carl. Next time we must ensure—'

'Next time?' Kleve snapped, cutting across the Baron. 'If you don't get out of here there won't be a "next time". Not for either of us. For God's sake listen to me: I've been summoned to appear before the Medical Council. What am I to say?'

'I'll come with you.'

'That would be madness. Let me do what I can.'

Frankenstein looked up at Kleve, his eyes blazing. 'I have nothing to fear from them,' he breathed. 'What can they prove?'

'They heard what Carl said.'

'And you expect me to run like a frightened rabbit because of what a dying man shouted to me? No. I'll come with you when you meet with them. Let them do their worst. And, if I have to, I'll bury them all.'

Sixty-Three

Seated at the head of the great long table around which sat the members of the Carlsbruck Medical Council, Frankenstein felt rather more at home than perhaps he should have done.

He was forced to suppress a smile as he looked at the faces of the men gathered at the table, all of them peering at him with a combination of irritation and wariness. Yes, sitting here in front of these doctors who would like to call themselves his equals appealed to Frankenstein's sense of irony. He also found it fitting that he should be in the position usually granted to the one who is looked upon as the most important in such a gathering. His place at the head of the table, he felt, was more than merited.

Sitting alongside him, Kleve looked less than assured and rarely met the gazes of the Council members. Frankenstein felt on more than one occasion that he should reach across, physically lift the younger man's head and remind him that these fools who confronted them were to be looked upon with contempt rather than fear. The Baron sniffed at the yellow rose in his lapel and waited for the babble of conversation among the Council members to die down.

Once he was sure that it had he cleared his throat, took a sip of water from the crystal glass before him and spoke, his words measured and deliberate as if he was speaking to someone who had trouble understanding what he said.

'Gentlemen, I deny it absolutely,' he said.

'You deny that your name is Frankenstein?' Hauser called from the other end of the table.

'Have you ever consulted a street directory, sir?' the Baron went on.

'I'm not with you,' Hauser murmured.

'If you look at any street directory for any town in Europe you will find dozens of Frankensteins,' the Baron informed him. 'I am a Frankenstein, I don't deny that.'

'So you admit it?' Molke snapped.

'I admit that I am a Frankenstein,' the Baron repeated. 'I also admit that I had heard of the Baron Frankenstein who supposedly created that monster some three years ago and naturally I didn't want to set up in practice here handicapped by that name. And so I changed it. I am sorry if you still find something sinister about that, gentlemen. I feel my reasons were more than valid.'

'But the resemblance,' Molke persisted. 'The uncanny resemblance – how do you explain that?'

It was Kleve who spoke next. 'This is a monstrous accusation,' he offered. 'Inspired by jealousy.'

'How dare you, Doctor Kleve?' Kiesel snapped. 'What have we to be jealous of?'

'You have treated Doctor Stein with mistrust and contempt ever since he arrived here in Carlsbruck because he refused to join this organisation,' Kleve said.

'All members of the medical profession who practise in this town join this Council,' Kiesel insisted. 'It is a matter of respect.'

'We are not here to discuss the rights or wrongs of this man's membership of this Council,' Molke said.

'Quite right,' Hauser agreed. Then he looked towards the head of the table. 'Baron Frankenstein.'

The Baron once again suppressed a smile. 'Doctor Stein,' he corrected.

'Doctor Stein,' Hauser said. 'How do you explain that wretched fellow calling you Frankenstein?'

'For the very same reason you did, I should imagine,' the Baron said.

'It is proof of who you really are,' Molke said flatly.

'It is no such thing,' Frankenstein snapped. 'Proof is what you do not have. You have nothing to support these accusations other than gossip and I venture that men of your supposed high standing in the community should require more than gossip before they begin hurling accusations around.'

'Again we see your lack of respect,' Molke hissed.

'Not so,' Frankenstein countered. 'I think a little proof rather than a lot of gossip would be advantageous to us all.' The Baron got to his feet, taking his top hat from the table in front of him and placing it on his head. 'Perhaps you would like to resume this conversation when you have some facts to lay before me rather than the hearsay and speculation that you seem content to rely on at present.'

'Now just a moment,' Molke snapped, also rising and shooting out a hand which he closed around Frankenstein's forearm.

Frankenstein looked down at Molke's hand, then met the man's gaze. He held it until Molke released his grip.

'Now, if you'll excuse me,' the Baron said curtly. 'I am a busy man. Good day, gentlemen.'

He turned and headed for the door, then left the room. Kleve too rose, preparing to join him.

'Doctor Kleve,' Hauser called. 'We have not yet questioned you.'

The younger man sighed and sat back down. 'I can tell you nothing more than Doctor Stein has already told you,' he said, wearily.

'Can't tell us or won't tell us?' Molke sneered.

'I have nothing to hide.'

'Unlike your companion and mentor,' hissed Molke.

'What did you learn from him that you could not have learned from any of us?' Hauser asked.

'How to reanimate the dead, perhaps?' Molke snapped. 'How to rob graves?'

'You go too far,' Kleve retorted.

'Not I, Doctor Kleve, but your colleague Doctor Frankenstein,' hissed Molke.

'He has already denied these charges you have levelled against him,' Kleve protested. 'And yet still you persist with this charade.'

'It is no charade, Doctor Kleve,' Hauser said. 'We are anxious to discover this man's true identity.'

'Why? So you can persecute him even more?'

'If he is who we suspect he is then who knows what kind of danger he might pose?' Molke snapped.

Kleve shook his head dismissively. 'Well, until you can prove your insane theories you should keep them to yourselves,' he added angrily.

'When we heard who this man might be,' Molke said, glaring at the younger man, 'we informed Inspector Schiller. He travelled to Innsbruck to inspect the grave of Baron Frankenstein. On police orders, the grave was opened. There were human remains inside but they were not those of Baron Victor Frankenstein.' He sat forward in his seat, his words now hard-edged. 'We were right: Frankenstein is not dead. As soon as Inspector Schiller returns he will arrest this man of whom you think so highly. And even if you warn him and he tries to run there isn't anywhere now that he'll be able to hide.'

Kleve looked in disgust at the other men seated around the table. 'Why didn't you confront him with this when he was here?' he asked. 'Or are you afraid of him as well as being envious of his genius?'

'Why should we be envious of a man like him?' Hauser snorted.

'We wanted to see if he would continue to lie,' Molke snapped. 'He did – so he obviously has something to hide.'

Kleve got to his feet and turned towards the door.

'Frankenstein asked for proof,' Molke went on. 'And now we have it.'

Sixty-Four

As Frankenstein closed the door of his surgery and stepped out into the corridor of the hospital he thought how quiet it was.

Normally there were sounds coming from the wards: subdued chatter from the patients or the noises generated by those who worked in the building. But on this particular morning it was almost unnaturally silent as the Baron made his way towards the double doors that opened into the first ward. As he walked, the sound of his footfalls echoed inside the corridor, reverberating from the stone floor and walls. He buttoned the last fastening on his long white coat, ran a hand through his immaculately coiffured hair and stepped through the ward doors.

The silence persisted.

Inside the large room every pair of eyes was turned in his direction and the expressions on all the occupants' faces seemed to be the same. Frankenstein could see something different in those looks today. Something he had not seen before – it seemed to him like anger. Not the fear and anxiety that he normally saw. It was as if every single one of the patients in the ward had been infected with the same emotion. They glared at him as he stood there in front of the doors calmly gazing back at them, aware of their piercing stares. Away to his right someone coughed and spat. Frankenstein wondered whether, if he had been standing closer, the projectile of phlegm would have been directed at him. Again he looked at the faces in front of him. Then, his jaw set in hard lines, he moved among them.

After all, what had he to fear from them? They needed him. They needed his expertise. Without him many of them would die. What right did they have to look at him with such disrespect and loathing? As he passed the man with the bandaged arm who had been sitting on his bed he got to his feet. But the movement was not a deferential one and he narrowed his eyes as he looked at Frankenstein who met his gaze and then moved on, passing another bed where the occupant was sitting up, staring at him.

For one fleeting second, Frankenstein felt like turning and asking them what they were staring at. But he suppressed that urge, moving across the ward towards a man with a bandaged head who eyed him suspiciously.

He was a big man in his fifties: bull-necked and with almost disproportionately large muscles in his arms that had been built up over many years of manual labour. Beside him a younger man balancing on one crutch also gazed fixedly at Frankenstein who consulted the chart at the end of the big man's bed before moving nearer to him.

'How's the head today?' he asked, reaching towards the dressing that was wound around the man's skull like a turban.

'Don't put your filthy hands on me,' the man snapped, brushing Frankenstein's hand away.

'Don't be a fool, man,' the Baron replied. 'I've got to look at it.'

'You heard me,' the man hissed. 'Keep your murdering hands off me, you bloody butcher.'

Frankenstein frowned.

'Do you hear?' the big man said. '*Frankenstein.*'

The word echoed around the ward and the Baron looked a little perturbed at the vehemence with which it was spoken.

'That's right,' the big man went on threateningly. 'That's what I said. Frankenstein. Fugitive from the guillotine. Murderer. Mutilator.'

'Murderer,' the younger man with the crutch repeated.

'Grave robber,' another voice intoned.

'Killer,' added yet another from the other side of the ward.

Frankenstein was still gazing at the man with the bandaged head when something flew past his own skull, missing him by inches. The bottle struck the wall next to the bed and shattered, broken glass spraying in all directions. The Baron jumped back in surprise and spun around to see who had launched the missile at him. Across the ward a bearded man was sneering angrily at him.

Someone else hurled a chamber pot, the contents splashing onto the Baron who recoiled, his own fury now rising. How dare they? He wasn't going to stand for this for one second longer. He turned away and headed back through the narrow gap along the aisle between the beds. But as he tried to pass several patients blocked his exit.

He thought about telling them to move but then decided to seek another way out.

As he turned he found a man blocking his path. Frankenstein saw that the man was holding a bottle, gripping it by the neck as if it was a kind of bludgeon.

He moved hastily past the man and headed off towards the other doors of the ward.

'Frankenstein,' someone said, the word spat out as if it was bitter on the tongue.

More of the patients called his name. It became a litany, spreading throughout the room.

'Frankenstein. Frankenstein.'

The sound built until it seemed that every patient in the ward was saying the word in perfect unison.

The Baron slipped between two more beds, intent now on reaching the safety of the corridor beyond the ward. His path was blocked by two men, one of whom raised a fist menacingly at him. He was about to push past the man when the first attack came.

From behind him the owner of a crutch swung the implement down with tremendous force. The blow caught Frankenstein on the top of the head, the impact so great that his legs buckled under him and he went sprawling on the cold stone floor. He rolled on to his back, aware that he was close to blacking out, but he fought the feeling, aware now of the pain that filled his head. When he tried to rise it swept over him like a wave and he slumped backwards once more.

Half a dozen of the patients were gathered around him now, looking down at him with expressions of pure hatred on their faces.

'Get him,' one of them shrieked and the onslaught began.

A foot was driven into Frankenstein's side, then another. At the same time a boot slammed into his face, cracking his cheekbone. The same crutch that had struck him before was driven into his face again and again, splintering the bridge of his nose. Blood burst from it and spilled over his face, while several ribs were shattered by the force of the blows hammering into his body. Someone jumped on his left leg, snapping the ankle, the crack of breaking bone clearly audible. Frankenstein raised his hands to try and protect himself but it was futile. The force and ferocity of the blows was incredible. Walking sticks and more crutches were used as weapons, all of them raining down upon him, along with fists and boots.

A shattered rib sheared through one of his lungs and blood filled his mouth, spilling over his lips to puddle beneath his head which had already been battered so badly that it looked like raw meat.

At first he had tried to fight unconsciousness but now he welcomed it as the rain of blows seemed to intensify.

Somewhere someone screamed and for a moment Frankenstein thought it was he himself who had uttered the shriek of pain and fear.

He was aware of someone crashing through the doors of the ward but who it was no longer seemed to matter. Nothing mattered any more.

The last thing he saw through a haze of blood and pain was the figure of Hans Kleve pushing furiously through the horde of patients that surrounded him and for a second Frankenstein wondered if the image was indeed real. Perhaps it was just a projection of the pain that filled every inch of his body, just the feeble imaginings of a brain now so close to death.

And yet he was aware of being lifted on to one of the beds and laid there by Kleve, the sounds around him now dying down to silence once again.

Frankenstein made a low gurgling noise in his throat and tried to speak but no words would come forth.

Blackness was closing in all around him and this time he didn't fight it.

Sixty-Five

It was all Hans Kleve could do to prevent himself from weeping.

Even his professional training could barely insulate him from the feelings that welled up within him as he stood in the underground laboratory, looking down at the body of Victor Frankenstein.

Stripped to the waist and lying on his back on the operating table, Frankenstein looked smaller and more vulnerable than Kleve had ever seen him before. He also looked as if a coach and horses had run over him. The injuries he had sustained were horrendous and, despite the fact that Kleve had spent the last hour or more cleaning them as best he could, the severity of the damage was incredible.

Kleve's shirt was soaked in gore, the floor around the operating table strewn with bloodied rags.

At least eight ribs had been broken and numerous other bones too. One of Frankenstein's lungs was punctured, the liver and spleen ruptured. One arm was broken, as was the lower jaw and both cheekbones. There were multiple fractures to the skull and one eye had been so badly damaged it was little more than a pool of viscous liquid in the battered socket. Kleve was amazed that Frankenstein was still alive, although the weak movements of his chest and his laboured breathing seemed to indicate that this condition would not persist for much longer. The younger man wiped more blood from his colleague's face.

'Hans,' Frankenstein gasped, somehow forcing the words from his swollen and bloodied lips.

'Don't talk,' Kleve told him, leaning closer to the dying man.

'It's no good,' Frankenstein went on, every word seemingly causing him immense pain. He coughed and flecks of bright blood sprayed from his mouth.

Kleve held one of his hands gently.

'You know what to do,' Frankenstein croaked.

'Yes,' Kleve said softly. 'I know.'

Before he'd even finished speaking, Kleve was dragging off his jacket, discarding it in favour of the long white laboratory coat that he would wear for the operation. He pulled it on, then reached beneath the table next to him and pulled out a large wooden box which he opened to expose his vast array of medical instruments. Moving quickly and efficiently, as he'd been taught, he laid the instruments out in the order that he would need them. Scalpels, saws, probes, scissors and tweezers all glinted in the dull light.

He glanced back at the immobile body of Frankenstein and noticed that the older man's chest was barely moving now. Each breath, laboured as it was, must be agony for him, Kleve thought. Time was running out rapidly.

*

Almost two hours had passed by the time Kleve gently lifted the brain of Baron Victor Frankenstein from the receptacle he had placed it in and slid it carefully into the jar of preservative fluid.

He wiped one bloodstained hand across his forehead, leaving a red slick there along with the perspiration that already beaded his flesh.

He looked back at the body and felt a moment of extreme sadness. He reached over and carefully pulled the sheet over the Baron's battered features as a final mark of respect. Then he turned back towards the brain, which was floating in the clear fluid. With infinite care, Kleve picked up the jar and carried it towards the rear of the large laboratory, passing through a curtained doorway.

Behind those curtains was a large upright tank and in that tank hung a bandage-shrouded body.

Waiting.

Kleve set the brain down and headed back into the laboratory.

As he did so he heard the sound of footsteps outside the door and he looked anxiously in that direction. Moments later there came several loud raps.

Kleve hesitated a moment, then hurried to unlock the door.

On the other side he saw some familiar faces.

'I have a warrant for the arrest of Victor Stein,' Inspector Schiller announced, holding up the piece of paper he was clutching as if to reinforce his words. Kleve stepped aside and beckoned him in, watching as the inspector looked warily around at the array of equipment.

Behind him Kleve could see the figures of Molke, Hauser and Kiesel. For a moment he thought he could detect a slight smile on the lips of Molke as he followed the policeman into the laboratory.

'Where is he?' Schiller enquired.

'This way,' Kleve said and the small group followed him towards the operating table where they could all see a shape hidden beneath a bloodstained sheet.

Kleve pulled the sheet back, holding it so that the others could see what lay beneath.

Schiller winced as he saw the damage that had been inflicted upon the body. 'What happened?' he asked.

'It was his patients in the hospital,' Kleve said. 'They went mad and practically tore him to pieces.'

Molke put a hand to his mouth. Kiesel turned away, shaking his head.

'Did they know who he was?' Schiller continued.

'I would think so,' Kleve said solemnly.

'It is a form of justice, I suppose,' Schiller said quietly.

Kleve shot the policeman an angry glance. 'I brought him here and operated in the hope of saving his life,' he explained. 'But it was useless.'

'Well, the body must be taken away and buried in unhallowed ground,' Schiller observed.

'As it should have been three years ago,' Molke added.

Kleve dropped the sheet, covering the Baron's lifeless face. 'You have what you wanted, gentlemen,' he said acidly. 'I would appreciate it if you would leave now.'

The little group turned as one and headed towards the door, shepherded out by Kleve who locked it behind them. He stood with his back to it, listening to their footsteps receding. When he was satisfied that they were gone he hurried back towards the rear of the laboratory, passing through to the curtained-off recess. For a second he stood gazing up at the bandaged, preserved body. Then he swallowed hard.

'Pray Heaven I've got the skill to do this,' Kleve murmured. 'Let's hope that you taught me well enough.'

He looked at the brain, still suspended in its preservative fluid.

What he must do would take, he estimated, close to four hours, perhaps longer. He checked his pocket watch and saw that it was almost ten p.m.

Outside, rain was beginning to fall.

Sixty-Six

LONDON

The mist that often rolled in from the river Thames on such cold days was particularly thick this day. It seemed to move through the narrow streets like a living thing. Some of those who lived in the city called it 'the breath of the river'.

This was one of the things that Doctor Hans Kleve had learned since his arrival in the English capital.

Despite the fact that he'd only been in London for the last four months he had already become fond of the place. He had found the English reserve that he'd heard so much about to be something of a myth. People from all walks of life, whether rich or poor, had welcomed him and he had found the transition between his own country and this new one virtually seamless. After all, he reasoned, what had he left behind? Persecution, anger and ignorance. At least here he had been able to begin anew. No one judged him, no one expected anything of him and no one was watching him constantly to see if he failed. He felt freer than he ever had before in his life, able to pursue his chosen career without distraction.

The journey from Carlsbruck had been a difficult and occasionally uncomfortable one. The long trek across country had taken him across parts of Switzerland, Germany and France until he had finally arrived at the port of Calais. The crossing of the English Channel had been one of the smoothest and least stressful parts of the trip. One of the sailors on board had warned him that he should not expect weather of a similar kind during his stay in England but Kleve had merely smiled good-naturedly as the man had talked. During the entire journey he had been content to keep himself to himself. Standing at the bow of the ship as it cut effortlessly through the water, he had felt a genuine thrill when he'd sighted the White Cliffs of Dover through a veil of mist early one morning.

They seemed to shine like a beacon, a wall of white rock that signalled not just the end of his journey but also the promise of a new life. Kleve could still remember that the sun had begun to poke out from behind the mist just as the ship had docked and he had taken this as a sign that his new life was to be somehow an improvement on his previous existence back in Carlsbruck. He had later rebuked himself for such fanciful thinking but, at the time, the incident had made him smile.

The journey from Dover to London had been relatively straightforward and once he'd arrived in the capital it had just been a matter of finding first somewhere to live and then a building where he could begin his work. That had not been too difficult and with the aid of a lawyer and estate agent in the area both tasks had been accomplished quickly and easily. He had left pretty much everything behind in Carlsbruck, preferring to start afresh. The only thing he'd taken with him had been a steamer trunk full of clothes and his medical instruments.

He didn't think about Carlsbruck much. Why should he? He had everything he wanted here in London. He didn't want to dwell on the past. His only plan was to build a more successful future.

Now Kleve stood looking out of the window of the Harley Street surgery, watching as a blue-uniformed policeman walked slowly by. The man saw Kleve standing at the window and touched the rim of his helmet respectfully.

The building where the practice had been established was a large converted town house with three large reception rooms on the ground floor. One of these had been set up as a surgery, another as a waiting room and the third as a consulting room. Since arriving, business had been very good and a steadily growing list of patients had been acquired, each of them wealthy and quite happy to spend some of their money on the services of a good physician. Kleve crossed to his desk and glanced at the large leatherbound diary propped open there. He drew his finger down the list of patients, checking to see who was next.

Lady Harcourt and her daughter Wendy.

Kleve smiled.

The Harcourt family, he had learned, was one of the wealthiest in London. Lord Harcourt was a Member of Parliament and also had a number of business interests. Through the family Kleve had built up a large part of his list of clients.

It was a world away from the day-to-day routine he'd been used to when he'd been working in the Hospital for the Poor in Carlsbruck, he mused. The smells he encountered in his surgery now were those of expensive perfume and fine soap, not of the sweat and bad breath that he'd become accustomed to. His work was confined to the needs of the rich and he was happy that was the case.

He crossed the office to a door that opened into a small bathroom. The man inside the room was washing his hands.

Kleve stood watching him for a moment. Then the man turned, drying his hands and replacing the towel with fastidious neatness on the rail beside the sink. He straightened up, inspecting his reflection in the mirror, brushing at his dark moustache with one index finger.

'You were an excellent pupil, Hans,' he said, leaning forward slightly to examine a slight blemish that ran from one temple to the other. 'This scar will hardly show.'

'I had the best teacher,' Kleve replied, smiling.

'Thank you, my friend,' the other man said.

Kleve helped him on with his jacket.

'I trust we have a full complement of patients again today?' the man said, brushing some dust from one sleeve.

'The practice is going from strength to strength,' Kleve assured him.

'Good. When the time is right we shall investigate more fully those other premises you looked at and begin to stock them with the equipment we shall need.'

Kleve nodded.

'But in the meantime . . .' the other man said, taking a red rose from a nearby vase. He sniffed it appreciatively and pushed it into the buttonhole of his jacket. 'The English Rose,' he said quietly. 'The most famous of them all.'

Kleve nodded. 'Your next patient is waiting, Doctor Franck,' he said, smiling again.

'Thank you, Hans,' the other man said, pulling open the white-painted double doors that led through into the surgery. As he stood there silhouetted in the doorway he reached into his waistcoat pocket, pulled out a monocle and screwed it into one eye. He smiled at the two figures who stood before him.

'Ah, Lady Harcourt and Wendy,' he exclaimed. 'How delightful to see you.' He stepped forward and Kleve started to close the doors gently behind him, preparing to leave him alone with his adoring patients.

Kleve felt a swell of pride and achievement of his own as he glanced at his companion briefly. The surgery that he had performed on the man had been faultless, the results stunning. It could not have gone better.

Just before the doors closed completely, the other man turned and glanced back at Kleve, a look of warmth and gratitude on his face.

Baron Victor Frankenstein was smiling.